CHANGING WAYS

JULIA TANNENBAUM

Julia Tannenbaum

Wicked Whale
Publishing

Tannenbaum, Julia

Changing Ways / by Julia Tannenbaum

Summary: A high school junior finds herself spiraling into mental illness and must travel the tough road to recovery with the help of her friends, family, and those like her she meets along the way.

ISBN: 978-1-7325554-0-2

Wicked Whale Publishing
P.O. Box 264
Sagamore Beach, MA 02562-9998

www.WickedWhalePublishing.com

Published in the United States of America

ADVANCED PRAISE

This is a brilliant debut novel from writer Julia Tannenbaum, a teenager who brings fact-based insight, amazing compassion and beautiful writing to her compelling story of mental health, specifically eating disorders. *Changing Ways* brings us on the real life journey to health with experiences, treatment challenges, friendships and struggles that make this novel a page-turner. We cheer for the teens and celebrate Tannenbaum's exceptional maturity and awesome talent.

Karin Stahl
Author, *The Option*

This book is dedicated to all the brave young people battling mental illness. Always remember that the war inside your mind does not define you. You are enough.

"I think the world is ending."

My mother stops what she's doing in the kitchen and peers around the corner into our TV room. There, I'm lounging on an old beige couch in grey sweats with my eyes glued to the television.

"Why are you watching the news?"

I shrug. "It was on. I was bored."

"Well, it's your last day of summer break. Don't get yourself all bummed over, uh," she squints at the tiny words projected at the bottom of the screen, "nuclear weapons."

"What else am I supposed to do?" I ask. "Nothing good is on."

"How 'bout you help me make dinner?" she suggests. "I could use an extra hand."

"Yeah, okay. What are you making?"

"Lasagna."

"Sweet."

Flipping off the television, I follow her into the kitchen. She hands me a knife and a cutting board, so I can start assembling a salad. Outside the window next to the sink, fat raindrops drench our peaceful little neighborhood in western Connecticut. It's been pouring ever since I woke up this morning and by the looks of it, it won't be stopping anytime soon.

"I hate this weather," I say as I'm methodically slicing a plump tomato.

"It could be worse," Mom responds. "If we still lived in California, we'd be in a drought."

"I'd take a drought over this any day."

"I wouldn't be so sure. I've seen photos on Facebook; it's pretty bad."

"Since when are you on Facebook?" I ask.

"Grace, I've had an account for two years. I've sent you a friend request three times."

"Oh . . . yeah, sorry 'bout that."

"It's all right," she says. "I understand being friends with your mother is embarrassing."

"It's not embarrassing, it's just . . ." I sigh. "Never mind. Forget it."

"Okay."

She continues spreading a thin layer of marinara sauce onto the lasagna while I peel skin off a cucumber. The rain has escalated to a downpour, like one thousand marbles are clattering against a metal floor.

I know rain is good for our environment or whatever, but this unexpected change in weather is screwing up my routine. I love the outdoors. As soon as the temperature reaches the sixties, I spend most of my free time taking walks around my block and reading horror novels beneath the beautiful maple tree in my backyard.

Not to mention that I was looking forward to wearing my

new white Converse tomorrow. But in these messy conditions, settling for my old Nikes is more sensible. Though they won't live up to the exemplary first-impression I'd hoped for for my junior year, it shouldn't be a big deal. After all, at my high school, styles range anywhere from skinny jeans and V-necks to dinosaur onesies and smiling poop emoji hats.

When I stepped through the daunting double doors of Chuck L. Everett High School two years ago, I had no idea what to expect. Prior to starting, I'd heard a number of things—some reassuring, some intriguing, and some downright intimidating. I'd heard that cliques are overrated, but that the afterschool activities you partake in determine your social status (i.e. don't join the Mathletes). I'd heard that as long as you do well on quizzes, most teachers don't care if you use your phone in class. I'd heard that you should always respect upperclassmen even if they're total dicks, because like clubs, they have the power to dictate whether you're liked or loathed. My neighbor Alex, who graduated last year, had even warned me to avoid the bathrooms in the C-Wing, because that's the most popular destination for getting stoned.

And while all this was true, high school was undoubtedly an improvement from my painfully awkward middle school experience. I can only hope it stays that way for what many students deem the "most stressful" year.

After I've dressed the salad with a balsamic vinaigrette, I place it on the table beside a bowl of steamed broccoli. "Can I leave?" I ask Mom.

She nods. "Yes. Thanks for the help."

"No problem."

I unplug my phone from its charger, grab my earbuds, and return to the TV room to listen to music. As I'm humming along to Coldplay's *Yellow*, a flash of orange beneath our dogwood tree catches my eye. I watch in fascination as a monarch butterfly lands on a fallen pink flower, unfazed by the brutal downpour that threatens to crush its delicate wings.

In the beginning of summer, butterflies were everywhere, but now that autumn's approaching, the only place I see them is in the community garden at the end of my street, fluttering around the shriveled roses and wilting lilies.

"See you next summer," I say, as if the butterfly can somehow hear me.

Then I recline into a stiff throw pillow, raise the volume on my phone to muffle the sound of raindrops steadily pounding against the roof, and close my eyes. I'm so exhausted, so bored of this lazy day, and so nervous about what tomorrow has in store that I wish I could just sleep until it's all over and everything is okay again.

New beginnings always make me anxious.

THE RAIN IS STILL GOING strong the next morning when I'm abruptly woken by my six-thirty alarm. I fumble around in the darkness for the OFF button, and when I can't find it, yank the cord out of its socket. The beeping stops.

"Thank God," I mumble.

I toss aside my covers and flip on my bedside lamp. Once my eyes have adjusted to the sudden brightness, I change into a navy shirt and dark-wash capris that are too snug in the waist. Had the temperature not been so abnormally cold for September, I'd have selected my favorite khaki short-shorts instead. But with a high of fifty-six, the capris will have to do.

In the bathroom, I add a couple strokes of mascara to my stubby eyelashes and rub concealer around my eyes to mask the

The girl rolls her eyes. "Asshole," I hear her mumble under her breath.

"Good going, Grace," Lou jokes. "C'mon, that's what this is for." She points at a four-by-six laminated paper that's stapled to a bulletin board outside the main office. "Now all we need to do is figure out where our advisories are, and we'll be good. Easy as pie."

"I can't believe you're so chill about this," I grumble.

Since her last name begins with a J and mine an E, as usual, we have different advisors. I find B-208, led by the notoriously strict French 3 teacher, Mademoiselle Rousseau, on the second floor, across from the restrooms. After claiming the desk farthest away from Mademoiselle, I insert my earbuds and stare out a nearby window, where dark clouds continue to dominate the colorless sky.

Students arrive at different intervals, so by the time the second bell rings, most of the seats are taken. I fling my bookbag on the desk to my left—amazingly the only one that's still unoccupied—as Mademoiselle stands at the Smartboard, patiently waiting for the chatter to cease.

Once the room is completely silent, she says in a thick accent, "Welcome back to Everett High School. Before we get started, I'm going to take attend—"

"Sorry I'm late." A boy bursts through the door, gasping for breath. "I missed my bus."

Everybody momentarily looks up from their phones to check out the boy, including me. When I see him—a well-built brunette with piercing blue eyes and sun-kissed skin—my jaw drops.

Holy shit. It's Liam Fisher.

Mademoiselle frowns disapprovingly, but doesn't chastise Liam for his tardiness. Instead, she points at the desk next to me and says, "You can sit there, uh . . ."

"Liam. And I promise I won't be late again."

"You'd better not," she warns. "Now, where was I?"

While she takes attendance, Liam maneuvers through the first two rows of desks and drops his backpack where my bookbag was. He's wearing a Florida Gators jersey and jorts that hang so low on his hips, I can see the waistline of his underwear.

"Hey, Grace. Long time no see." He grins.

I force myself to return my ex-friend's charismatic smile. "When'd you get back?"

"A couple weeks ago. My aunt's in the hospital again, so my dad wanted to be close to her for moral support or something."

"I'm sorry."

"Me too. Depression sucks."

"Grace Edwards?" Mademoiselle calls.

"Here!"

"How's Lou?" he asks while she moves onto the Fs.

"Good. She's dating Cassie Myers now."

"The principal's daughter?" He chuckles. "I see she hasn't changed much."

"Yeah. So, are you seeing anyone?"

"Not currently," he says, "but there's this girl on my block, Bianca Sanchez. She's fine as hell."

"Santos."

"Huh?"

"It's Santos, not Sanchez."

"Oh. Do you know her?"

"Everyone knows Bianca. She's, like, the most popular girl in the grade. Good luck getting with her."

"Keep your luck," he responds. "She gave me her number this morning."

"I'm passing around the rulebooks," Mademoiselle

"At least you weren't asked if you were on the IBTC all of ninth grade," I say.

"IBTC?" Cassie asks.

"Itty Bitty Titty Committee."

She laughs. "That's hilarious."

"I didn't think it was funny. It was mean. And hurtful."

"Freshmen are dumb. By the time you're a junior, everyone's far too preoccupied with college and grades and stuff like that to give a damn about the size of your boobs."

"Thank God. So, what class do you have next?"

"Painting," they simultaneously respond.

"Since when do you paint?" I ask Lou.

"Since it's the only elective that fits into both of our schedules," Lou responds. "That, and it's an easy A."

"Well, gym doesn't start until next week," I say, "so I have a free period. I think I'll just hang out in the library, maybe find a book or something."

"A book?" Lou snorts. "If you're bored, just text me. I've gotten pretty good at pocket texting."

"You're kidding, right?" I ask. "You can't pocket text to save your life!"

"Yes, I can!"

"Uh-huh. Cass, check this out." I hand her my phone, where I've screenshotted a text Lou sent me over the weekend when she was eating lunch with her family.

Lou: dad wont stop panting about his dump job. its literary driving me crayon. wanna bang later? i knee to escape this ducking mouse!

Cassie laughs so hard, she nearly chokes on her strawberry milk. "Wanna bang? Should I be jealous?"

"I meant 'hang,'" Lou insists. "It's autocorrect's fault."

"Sure. Blame autocorrect." The bell rings, and Cassie says, "C'mon, I'll show you where the art wing is. See ya, Grace."

"Bye."

I gather my garbage—my empty popcorn bag, a can of lime seltzer, an apple core, and the rest of my sandwich—and toss them into the heaping trashcan on my way out the door. The halls are less crowded than they were earlier, so I have little trouble navigating to the library.

At the computer, I enter my six-digit ID code and head to the "Quiet Learning" corner near the Emergency Exit, where students rarely hang out. I settle onto a tattered red couch, plug my earbuds into my phone, and quietly hum along to *Californication*.

Sometimes, I miss California almost as much as I miss my father. Beach life was so simple compared to the constant commotion of the suburbs. Snapshot memories like walking barefoot in the sand, watching the sun set over turquoise waves, and eating apricots from the small tree in our backyard have stuck with me to this day. Although I've spent the last six years in Connecticut, my heart will forever be loyal to the West Coast. It doesn't matter how many places you visit or how many houses you own, because in the end, you only have one true home.

The rest of school is a monotonous blur of teachers reiterating rules we're all very accustomed to and reviewing syllabuses, three of which Mom must sign by the end of the week. I return home at two-forty on the dot, thanks to Mrs. Jackson's timely pick up.

"Hello? Mom?" I was initially surprised to see her car in our driveway, as her afternoon shift usually ends no sooner than five, until I remembered Jamie's appointment.

"Hi, hon." Mom is sitting at the table, skimming through a weekly Stop&Shop flyer while she simultaneously noshes on an old-fashioned doughnut.

"Where'd you get the doughnuts?"

"Retirement party at work. My boss said I could bring the leftovers home. Want one?"

"Yeah. I think I'll only have half though. I had a big lunch."

"Okay."

After careful consideration of the remaining doughnuts, I select a glazed jelly. I divide it into two pieces with a butter knife, then place the larger one back in the box. "Mom, do you think I'm fat?"

Mom shoots me an incredulous look. "You? God no. Why do you ask?"

"No reason."

"Well, I think you look great." She glances at her watch and makes an annoyed clucking sound with her tongue. "I swear, if your brother isn't home in the next two minutes, I'll—"

As if on cue, Jamie strolls through the door. "Ooh, dough-nuts!" He drops his magenta backpack onto the floor and eagerly reaches for a strawberry frosted. "Thanks, Mom!"

"Not so fast, mister. You'll have to wait until after the dentist."

"But—"

"No buts," she interrupts. "I don't want to pay for another cavity."

With a sigh, Jamie reluctantly retracts his hand. "Okay."

"We shouldn't be gone more than an hour, Grace," Mom says as she's rummaging through her purse. "Call me if you need anything."

"I'm sixteen," I respond. "I'll be fine."

"Right. Jamie, put that down!" She wrangles the doughnut from his grip as he's about to take a bite. "What did I say about cavities?"

"Sorry."

"Go wait by the car. Now, if I could only find my damn keys . . ."

"Check your pocket," I suggest, and sure enough, they're there.

"Thanks, hon. I can be so forgetful sometimes."

"It's cool. Are you going back to work?"

Mom nods. "I'll drop Jamie off after his appointment. He's allowed to have one doughnut—that's it. You know how he gets if he has too much sugar."

"Yeah, I know."

As Mom bends down to kiss my cheek, she whispers, "But you can have two."

"Thanks."

Once they're gone, I finish the last bite of my doughnut and wander into the TV room to see if anything interesting is on. I'm halfway through a *Modern Family* rerun when my phone buzzes.

Lou: hey. wanna hang out?

I check the clock—three thirty-six—before replying; *ok but can i come over to ur house? M and J will be home soon.*

Lou: yeah thats fine.

Grace: cool. see u in 10.

Lou: see ya!

Pocketing my phone, I turn off the television and return to the kitchen. I find a sticky note in the drawer beneath the snack cabinet and scribble *at Lou's be back soon* in blue Sharpie. I place it on the center of the table, where I know Jamie will see it, then lace up my sneakers, grab my key, and begin the mile-long jog to Lou's house. The asphalt is still damp from the rain, though the thunderclouds have cleared overhead. It is a good thing too. I'd prefer blue to grey any day of the week.

The Jackson's are wealthier than my family, therefore their

property, from their elegant Dutch Colonial to their impeccably-cut lawn to the row of tulips lining the stone pathway leading to their front door, is nicer than mine. Lou's lived here her entire life, ever since her mother gave birth to her on a burgundy couch that they now stash in the basement with other random junk, like boxes of 80s hair metal CDs and bizarre abstract paintings. Until I saw their lower level, I would have never guessed that the Jacksons' were hoarders.

"Hello, Grace," Mrs. Jackson greets me when I let myself in with the spare key they keep under their *Home Is Where the Heart Is* welcome mat. She's hunched over the oven, tending to a chicken pot pie. "How was school?"

I shrug. "Fine. I like your scarf."

Mrs. Jackson touches the sheer olive fabric wrapped around her head. "Are you sure? Lou said it looked tacky."

"Have you seen Lou's wardrobe?" I joke. "I think it looks great."

She smiles. "Thanks, dear. You're a doll."

One year ago as of November, Mrs. Jackson was diagnosed with stage four breast cancer. Since then, she's undergone numerous treatments with the hope of beating the tumor that has made her life—and her family's—a living nightmare. Sadly, none have been very successful.

But despite everything she continues to go through, cancer has failed to destroy Mrs. Jackson's optimism. She's always so cheerful when I'm around, cracking jokes about her quirky treatment team and asking if I'd like to see her newest wig or head-wear (of course, I consent).

"For whatever reason, God intended for this to happen," she once told me. "I must accept His plan and continue living my life to the fullest, because even if I don't always understand it, I know it's what He'd want."

Growing up as an atheist, I could never fathom why people place their fate in the hands of an imaginary being like God. But I respected Mrs. Jackson's beliefs nevertheless. If her faith helps her answer questions doctors and nurses fail to, who am I to tell her otherwise? After all, life isn't about understanding; it's about accepting.

"Hey, girl." Lou saunters into the kitchen, munching from a bag of Nacho Cheese Doritos. Her fingertips are stained bright red. "When'd you get here?"

"A couple minutes ago. I was talking to your mom."

"Well, sorry to interrupt, but *Supernatural* is rerunning any minute, and we need to get caught up before October."

"October?" Mrs. Jackson asks.

"That's when the next season starts, Ma. Duh." Lou grabs my hand and drags me away from her mother, who rolls her eyes.

"Enjoy your show, girls. Are you staying for dinner, Grace?"

I shake my head. "Mom's going back to the hospital, so I have to make something for Jamie and me."

"Let me guess; pasta again?" When I nod, Lou wrinkles her nose. "Aren't you sick of it yet?"

"Pasta's easy," I say, "and affordable, and Jamie likes it. What's the big deal?"

"I'm just saying, you outta shake it up. Variety is the spice of life." Lou closes the door to her room and flips on her miniature television as an episode of *Riverdale* is ending. "Perfect timing."

We recline onto the massive beanbag chair her grandfather bought for her seventeenth birthday in July. Its soft olive fabric is almost the exact color of her mother's scarf.

"Your mom seems better," I say.

"Shh. The episode's starting."

"Sorry."

We immerse ourselves in the fictitious world of *Supernatural* for the next hour, muting the television during commercial breaks to discuss our days. Lou says that despite having no interest in painting, the class isn't half-bad.

"It's the kids. They're so down-to-earth and just . . . I don't know, real. Like, they know they're different, but they don't care. It's no wonder Cass likes it."

"I wish my classmates were that way," I say. "They're all so judgy and fake."

"That's society for you. It's like Tupac says; 'some things never change.'" She begins rapping *Changes* under her breath, tapping the heel of her black ankle boot to the beat.

"Well, that's reassuring."

"I'm just being honest. I mean, you've seen the stuff people write in the bathroom." Lou laughs. "Although, a lot of it's actually pretty funny."

"I doubt you'd feel that way if it was your name on the stall," I say.

"Right. IBTC."

"Among other things," I remind her.

"Well, haters can fuck off. They're just insecure assholes who think they can boss us around because they have hot bodies and date jocks. Want some Doritos?" She waves the bag in my face, but I shake my head.

"No, thanks. I had food at home."

"Suit yourself."

The sexy woman onscreen mouths the familiar catchphrase, "Ask your doctor if Viagra is right for you," and the screen darkens momentarily before *Supernatural* resumes. We watch the final segment with bated breath, and when it ends, we move onto a season nine rerun. By the time the latter wraps up, it's almost six o'clock.

"You sure you can't stay a little longer?" Lou asks.

I shake my head. "Jamie doesn't like being home alone for too long."

"Well, say hi to the little bro for me. I'll text you later."

"All right. Oh, and this time wait until you're not eating to send that text."

"Fuck off."

I smirk. "Will do. See you tomorrow."

"Do you need another ride?"

"Maybe. I'll let you know in the morning."

"Okie-doke."

Lou holds the door for me while I finish double-knotting my laces. It's darker outside now that the days are becoming shorter. Autumn's still three weeks away, though by the newspaper ads promoting discount Halloween costumes and the colorful leaves dangling from every tree in sight, one might assume it's already here.

I've just reached the end of her driveway when I hear Lou bellow, "Ma, I'm starving! When's the chicken gonna be ready?"

I'll occasionally wonder how it's possible that someone so extroverted and confident like Lou could be compatible with an insecure wallflower like me. We're complete opposites, and yet we're also the closest thing either of us have to a sister—minus the sibling rivalry, that is.

I love Lou. I love that she makes me smile when I'm feeling sad and laugh when I want to cry. I love that she doesn't hesitate to stand up for what she believes in, no matter the consequences. I love that she's pushed me out of my comfort zone time and time again with venturesome activities like tree climbing and egging mean Ms. Crawford's house, because she knew in hindsight I'd enjoy them. And above all, I love that she's never given up on me—even when I've given up on myself.

I used to love Liam too. Maybe I still do—not that I'd ever

admit it. We met the summer before sixth grade when we both attended the town's coed soccer league, though unlike Lou and me, our relationship took time to develop. We were competitors, eager to claim the trivial candy prizes our coaches awarded to the victorious team. I'll always remember our final scrimmage; how his jaw dropped when I, the scrawny blonde girl who'd barely said a word for the entire two weeks, scored the winning goal from just beyond half-field.

After our teams had shaken hands, he approached me by the bench. "That was, uh, a nice shot."

"Thanks. You play good too."

He laughed awkwardly. "I mean, if you call getting your butt kicked by a girl 'good.'"

"I'm not just a girl," I responded emphatically. "I'm an athlete. Learn the difference."

"Okay, jeez. I didn't mean to offend you. I'm Liam, by the way."

"Grace."

"You playing this fall, Grace?"

I nodded. "You?"

"Yeah."

"If you want, we can, you know, get together and practice sometime," I offered.

"I mean, I guess that'd be all right. Here's my number." Grabbing the pen we used to check in, Liam jotted seven digits onto the back of my hand. They were messy, but still legible. "Call me."

"Okay. Maybe I will."

That day, I returned home with a bag full of sweets and a new friend. We hung out a lot that summer—and not only to sharpen our soccer skills. I invited Liam to Six Flags after Lou bailed to attend a family gathering. Liam's father took us on a fishing trip, where we swam in murky water and ate sandy grilled cheese sandwiches while Mr. Fisher patiently waited for the bass to bite.

They never did.

Liam told me that he had an older sister who was a ballerina at Julliard, and that when she lived at home, he'd secretly sneak into her room and dance to *Dancing Queen* in her ballet slippers.

I told him that in California, after my lab was hit by a car, I'd sit beneath her favorite hibiscus tree and sing *You'll Be in My Heart* because I somehow knew that she was listening.

I liked him even more when he didn't laugh.

Lou would sometimes hang out with us too. Although she was initially jealous of my closeness with Liam, she soon found that he was too charismatic to dislike.

"He's an okay dude," she once said. "It's no wonder you're crushing on him."

"I'm not crushing on Liam," I insisted. "We're just friends —that's all."

"We'll see about that," was her response.

I arrive home at six-ten drenched in sweat. Jamie is in his bedroom playing an upbeat song on his clarinet. He doesn't hear me the first time I knock on his door, so I try again.

"I'm practicing for my Jazz Band audition," he explains. "It's in two days, and I really want a spot."

"You're good," I assure him. "The teacher would be crazy not to give you one."

Jamie beams. "Thanks."

"So, are you ready for dinner?" I ask. "It's cool if you want to practice more."

"Are you kidding? I'm starving!" Jamie rubs his stomach. "Can I choose the pasta?"

"Actually, I was thinking I'd make grilled cheese tonight. Is that okay with you?"

"I'd love grilled cheese."

Pleased by his enthusiasm, I smile. "Great. Then grilled cheese it is."

3

"Take the damn shot!" Coach Cooper, Chuckle's reputedly cutthroat senior gym teacher, screams from the sidelines. Mr. Lipschitz stands beside him jotting down notes on a clipboard. He's dressed in bright orange shorts and a grey sweatshirt that reads *Keep Calm and Play On.*

Eileen Miller lifts her foot, but before she can make contact, I steal the ball from her and pass it to Laurie Matthews. She takes two dribbles, then sets up Kaya Brinkley inside the penalty box, who pops the ball above the goalie's head and into the net. My team erupts in cheers.

"All right, settle down," Coach Cooper orders. "Excellent ball handling, Laurie. Keep up the good work, and we're lookin' at our new captain."

Laurie grins. "Sweet."

"Grace, that was a nice pass," he continues to my delight. "Next time, however, I'd like to see more dribbling, okay?"

In a split-second, that delight becomes disappointment. "Okay, Coach."

"Let's go, girls!" Coach Cooper calls to the group gossiping by the sidelines. "We've still got fifteen minutes left!"

Even though I'm physically exhausted from over an hour of nonstop drills, I take a deep breath and remind myself that the harder I work now, the greater the chance I'll have of making Varsity. So, I power through the pain until four-thirty, and when we "cool down" with two laps around the field, I sprint the entire way, placing second behind Laurie. As the co-captain of the girls' track team, it isn't surprising that she's a strong runner.

"Good work, girls," Coach Cooper says as we're gathering our belongings. "I'll email you the roster tomorrow. For those of you who don't make the team, I'd recommend looking into the town league. Link's on my page."

"Man, he's hardcore," Lou says when I join her by the bleachers.

"No kidding." She hands me my water bottle, and I gulp it down in ten seconds flat. "How'd I do?"

"Fantastic."

"Good enough for Varsity?"

"Girl, you kicked ass. You're definitely Varsity material."

"Thanks. Do you wanna hang out after I change?"

Lou shakes her head. "I promised Cass I'd go with her to some art exhibit in the Center. If you want, you can come too."

"And be a third wheel? I'll pass."

"All right, well, I'll see you tomorrow—unless you need a ride."

I shake my head. "Mom's off early today. I'll ask her to pick me up."

"Cool. Later."

"Later." Waving goodbye with one hand, I use the other to compose a text to Mom, letting her know that tryouts are over. She responds ten seconds later.

Mom: be there in five

While I wait for her, I open Instagram and scroll through the latest pictures my followers have posted. Beaches, landmarks, and foreign destinations captioned *sad to WAVE goodbye* and *vaycay wya?* are the most popular tags. It looks like I'm not the only person who's already having vacation withdrawal.

When Dad was around, summer vacations were fantastic. His sizable salary made traveling as simple as precheck at LAX. We'd visit national parks or explore European cities or enjoy the slow-paced island aura of the Bahamas or Jamaica. One summer, we traveled to Reykjavik to stay with his college friend Amundi in his villa. That was a trip I'll never forget.

After Dad left and we moved to Connecticut, summers changed drastically. We no longer had the luxury of traveling wherever we wanted to anymore, because it was difficult for Mom to save up enough money for Six Flags, much less a five-hour flight to the West Coast.

This summer was no different. Besides a day trip to Boston, I spent most of vacation pent up in my house with only my phone and gym membership to keep me occupied. Even Lou, a notorious homebody, had more fun than me visiting her relatives in Louisiana and Florida. We Snapchatted daily, though the pictures she sent of her endeavors merely intensified my jealousy. I wanted to be there with her; to swim in the warm waves of Miami Beach and dance to jazz music at festivals in New Orleans. I wanted to remember what it felt like to enjoy life.

On the drive home, Mom asks, "So, how were tryouts?"

"I think I played good," I respond, "but I don't know if it was enough to make Varsity."

"Well."

"Huh?"

"You played well, and I'm sure by doing so, you impressed

your coach. You're a strong athlete, Grace. If I were a coach, I'd want you on my team without a doubt."

"Except you're not."

"I used to be. I co-coached you in Rec for two years, remember?"

"How could I forget? You benched me for the playoffs. Twice!"

"Maybe if you weren't so aggressive, I wouldn't have had to. You were always so competitive. You still are."

"Is that a bad thing?"

"It's not bad or good. It's just the way it is. Some things you can't change."

I hear the engine of Dad's Jaguar; feel the coolness of the glass as I press my forehead against my bedroom window and watch him speed down Seaside Boulevard.

"I know what you mean."

When we pull into the driveway, Jamie is sitting on the front step of our house, playing Candy Crush on his phone.

"Jamie, what are you doing out here?" Mom asks.

"I forgot my key," he responds. "How were tryouts, Grace?"

"Pretty good, I think."

"Did you make Varsity?"

"I'll find out when the coach emails the rosters tomorrow."

"Oh. Cool."

"Come on, you two. It's getting late," Mom says. "What would you like for dinner?"

"Mozzarella sticks," Jamie responds enthusiastically.

"Grace?"

I shrug. "Works for me."

"Great. I'll get started after I change my clothes. These damn pants feel like they're made of sandpaper."

She pats my shoulder and walks inside, kicking off her heels next to the counter. I leave my sweaty cleats beside them, then head to the bathroom to freshen up for dinner. As I'm washing my hands, I stare at my reflection in the mirror. My wavy dirty-blonde hair is matted with sweat, and my makeup is smudged beneath my hazel eyes. I'm pale, but not ghostly, and fit, but not thin. My nose is too large for my narrow face, but my salmon-colored lips are shaped perfectly. It's a shame they don't get any action.

I've never been satisfied with how I look—even when I was younger, I was self-conscious of my appearance. Now that I'm older, those insecurities are more profound than ever. I see girls at Chuckles or around town and long for their thin bodies, their golden skin, their silky hair, and their flawless complexions, hopelessly wishing that maybe someday, I could be like them. I could be a pretty girl too.

"I hate you," I tell my reflection.

Then I dry my hands on a towel and leave the bathroom to join my family for dinner, not once looking back.

* * *

"GRACE, HAVE YOU SEEN THE CHEERIOS?" Jamie walks into the bathroom, where I'm applying a subtle pink eyeshadow to my eyelids. "They're not in the cereal cabinet."

"Did you check the pantry?"

"Yes."

"Then we must be out. Sorry, kiddo. Guess you'll have to eat something else."

"Can you make me a bagel?"

"Make it yourself. I'm busy."

Jamie scowls. "Fine. I'll have stupid Special K."

He walks away in a huff while I move onto my eyebrows. If

I had more time, I'd pluck them, but Mrs. Jackson will be here in ten minutes, and I still haven't eaten breakfast. So, after filling them in with a light-brown pencil, I join Jamie in the kitchen.

"I'll text Mom to pick up Cheerios on her way home," I say. "Sound good?"

"Uh-huh."

"What's going on?" I pour myself a small bowl of Rice Krispies, add a splash of milk, and sit down beside him. "You're not usually this quiet."

"Just some stuff at school. It's no big deal."

"Well, let me know if I can help. I know how tricky eighth grade can be with schoolwork and friendships and—"

"I said it's no big deal," he interrupts.

"Okay. Jeez, I'm sorry."

"Whatever." He plays with his cereal, but doesn't attempt to eat it, which really bothers me for some reason.

"Aren't you hungry?"

He shakes his head. "I'm gonna get dressed. I wanna look good for picture day."

"You shouldn't waste food."

"It's just cereal, Grace. You don't need to get all butthurt."

"Jamie—" I sigh. "Never mind. I'm not really hungry either."

School crawls by at a snail's pace. I check my email four times throughout the morning—once while I'm waiting for American Literature to begin, twice during my free period, and once more at lunch.

Lou snatches my phone from me. "Stop it. You're gonna drive yourself crazy."

"Have you ever wanted something so badly, you'd do anything for it?" I ask.

Lou considers this. "Florida's Key Lime Pie," she says finally.

"I'd walk to Miami on foot just to have another slice—that's how ah-mazing it is."

"Great analogy," I respond sarcastically.

"Oh, come on. It's no better than obsessing over a silly sport."

"I want to play professionally," I say, "and coaches look at your high school profile. That shit matters to them."

"If you say so."

I hold out my hand, and she reluctantly returns my phone. "I do."

Lou stuffs a fistful of Smartfood popcorn in her mouth. As she's chewing, she says, "I wish I was as motivated as you, Grace. It's actually pretty annoying sometimes."

"How come?"

"Because you're so damn good at everything you do. But me? I can't even paint a bowl of fruit without fucking it up."

"Well, I wish I had your confidence," I respond. "Being friends with someone who always has their shit together can be annoying too."

"It's all about mentality. If you think happy thoughts, then acting happy is easy. The same goes for any emotion—excitement, sadness, anger."

"Fear," I say.

"Yeah. You don't want people thinking you're a pussy."

"Like you on roller coasters?"

Lou scowls. "It's perfectly normal to be scared of roller coasters. I bet if you polled the school, at least fifty percent would agree with me."

"Wanna bet?"

"Are you seriously gonna send out one of those stupid surveys?"

"Zack Ackerman?"

"This guy in my band class. He says clarinets are girly instruments."

"Ignore him. He's probably just jealous that you're better than he is."

"He does suck," Jamie agrees. "So, what are you gonna make for dinner?"

"I was thinking about tofu steaks," I say. "I know we don't usually have them, but tonight I'm celebrating."

"Celebrating what?"

"Making Varsity."

Jamie gives me a high five. "Awesome. I knew you'd do it."

"Thanks, kiddo. Do you have homework?"

"Just some science vocab. It shouldn't take long."

"Get started on that," I say, "and I'll be down in a couple minutes to start dinner. You can help with the salad."

Jamie wrinkles his nose. "I hate vegetables."

"You won't when they make you big and strong."

"Vegetables can do that?"

"Definitely. They're loaded with tons of important nutrients. I'm sure you'll learn all about it in health."

"Apparently I'll be learning a lot of stuff in health this year," he says. "This kid Matteo, who's repeating eighth grade, said the videos we watch are, like, lowkey pornos."

"Is that bad?"

"It is when your teacher reminds you of Grandma."

"You have Ms. Clermont?" When he nods, I say, "I remember her. If it makes you feel better, I bet everyone else will be super weirded out too."

"Well, it can't be badder than gym."

"Worse."

"Huh?"

"It's worse," I clarify. "Not badder."

"You are literally turning into Mom," he says.

I shove him playfully. "Say that again, and you're dead."

Jamie laughs. "Can you make oven fries with the tofu? Mom made some for me the other day, and they were good!"

"Yeah, sure. I probably won't want any, but I can make them for you."

"Cool. Thanks."

He leaves my room, closing the door behind him. I wait until he's gone to swap my jeans and blouse with pajama pants and a UConn sweatshirt. I'm still smiling as I skip downstairs to prepare tonight's celebratory dinner.

If this is what it feels like to be on top of the world, I think, *I never want to come down.*

4

I've always been an anxious person. Mom says it runs in our family; that her father, my grandad, would have panic attacks when he was younger. After Dad left, I also began suffering from intense anxiety. It became so bad that Mom took me to a psychiatrist, who prescribed Prozac, then Zoloft when Prozac didn't work, then Lexapro when Zoloft was unsuccessful as well. And those are the ones I remember.

As the years passed and I became better at repressing my memories of Dad, I was gradually taken off the medication. But that doesn't mean I no longer have anxiety. On some days, it's easy to ignore, while on other days, it's more evident, but regardless it's always there, like an obnoxious mosquito that keeps nipping at my skin no matter how many times I swat it away.

Walking on the field for my first practice with Varsity induces the most profound anxiety I've felt in a while. My teammates are huddled together by the net, quietly conversing with each other.

"Hi, guys," I say.

One of the girls—a petite brunette named Katie—offers me a polite smile while the rest briefly glance my way before continuing their conversation.

"Did you see that shirt Mr. Starr was wearing today?" Tessa asks. "Goddamn."

"I know, right?" Laurie agrees. "He's, like, so swole."

Tessa nods. "Totally."

"Who's Mr. Starr?" I ask.

"Only the hottest sub ever," Kaya responds. "How have you not heard of him?"

"I don't know. I guess I've just never had him."

"You're a senior, right?"

"Junior."

Kaya arches an eyebrow. "And they let you on the team? That's surprising."

I can't tell if she's complimenting or mocking me, so I don't respond. Kaya takes this as a sign that we're done talking, because she averts her attention to an image on McKenna's phone.

"Holy shit. Is that a six-pack?"

"Sure is."

"Do you think if I followed him he'd follow me back?" Caroline asks. "Because if he did, that would be ah-mazing."

"Desperate much?" Laurie jokes, and everyone erupts in laughter. Well, everyone except me.

"All right, enough chitchat." Coach Cooper joins us at the net with a bag of soccer balls and a stack of orange cones. "For those of you who weren't on the team last year, welcome to Varsity. I hope you trained hard over the summer, because this is going to be an intense season. We're up against some tough competitors, so I expect to see one-hundred-and-ten percent from every one of you. Got it?"

"Yes, Coach," my teammates and I respond.

"Great. While I set up our first drill, Laurie will lead you in two laps around the field—and stick together. We are a team, after all."

Following his instructions, my teammates and I trail behind Laurie as she sets the pace for our first lap. We've been jogging for no more than ten seconds when they resume their conversation about Mr. Starr's shirtless Instagram pictures. As much as I want to contribute—no, as much as I want to belong—words fail me. I simply cannot understand why teenage girls fantasize about men who are twice their age. It's just weird.

After we've completed our laps, we transition to drills. Coach Cooper keeps us busy with cone dribbling, one-touch passing, two-v-two, and wind sprints until the final five minutes, when we breathlessly gather around him so he can hand out our schedules.

"These are the dates of our games. Let me know ahead of time if you can't make it. Also, if you'd like to sharpen your skills, a friend of mine is running a workshop this weekend. I'll email you the details later. See you tomorrow!"

Mumbling "goodbyes" and "thanks, coaches," we trudge off the field to collect our belongings from the locker room. Fifteen minutes later, as I wait with Mom in a lengthy lineup of parents and students eager to leave Chuckles, I open Instagram and type S-T-A-R-R into the search bar. I wish I knew his first name, but I hadn't had the opportunity to ask my teammates.

"You're awfully quiet," Mom observes. "Was practice okay?"

"Uh-huh," I respond without looking up. Michael Starr, Joseph Starr, and Burt Starr are all too old to be contenders, not to mention that one lives in Utah and the other two in New York.

"Do you like your teammates?"

"Uh-huh."

"Grace, put that thing away. I'm trying to talk to you."

"I'm tired, Mom," I say. "I don't feel like talking right now, so just please respect that."

"Okay, I'm sorry."

"Whatever. It's fine." To avoid any awkward silence, I turn on the radio, and The Wallflower's *One Headlight* blasts through the speakers.

"I was in medical school when this song came out, studying to be an oncologist—believe it or not." Mom chuckles. "I thought if I applied myself enough, I could cure cancer. That dream died a long time ago."

Matthew; that's Mr. Starr's first name. I've seen him around school, talking to Mr. Chadwick in the library. It's true that he's an attractive man—and also taken, made known by the heart emoji beside someone named Jordyn Brown.

I snort. "Idiots."

"What was that?"

"Nothing. Just thinking out loud."

"Okay." She raises the volume on the radio and begins to sing along to *One Headlight*, unaware that she's painfully off-key.

I sigh. Dad had a much better voice.

Thanks to a three-car accident on Chestnut Street, we don't get home until a quarter to six.

"Are you hungry?" Mom asks. "The pizza won't be ready for thirty minutes, so if you are, you should have something now."

"Actually, I think I'm gonna lie down," I say. "I'm not feeling so well."

"What's wrong?"

"Cramps," I lie. "I guess it's that time of the month."

"There's a heating pad in my closet if you need it," Mom says.

"I'll leave a couple slices in the microwave for when you're feeling better."

"Thanks."

Gripping my abdomen dramatically, I limp upstairs and close my door. I hear Jamie watching a video through the wall connecting our rooms. If I listen closely, I'm able to catch certain words; "igneous," "sedimentary," "metamorphic," "crystallization." He must have begun his rock unit in science.

I should probably do my homework too, I think. I pick up *Macbeth*, my first assigned reading for American Lit, skim through a couple paragraphs, then set it back down beside my factoring worksheet. *Nah, I'll do it tomorrow.*

So, after changing out of my sweaty soccer clothes, I crawl into bed and wrap my covers around me. With the lyrics to *One Headlight* still looping through my head, I close my eyes and drift into oblivion.

"GRACE! WAKE UP!"

When I raise my head from my pillow, I'm blinded by sunlight seeping through my curtains. I blink twice, and Jamie's face fades into focus. "What time is it?"

"Seven-fifteen."

"You're kidding." I glance at my clock and, to my dismay, he's right. "Fuck! Why didn't Mom wake me?"

"She's been gone since six," he responds. "I guess she assumed you set your alarm."

"Well, the button's broken. I told her that two days ago." I throw off my covers and hurry to my dresser, where I grab a pair of grey skinny jeans and a black long-sleeved shirt with a sizable hole near the collar. "Jamie, get out. I need to change."

"Okay. Are you gonna have breakfast with me?"

"Don't have time." I yank the shirt over my head and wiggle into the pants. I'm too rushed to brush my hair, so I settle for a messy bun. "Cheerios are in the pantry by the way. First shelf, next to the pasta."

He trails behind me as I run downstairs, narrowly avoiding tripping on our wobbly second-to-last step. "Are you feeling better?"

"Huh?"

"Mom said you had a stomach ache, and that's why you couldn't eat dinner with us."

"Oh, yeah. I'm fine." Through the kitchen window, I watch Mrs. Jackson's Pathfinder pull up beside our house. "My ride's here. See ya."

"Bye."

I shove on my sneakers, grab my bookbag, and sprint down our driveway. With every step, my bulky algebra textbook thumps against my back. Of course Mr. Lipschitz would be the only teacher adamant on making us bring it to and from school.

"You all right?" Lou asks when I breathlessly slide in beside her.

"Yeah. Just had a little trouble getting up."

"You're not the only one," Mrs. Jackson says. "Some days, it's nearly impossible to get Lulu out of bed."

"Ma, you know I hate it when you call me that."

"And you know I hate it when you miss breakfast," Mrs. Jackson responds. "It's the most important meal of the day, after all."

As if on cue, my stomach lets out an angry growl.

"Speaking of missing breakfast," Lou jokes. "Girl, you really are a mess. And what's with the outfit? Are you going goth on me or something?"

"Can it, Lou," I snap. "I'm not in the mood."

Lou's dark eyes grow wide with surprise. "Sorry. I was just kidding."

"No, it's not your fault." I sigh. "I'm just really tired and—"

"You don't have to explain," she interrupts. "If I had your life, I'd be tired too."

A second sigh escapes my lips. "Tell me about it."

When we arrive at school, she heads to the H-Wing for AP Government while I walk to A104 for American Literature. Mrs. Perkenson is absent today, and filling in for her is an elderly female substitute. She distributes vocabulary worksheets and warns us that she will impose detentions if she hears talking.

Thankfully, my class would rather exchange notes than words. Scraps of paper travel around the room while she flips through *The New Yorker* at Mrs. P's desk, unaware of the comments about her see-through blouse that are spreading faster than influenza in the winter.

I finish the worksheet with ten minutes to spare and spend the remainder of the period listening to music. My next two classes, AP European History and Spanish, are also strangely low-pressure. After Señora Martinez has wrapped up her lesson on *conjugación de verbo*, I walk downstairs to the gymnasium for physical education. It's my first gym class of the year, as the notorious College Prep assembly occupied both Monday and Thursday of last week, and I'm not looking forward to it.

The locker room, as usual, is not a pleasant sight. Reeking of perfume and sweat and crowded with twenty half-naked girls, I feel overwhelmed simply entering. In the third aisle, several lockers away from mine, Bianca Santos and her equally pompous friends Jess Bishops and Tiffany Frasier gossip and giggle amongst themselves.

While I rummage through my bookbag for the lock I

purchased this weekend, I steal occasional glances at them. All three wear push-up bras and lacey thongs that leave little to the imagination—not that they have anything to be ashamed of. Their legs are toned and golden, and their washboard abs are to die for.

"You checking us out?" Bianca taunts.

I quickly avert my gaze. "No."

"Oh, she totally was," Jess says. "Who knew you and Lou had so much in common?" Another high-pitched giggle escapes her ruby lips.

Bianca elbows Jess, silencing her. "And I thought you only had eyes for my boyfriend."

"Liam's your boyfriend?" I ask.

Bianca answers my question with a disclosing smirk. "C'mon, girls. Leave the freak." As she and her clique flaunt by me, she whispers, "You're too ugly to be his type, so back off. There's no point wanting what you'll never have."

I try to think of something clever to say in response, but when words fail me, I grab my gym clothes and retreat to the bathroom stall. Tears pool in my eyes.

Don't cry, don't cry, don't cry, don't cry.

I close my eyes and inhale deeply. Once my anxiety has subsided, I change into my shorts, but as I'm adjusting the waistband, I bang my knee into the toilet paper dispenser. "Fuck!" I exclaim. "Dammit!"

I'm beginning to wish I hadn't gotten out of bed this morning.

The locker room is empty when I reemerge from the stall; everyone else must already be in the gymnasium with Coach Berger. Just as I'm about to join them, I hear him exclaim, "Settle down, students. For our first unit, we'll be—hey, you in the back! I said settle down!"

I sigh. Great. On top of everything else, now I'm going to be late.

I take another deep breath, then briskly leave the locker room in my shorts and untied sneakers. My mind is spinning with a thousand thoughts as I navigate through the empty halls to the library, so I can relax until the period ends.

But when the bell rings half an hour later, I remain seated. I don't want to go to lunch either; I want to stay here, where the "no food or drink" rule prevents me from gorging on the sesame bagel with cream cheese I packed last night. I want to prove to Bianca, to myself, to *everyone* that I'm not ugly or weak or undesirable.

But after skipping dinner and then being in too much of a rush to eat breakfast, my stomach is already upset with me. Not even The Counting Crows can silence its noisy complaints as I toss my untouched lunch into the trashcan on my way to chemistry.

When I enter the classroom, Lou is seated in the back with her feet propped up on the desk we share. She's so captivated by whatever mindless game she's playing on her phone, that she doesn't notice me approaching her.

"Hey. Can you move your stuff?"

She shoves her binder into her overflowing backpack, making room for me to slide in beside her. "Where were you? I didn't see you at lunch."

"I was studying. Sorry."

"No worries. So, what were you studying for?"

"Math," I respond, which isn't a total lie. Mr. Lipschitz did hint at a pop quiz on Monday.

"I don't know what's worse; math or Mr. Dipshit," she gripes. "You're so lucky you made Varsity."

"Yeah, I'm the luckiest girl in the world."

Lou shoots me a strange look. "Grace, are you—"

"Phone's away, students!" Ms. Lloyd, our overly-enthusiastic teacher, claps her hands twice to catch our attention. "Today we'll be beginning our unit on atomic structure. Can anyone explain what an atom is? Yes, Eli?"

While Eli Doherty responds to Ms. Lloyd's question, I stare out the nearest window, where three girls are sharing a box of Cocoa Puffs beneath an oak tree. I watch as one of them—a full-figured blonde—snickers at a remark her friend makes. Forget math and science; the subject Chuckles' girls genuinely excel at is the art of spreading rumors.

Lou nudges me. "Hey, wanna be partners?"

"What for?"

"This." She waves a worksheet titled *Unit 2: Basic Atomic Structure* in my face. "Weren't you listening?"

"Sorry," I apologize. "I don't know what's going on with me today."

"You sure it's just today?" She laughs at her own joke. "JK. We've all had shitty mornings. I mean, you heard my mom. I'm, like, the queen of lethargy."

"Yeah. So, what are we supposed to be doing?"

"Filling in the table, I think. It says we need a textbook. I'll go ask Ms. Lloyd for one."

"Okay." I wait until she's out of earshot to yawn loudly.

"Very attractive," Matt, who's sitting with Eli at the desk to our left, says sarcastically.

I roll my eyes. "Whatever."

Ninety miserable minutes later, I return home to an empty house, where the silence is more intimidating than relaxing. The cloudy sky casts shadows against the kitchen walls. They dance to the rhythm of the wind, which despite rustling the browning leaves, is no louder than a whisper.

I find a bag of Red Delicious apples in the refrigerator and divide one into eight slivers with a knife. Its blade glistens in the dim lighting as I run my fingers along the cutting edge.

"Use me," it seems to say.

The knife slips through my hands and clatters against the floor. Tiny beads of blood appear on the tips of my index and middle finger. The flashbacks are strong—dizzying; holding the aqua sea glass against my wrist, biting my lip to stifle my scream. Press, drag, repeat. Press, drag, repeat.

"It's Mrs. Anderson's cat, Mom. She's got really sharp claws."

Once the kitchen stops spinning, I rinse blood off the knife and place it in the dishwasher, then hurry upstairs before I'm tempted to act on another impulse. I'm partially through Shmooping the second chapter of *Macbeth* when I realize that in my haste to leave, I'd forgotten about my apple.

I leave my computer on sleep mode and drag myself back to the kitchen. But unbeknownst to me, Jamie has returned home from school and is sitting at the table with his nose buried in *Harry Potter and the Prisoner of Azkaban*. He dips an apple sliver into a jar of peanut butter and pops it in his mouth.

"I thought you had band practice," I say.

Jamie shakes his head. "Cancelled. The teacher was sick. What about soccer?"

"Cancelled too. It's supposed to rain."

"Oh. I think I felt a couple drops when I got off the bus."

"Do you mind if I have one?" I point at the apples.

"Sure." He holds out the plate, and I select a slice. "Do you want peanut butter?"

I shake my head. "No, thanks. So, how was school?"

"Okay, I guess."

"Did you see the Rice Krispy Treat I put in your lunchbox?"

"Yeah, but I didn't get to eat it. Zack Ackerman stole it while I was in the bathroom."

"This Zack Ackerman seems like a real dick."

"It doesn't make sense," Jamie says. "Why is he mean to me if I didn't do anything to him?"

You're too ugly to be his type.

"Because bullies are insecure," I respond, "so treating others like crap makes them feel better about themselves."

"Are you bullied, Grace?"

There's no point wanting what you'll never have.

Clearing my throat uncomfortably, I say, "I should finish my homework. But, Jamie?"

"Yeah?"

"The next time Zack tries to push you around, give him a piece of your mind. You have a voice for a reason. Use it."

"I will, Gracie."

"Grace," I correct. "It's just Grace."

Back upstairs, I boot up my computer to finish analyzing Shakespeare's antiquated writing. I've just begun chapter three when an Instagram notification pops onto my lockscreen. *Liam Fisher has sent you a follower request,* it says.

I open Instagram and click on Liam's profile. His account isn't locked, so I'm able to access his posts without having to follow him back. His photos, most of which were taken in Florida, date back a little over three years; eating ice cream with a couple shirtless guys, waiting in line for *The Forbidden Journey* at Universal Studios, hiking through Blackwater River State Forest, and posing by a surf shop with his younger sister on National Siblings Day to name a few.

He's posted two pictures since he returned to Connecticut. The first, from three weeks ago, is of him standing in front of his house. *My home away from home,* the caption reads. He posted the second earlier this week. In it, he's wearing his football uniform—sweaty and grinning, as his team had won their first game of the season—and his arm is wrapped around Bianca's waist. If I look closely, I can see her fuchsia underwear peeking out from beneath her fitted cheerleader uniform.

Even worse than the photo itself is his caption; *you make me smile #bae #couplegoals*

So, Bianca wasn't lying to make me jealous; they really are an item. Jealousy bubbles up inside me like molten lava rising within an active volcano. I want to scream, and I want to cry, and I want to call Liam right now and tell him that he's making a terrible mistake by dating a bitter bitch like Bianca.

But I don't. Instead, I sit down at my desk and take Mr. Lipschitz's factoring worksheet out of my homework folder with the hope that the challenging problems will distract me. Yet no matter how hard I focus, not even the brutal quadratic formula can abate my maddening thoughts. They're still there, getting louder every minute.

5

"So, do you think I should go with strapless or halter top?" Tessa asks. She passes the ball to Kaya, who passes it to me. "I know Jason likes strapless, but I'm only a 34A, and I don't want to have a nip-slip at HOCO."

"Go with the halter top then," Kaya responds. "It's so not cool when girls are always adjusting their boobs."

"True. What about the color though? I can't decide between blue or purple."

"He's a jock, right?" I ask.

"Uh-huh."

"Wear the purple one. He'll appreciate the school spirit."

Kaya rolls her eyes. "That's dumb."

"Sorry," I mumble. "I'm just trying to help."

"I think I'll go with blue," Tessa says. "It matches my eyes."

"Pick up the pace, girls!" Coach Cooper barks. "If you're not talking about soccer, your lips shouldn't be moving."

"Okay, Coach," Kaya responds. She waits until he's out of

earshot to say to Tessa, "Send me a Snap later. I bet it looks hella hot on you."

Tessa grins. "I hope Jason thinks so too."

"At least you have a date. I'm still waiting for Kyle to ask me."

"Ask him," I suggest.

Kaya laughs, as if I've made a joke. "That's the stupidest idea I've heard all day."

I'm about to respond when Coach Cooper blows his whistle. "Bring it in!"

"Think he's gonna give us the lineup?" Tessa asks.

"He'd better," Kaya responds. "Like, I'm almost positive I'm a starter, but it'd be nice to get some confirmation, you know?"

I cannot help but envy Kaya's confidence. I know I deserve a spot on Friday's lineup too. After all, I'm one of the most dedicated people on the team; I show up on time, I always remember my gear, and I work my ass off even on the days when I'm physically spent.

Whether or not he knows it, however, is a different story.

Sure enough, once we've gathered around him, he takes a loose-leaf paper out of the pocket of his sweats and unfolds it. "Here's the starting lineup for Friday. Listen for your name."

I cross my fingers behind my back. *Please be me, please me be, please be me.*

"Laurie and Amara, you're strikers. Katie and Emma are center-mids with Eileen on the right and Tessa on the left."

Please be me, please be me.

"For defense, I have McKenna as stopper, Kaya as sweeper, and Ashley and Syd covering the sides. Nikki, you're goalie. As for the rest of you," he turns to the five of us who weren't included, "this isn't a definitive list. Changes will be made if I feel they're necessary. Understand?"

"Yes, Coach," we mumble dejectedly.

"Great. We don't have practice tomorrow, so I expect to see you here Friday at four sharp for warmups. Get some rest, eat a good dinner, and hydrate hydrate hydrate! It's gonna be a hot one."

While my teammates are gathering their belongings, I approach him. "Uh, Coach? Can I talk to you for a sec?"

"Sure, Grace. What is it?"

"I was just, uh, wondering when I'd be able to play. I think if you gave me a chance, I'd—"

"Grace, as much as I appreciate your enthusiasm," he interrupts, "you're still our youngest and least experienced player. This isn't JV anymore. We do things differently on Varsity."

"I know, but—"

"I'm sorry, Grace. I've made my decision." Offering me an apologetic nod, he grabs his ballbag and heads towards the parking lot, calling over his shoulder, "Have a good night!"

"What was that about?" Mom asks when I join her in the car a few minutes later.

"Nothing," I lie. "Can we just go? I'm tired."

"Radio on or off?"

"On."

While she hums along to Alanis Morissette's *You Oughta Know*, I gaze out my window at the luxurious ranch-style houses we're driving by. They remind me of my old home in California —my real home. Our next-door neighbors had a daughter my age, who I'd often hang out with. We'd run through sprinklers in our matching tankinis and devour kumquats from the tree in her backyard and walk through our neighborhood, pretending we were collecting money for charity so we could buy Choco Tacos from Otto the Ice Cream Truck man. Her name was Jenna. She was my first best friend.

I can only image how different my life would be if we hadn't moved to Connecticut. I would have grown up with Jenna, not Lou. Jamie and I would be private school kids at Connelly Academy dressed in ugly plaid uniforms like the rest of our homogenous peers. We'd probably have had to move to another neighborhood, since Mom made less money than my father did, but at least we'd still be surrounded by palm trees and warm ocean breeze rather than dying oaks and bone-chilling wind.

But Connecticut was Mom's way to escape the memories of Dad, so that's where we wound up, less than thirty minutes away from her own childhood home. It was the first time she'd returned since she graduated high school and moved across the country to study pre-med at UCLA.

She met my father when she was a sophomore, and they casually dated for four years until she discovered she was pregnant with me. From that point on, it was goodbye oncology and hello baby preparations. Dad never left her side. He attended parenting classes with her and, due to his wealthy upbringing, was able to afford a nice house in a nice neighborhood where I ran through sprinklers with Jenna and ate Choco Tacos until my stomach ached. They never officially got married, which turned out to be a good thing in the years to come.

"Separation" is a much nicer word than "divorce" is.

THE NERVOUS ENERGY coursing through my teammates' blood, specifically the eleven lucky starters, is palpable as Laurie leads us in a warmup jog for our game against the Angels from St. Bronwyn Convent. For a school comprised of preppy Catholic girls, they appear surprisingly tough. They're bigger than we are anyway—more muscular too. I bet they eat a lot of carbs.

"Huddle up!" Coach Cooper calls once we've finished our

second lap. "I have a few pointers before we start. Firstly, the Angels are strong and fast, therefore you need to execute the defensive positions we practiced last week. Stance is everything. If you move, the ref will call a foul.

"Also, I want you to hold onto the ball when you receive it. Don't pass immediately. Show me you know how to dribble—especially you three." He turns towards Katie, Tessa, and Eileen, our midfielders, and asks, "Can you do that?"

"Yes, Coach," they respond.

"Excellent. Now, let's get out there and show 'em what we got! Laurie, lead us in a chant."

Laurie extends her arm with her palm face-down into the middle of the circle. She waits until we've reciprocated to say, "Woodpeckers on three. One . . . two . . . three . . ."

"Woodpeckers!"

The starters jog onto the field while the rest of us squeeze beside each other on the bench. It's a warm day—seventy-nine degrees, according to my phone—with no breeze and the blistering sun beating down overhead. As Laurie and Amara approach the center line for kick-off, Laurie wipes sweat off the back of her neck. She mouths, "It's so fucking hot."

Maybe they'll get overheated, I think, *and will have to sub out*. I know it's not a kind thought, but I'm too frustrated with Coach Cooper and his biased lineup to care. How am I going to become a better player if I'm not even given a chance to prove my worth?

However, despite the intense heat, the starters persist through the entire game, breaking only at half-time to chug their beverages. The Vitamin Water Mom packed me remains untouched in my backpack. I don't see the point of drinking it when the likelihood of me burning off the calories is nil.

We end up beating the Angels 1-0 with Katie scoring the

winning goal in the final two minutes. After we've shaken hands with them, she limps off the field and collapses beneath the shade of a sycamore tree.

"Nice goal," I say.

Katie downs the last sip of her Gatorade and wipes her upper lip. "Thanks. It was really a team effort."

I'm about to argue otherwise when my phone buzzes with a text from Mom.

Mom: something came up. is there anyone u can get a ride from?

"Uh, Katie?"

"Yeah?"

"I know it's last minute, but my mom's busy and—"

"You need a ride," she finishes. "No problem. My car's this way."

"You drive?"

Katie nods. "I've had my license for a year. How 'bout you?"

"I got my permit a couple months ago, but I haven't taken lessons yet. I'll probably take a class over the summer."

"Good luck. They're a pain in the ass."

"Were you on Varsity last year?" I ask as she unlocks a navy sedan.

Katie shakes her head. "I tried out, but I didn't make it. Juniors usually don't."

"Yeah, I've heard."

"Just wait until next year. Everything will be better then."

"Next year," I repeat. "Right."

Minus several isolated remarks about the weather and a muttered "asshole" at the expense of a speeding SUV, Katie and I talk very little as Siri directs her to my house. Once we've arrived, she says, "I'll see you Monday."

"See ya."

While she drives away, I head up my driveway and unlock the

door. Mom is sitting at the table wearing her formal work outfit and grey Under Armour socks.

"Hello, Grace," she greets me flatly.

I can tell by the tone of her voice that something is wrong. "H—hi, Mom."

"How was the game?"

"Fine. We won."

"Congratulations. Sit down, I want to talk to you." She waits until I'm seated in the chair across from her to proceed. "Jamie's principal called me this afternoon. He was in a fight."

"Oh my God. Is he all right?"

"He will be. He'd hurt his lip, so I had to take him to the ER for stiches. That's why I couldn't pick you up."

"How—how'd it happen?"

"A couple boys were picking on him at recess. Apparently, he said something that pissed them off, and as a result, they beat him up. When we were driving home from the ER, I asked him why he didn't go to a teacher for help, and do you know what he said?"

I shake my head.

"He said 'Grace told me to give them a piece of my mind.'"

The gum I'm chewing lodges in my throat. "Mom, I didn't mean—"

"His doctor says he can't play the clarinet for at least two weeks," she interrupts. "That damn instrument is his passion, Grace! It's the only reason he tolerates school."

"I'm so sorry," I apologize. "I was just trying to help."

Mom sighs. "Next time, try thinking before you speak. You're a smart girl, but sometimes you can be so damn thick-headed."

"Can I talk to him? You know, tell him how sorry I am?"

"He's sleeping now," she responds. "You'll see him in the morning."

"Oh, okay."

"There are leftovers in the fridge if you're hungry. I was planning on making enchiladas but . . . you know." Sighing once more, she walks out of the kitchen without another word, leaving me alone with vicious thoughts invading my mind.

You're a horrible sister, they tell me. *You're stupid and ugly and fat and a horrible person who doesn't deserve to be happy after what you did.*

My body is trembling as I rummage through the disorganized drawers for a knife. I eventually find one nestled with a pile of chopsticks that none of us are patient enough to master the technique of. I hold it in my hand, waiting for the moment to pass, for my thoughts to subside.

But they don't.

Do it! Do it, you worthless piece of shit!

Unable to resist anymore, I squeeze my eyes shut and press the blade against my wrist until it punctures my soft skin. Blood trickles down my arm, spilling onto the ivory countertop in small crimson blotches. I bite my lip to stifle the shriek rising in my throat.

"It's okay, it's okay, it's okay, it's okay."

I fumble for a dishtowel to clean the counter. I'm still shaking, though my emotions have dulled significantly. Gone is the sadness, the indignation—even the shame is nonexistent as I rinse blood off the blade of the knife. Instead, I'm just . . . numb.

I'd forgotten what a wonderful feeling it is to feel nothing at all.

I GROGGILY RISE the next morning after a meager four hours of sleep, most of which was dominated by vivid nightmares. The sunlight seeping through my curtains blinds me as I rub my eyes.

"Saturday," I mumble. "Thank God."

In the bathroom, I stand in front of the mirror and mindlessly rub my toothbrush around the same tooth for five minutes. My arm throbs horribly, but I wait until I've rinsed and spat to take a peek. I'd foolishly forgotten to cover my cut with a Band-Aid before I fell asleep, so bits of fleece from my blanket adhere to its raw surface. I methodically remove them with a tweezer and apply bacitracin while questions I'd neglected to consider yesterday race through my mind;

What if someone notices?
What if it gets infected?
Will I have to wear an undershirt with my soccer uniform?
Or long sleeves in gym class?
Does this mean I have to go back to changing in a stall?
What if I want to do it again?

I pull on a grey turtleneck and tell myself not to worry, that everything is going to be okay. But no matter how hard I try, I can't ignore a nagging thought in the back of my mind that taunts, *Oh, you silly girl. This is just the beginning.*

I jog over to Lou's at ten o'clock after scarfing down half a cup of low-fat vanilla yogurt. Her house is unusually quiet for Saturday morning. Usually, Mr. Jackson would be sitting at the table reading the newspaper while his wife flipped pancakes at the stove and simultaneously yelled at Lou to "get your lazy butt out of bed!"

"Where are your parents?" I ask Lou. She's lounging on the sofa watching *The Simpsons* in a pink sweatshirt and pizza-patterned pajama bottoms.

"CTC. Pa took Ma for her weekly checkup."

"And you didn't go with them?"

Lou shakes her head. "I don't like hospitals. Everybody there is so sick and sad, and it's just a lot, you know?"

Even though I don't, I nod. "Totally."

"You want something to eat?" she asks. "We've got a fuckton of leftovers in the fridge."

"No, thanks. I already had breakfast."

"Suit yourself. *I'm* craving some General Tso's Chicken."

"It's ten o'clock in the morning," I say.

"So? It's dinnertime in China."

I roll my eyes. "You're so weird."

"Oh, quit judging me, At least I actually eat normal food."

"What's that supposed to mean?"

"Seriously?" When I shrug, she says, "Grace, I haven't seen you eat anything other than salad all week. Don't tell me you're still obsessing over Liam and his anorexic girlfriend of the month."

"Not everything is about Bianca," I insist. "I haven't been hungry—that's all."

"Well, I'm gonna heat up my amazing chicken because I'm hungry as fuck. You wanna watch TV?"

"Not if all that's on is cartoons."

"Well, there is the news, but that's hella depressing. I know; let's play a game!"

"Do you still have *Life*?"

"I think so. You'll have to check the storage room." She grimaces. "Apologies in advance."

The Jackson's storage room, which I've bravely ventured into twice before, remarkably makes their basement seem tame. From an outdated boombox to a busted boogie board to a rack of fur jackets, junk is everywhere. After some thorough rummaging around, I finally find the game buried beneath a box of busted Barbie Dolls and set it up at the kitchen table while Lou is preparing her "breakfast."

Honoring Chuckle's eighty-nine-percent college attendance rate, we both opt for college. One turn later, Lou becomes a doctor with a ninety-thousand-dollar salary while I'm forced to settle for an artist with fifty thousand. But my misfortune doesn't end there. I get in a ski accident, lose my stock card, buy an unreasonably expensive lakeside cabin, and have my Deals on Wheels Realty struck by a tornado because I forgot to purchase insurance.

By the end of the game, Lou is a multi-millionaire with three stocks and the Nobel Peace Prize under her belt. I'm a mother of four who's changed careers twice and is ten thousand dollars short of five hundred thousand.

Lou beams. "Good game."

"You're just saying that 'cause you won."

"Oh, don't be a sore loser. Life isn't only about winning."

"Yes, it is."

"Whatever you say, Miss Competitive," she responds, nudging me playfully. "So, what do you wanna do now?"

"Go to the bathroom," I say. "Like, badly."

"The flusher's busted down here. Use the one in my parents' room."

"Okay."

While she continues gloating over her victory, I make my way upstairs and into Mr. and Mrs. Jackson's bedroom. Their bathroom is located to the left of their master bed next to a window that overlooks their massive backyard. They must have renovated it recently, because it's more modern than the rest of their house. Even the toilet is oddly contemporary.

As I'm relieving myself, I notice a scale tucked beneath the sink. The rational part of my brain urges me to walk away; to rejoin my unsuspecting friend downstairs and challenge her to a rematch of *Life*. But another part of my brain—the part that feeds off temptation—coerces me to strip down to my underwear and drag the scale to the center of the bathroom, where the tiles provide an even surface. I hold my breath, anxiously watching as the numbers steadily rise.

They stop.

I stare at my weight for a minute or two, trying to decide how I feel about it. I've done enough research to know about BMI and the numbers and percentages that determine whether you're over, under, or somewhere in the middle, like I am.

But being average doesn't dismiss the insecurities I have when I look in the mirror or compare my body to the idealistic physiques of girls like Jess and Bianca. If wanting to be skinny is a crime, why does the media glamorize women who look like they haven't eaten in weeks? It's not people who are fucked up; it's society. Because accepting yourself is really damn hard to do when you're constantly being reminded that you aren't good enough.

"Well, that took a while," Lou remarks when I return to the kitchen. "I'm telling you; it's that vegetarian crap you eat. Really clogs you up."

If the circumstances had been different, I'd immediately rebut her claim with the scientifically proven fact that beef is harder to digest than soy. But since I'm not in the mood to argue, I say, "I'm not feeling so good. I think I'm gonna go home and take a nap."

"You sure you don't just wanna crash in my bed?"

I shake my head. "I'll pass. Jamie's probably wondering where I am anyway."

"How's the little nugget doing?"

"He's okay," I lie. "He hates school, but then again, who doesn't?"

"I don't."

"Well, aren't you lucky?" I respond sarcastically. "I'll text you later, okay?"

"Uh-huh." Lou glances out the window, where threatening thunderclouds loom in the grey sky. "You sure you can't stay longer? It looks like it's gonna rain."

"That's what warm showers are for," I say.

"Well, just don't get a cold, okay? You know I can't have you over if you're sick. At least not until Mom's WBC is stable."

"I'll be fine," I assure her. "I always am."

When I return home eight minutes later—soaking wet, as Lou had forewarned—Jamie is sitting at the table eating a bowl of cereal. Just looking at him, at what Zack and his asshole friends have done to his beautiful face, brings tears to my eyes.

"Oh, Jamie. I'm so sorry."

"It's okay," he says. "It doesn't even hurt that much anymore."

"This is all my fault. I shouldn't have given you that stupid advice." I gently touch the purplish bruise encircling his right eye. "They really did a number on you, didn't they?"

He sighs shakily. "Grace, I can't go back to school. I'm so scared."

"It'll be okay. I heard Mom on the phone with your principal this morning. She's trying to get them expelled."

"Really?"

I nod. "She's not gonna let anyone hurt you again, Jamie. Neither am I."

"I love you, Grace."

"Love you too, kiddo," I say, playfully tousling his messy hair. "So, what did you tell Zack to make him so angry?"

I laugh. "I don't know. It might not be that bad."

"Hopefully, I won't have to find out. Are you gonna eat that?" She points at the chocolate chip energy bar Mom slipped in my bookbag this morning when she saw how tired I was.

"Go ahead," I say. "It's all yours."

While she heads to painting, I trudge downstairs to the girls' locker room fueled by a salad and Honest Kids juice pouch and lock myself inside the stall to change. Some idiot has left a used maxi pad in the toilet, so even after I've flushed twice, the stench remains.

Plugging my nose, I swap my jeans and sweater with a long-sleeve shirt and lycra leggings, adjusting the sleeves so they cover the two new cuts on my wrist. Then I flush the toilet once more and join my classmates outside to begin our fall sports unit.

Coach Berger has us run a lap around the track, and afterwards we gather by the football field to play flag football. He hands out yellow pinnies, then goes over the simple rules in so much detail that by the time he's finished explaining them, there's only twenty minutes left of class.

"Play safe! Don't hurt each other!"

But his last words fall on deaf ears, as barely one minute later, Matt Durham headbutts Tommy Kershaw as he lunges for his flag. Tommy dramatically collapses onto the turf, crying out in pain.

"My nose! I think it's broken!"

Coach Berger rushes to his side. "It's not broken," he assures Tommy, "but if you'd like to go to the Nurse's Office for ice, you can."

"O—okay, Coach." Tommy hobbles off the fields, intentionally elbowing Matt in the gut when he passes him. "You're gonna pay," I hear him threaten under his breath.

"Oh, don't be such a pussy," Matt responds.

Bianca, Jess, and Tiffany, who are huddled between the fortieth and fiftieth yard line, are also quietly conversing with each other.

I hope they're not talking about me," I think. I adjust my shirt so it covers my bottom and the uppermost part of my gross thighs. I knew I should have stuck with sweats.

"All right, students! Let's take two!"

Coach Berger blows his whistle, and the game resumes. By the time we return to our respective locker rooms—injury free, thankfully—I'm one of three people to still have their flag. I smile. It may be only a meaningless gym game, but I still really like to win.

I arrive at chemistry two minutes late after waiting in a line of fidgety girls to use the stall. Ms. Lloyd is in the process of reviewing test etiquette when I hurry through the door.

"Sorry," I say. "I was in the bathroom."

She sighs. "Take your seat. We're just about to begin."

I slide in beside Lou, who's reviewing her flashcards for the hundredth time. "Ready?"

"I think so. How was gym?"

"Okay. I won flag football."

"Sweet. Are you more awake now?"

I nod. "It's brisk out there, so that helped."

"Maybe if you had a little more meat on your bones, you wouldn't be so cold." She pinches my stomach, laughing when I swat her hand away. "Just saying."

"Settle down, students," Ms. Lloyd orders. "I'm passing around the tests, so I expect no talking until the end of the period."

She hands me my test, and I glance at the first question:

Which of the following particles has the least mass?
a. neutron
b. proton
c. electron
d. hydrogen nucleus

I remember reading about this in the textbook last week, however no matter how hard I rack my brain, I cannot recall the correct answer. A sudden wave of anxiety overcomes me. *What am I going to do?* I wonder. *I can't fail.*

My eyes travel to Lou's paper. She's circling her answers with a bright pink pen, so if I squint, I can easily see them. But I'm not a cheater, so I avert my gaze to my own quiz and uncertainly circle letter B. Protons are light . . . right?

Right. With a sigh, I move onto the next question.

All atoms of an element have the same . . .?
a. number of neutrons
b. atomic mass
c. atomic number
d. mass number

Fuck, I'm so screwed.

"Time's up!" Ms. Lloyd calls a minute before the period ends. "Pass your papers forward. I'll have them in PowerSchool by tomorrow."

"That wasn't so bad," Lou says. "For once, studying actually paid off."

"Uh-huh."

"How do you think you did?"

"Me? I, uh . . ." I laugh nervously. "Pretty awful, to be honest."

"Oh, give me a break. I can't remember the last time you did bad on a test."

"I flunked my math test," I say. "Fifty-four percent—well, fifty-eight with the curve."

Lou cringes. "Yikes. You gonna retake it?"

"Fifth period tomorrow, so I probably won't eat with you."

"It's cool," she says. "I mean, it's not like this is the first time you've ditched me at lunch."

"Lou—"

"Forget it, Grace." She shoves her binder and spiral notebook into her backpack and stands up as the bell rings. "Good luck on your quiz."

"Thanks," I mumble. "I'm gonna need it."

MY EYES ARE CLOSED; my body is still. The shrill *beep beep beep* of the Jackson's scale is stifled by the running faucet I left on when I washed my hands. The likelihood of Lou hearing me from her TV room is slim, but I'm not about to take any chances.

I hear her voice in my head asking, *"Since when do you give a damn about how you look?"*

Everyone, to some extent, has body insecurities. For years, I've listened to Lou complain about how big her breasts are or the fact that her thighs are too curvy to squeeze into "skinny sizes." I've listened, and I've sympathized, and I've thanked her when she'd compliment my body even though I was—and still am—very dissatisfied with it.

Once I've mentally recorded my new and improved weight, I slide the scale under the sink and head downstairs to rejoin Lou.

"You know, the bathroom down here is working fine," she says.

"Well, uh, I like your parents' more. It's . . . cleaner." While I talk, I pace behind the couch she's lounging on. The television is muted on TNT, as we'd just finished watching a *Supernatural* episode.

"You calling me dirty?" she asks.

"Not unless we're talking about your mouth."

"Fuck you."

"See! And anyway, it's a personal preference. Don't worry."

"I'm not worried," she assures me. "I'm too excited to be worried."

"Why are you excited?"

Lou turns around to shoot me an incredulous look. "It's October first, which means Halloween is only a month away. Grace, this year's gonna be so lit! Cassie's friend Sam is hosting a costume party, and she said we can come!"

"Do you know what you're going to be?" I ask.

Lou nods. "Cass and I are going as Taystee and Alex from *Orange is the New Black*. You can be Piper, since you're blonde and thin."

"You think I'm thin?"

"Please tell me you're not talking about that ridiculous show again," Mrs. Jackson interjects, having overheard our conversation from the kitchen. "I can't believe your friend's mother lets her watch such obscenity."

"Oh, give me a break, Ma. Those crime shows you and Pa go crazy for are just as graphic."

"It's different."

"Yeah, 'cause guns are *so* much better than butts," Lou responds sarcastically. Lowering her voice, she says to me, "You're lucky your mom isn't a total prude."

"Does she still think Cassie is just your friend?" I ask.

Lou shakes her head. "She knows she isn't. She just doesn't want to admit it."

"That sucks."

"It could be worse. This lady who goes to our church sent her son to a conversion therapy camp when she caught him making out with an altar boy. Talk about fucked up!"

"Totally."

"I'll never understand why some people think different means less than," she continues. "The world would be a hella boring place if we were all the same."

"People are idiots," I say. "Just look at ninety-five percent of our classmates."

"No kidding. Are those girls on your soccer team still treating you like shit?"

"Not as much as they used to. They've started calling me by my real name instead of 'newbie,' so I guess that's progress."

"And Bianca?"

"Bianca's still Bianca," I say. "I don't get it. She's, like, the meanest girl I've ever met, yet for some reason, everyone seems to adore her."

"It's because she's a player. I don't know what's more fake; her tits or her personality."

"I dunno. That's a tough call."

"I hope I'm not interrupting." Mrs. Jackson bustles into the room with a plate of freshly-baked chocolate chip cookies in her hands. She sets it down on the coffee table. "Enjoy, girls."

"Thanks, Ma!" Lou snatches a cookie off the plate and crams half of it in her mouth. As she's chewing, she says, "Mmm. These are so good. Grace, you gotta have one."

"Oh, uh—"

"And sit down, for God's sake. All this pacing is stressing me out."

So, I take a seat beside her and stare at the cookies with my arms frozen at my sides. If there's one thing I know about Mrs. Jackson, it's that she loves food. She even has a sign above the kitchen sink quoting Julia Child's declaration, "With enough butter, anything is good." Just imagining the sinful ingredients she used to make them taste so scrumptious unleashes a swarm of butterflies in my stomach.

"Yo, Grace?" Lou snaps her fingers to catch my attention. "You all right?"

"What? Yeah." Then ignoring the thoughts that urge me otherwise, I grab the smallest cookie and take a bite. "Yum."

"I know, right? I'm on my second one!"

"Your mom's a good cook," I say. "Think she could give me the recipe sometime?"

"Why? I thought you hated baking."

"Yeah, but I've been watching a lot of the Food Network lately, and that got me thinking that maybe it'd be fun to learn some stuff."

"I love the Food Network!" she exclaims enthusiastically. "*Chopped* is my favorite."

"Mine too. So, do you think you could ask her to send me the recipe?"

"Sure. I'll have her text it to your mom later."

"If she could just text it to me, that'd be better."

Lou shrugs. "All right."

"Thanks."

I'm halfway through my cookie when Lou announces that she needs to use the bathroom, so I wait until she's gone to slip the remaining half in my pocket. My thoughts applaud me. My stomach condemns me. I feel kind of badly knowing Mrs. Jackson worked hard to make them, but numbers don't lie; not with the calories, nor with the scale. Giving into temptation now when I'm doing so well resisting it would be foolish—and I can't be foolish. I have to be smart. I have to be in control.

When Lou returns from the bathroom, I'm curled into a ball beneath her gramma's quilt, softly crying into the threadbare fabric. She sits beside me and holds my hand, rubbing her thumb over my clammy skin.

"I'm sorry," I whisper.

"You don't have to apologize," she responds. "Grace, don't take this the wrong way, but are you, like, depressed?"

"I—I don't think so."

"Well, is something else going on? Are you PMSing?"

"Maybe. I'm a little late."

"How late?"

"Uh . . . four days, I think."

"Oh, then that's probably it. But, Grace?"

"Yeah?"

"You'd let me know if something was wrong, right? Like, if you actually were depressed?"

"Of course."

"Good. Because everybody knows that secrets screw up friendships." After a brief pause, filled solely by the sound of my sniffles, she asks, "Do you want another cookie? Cookies always make everything better."

As much as I'm tempted by her offer, I shake my head. "No, thanks. I'm not hungry."

7

"I'm stuck, Mom."

Mom glances up from the counter, where she's dicing vegetables for tonight's salad, and nods in agreement. "I've noticed. You do seem to have fallen into a rut lately."

"What? No, I'm not talking about that. It's these stupid pants." I gesture to the jeans she bought me at Marshalls the other day. After soccer practice while she began preparing dinner, I tried them on, and now I can't wrangle my left foot out of the tiny leg hole. "They're too tight."

"Do you need help?"

I try again, and when I still don't succeed, collapse onto the floor. "I hate this. I'm so fat!"

"Grace, of course you're not fat. You just have large feet. Here, let me help." She grabs hold of the jeans with both her hands and pulls until they uncomfortably slide off. "I'm sorry they don't work. They seemed awfully cute on the rack."

A tear slips down my cheek. "Well, they weren't cute on me."

"Oh, Grace. There's no need to cry over clothing."

"I know, I'm sorry." I use the sleeve of my sweatshirt to dry my eyes. "I'm just really tired."

"Hopefully dinner will make you feel better. Once I've dressed the salad, we'll eat."

"Did you buy more tomato soup?"

She shakes her head. "I didn't have time to go food shopping, so I made soy nuggets instead."

"But I want soup," I say.

"I'm sorry, Grace. I don't have soup."

"Why not?"

"Because I'm busy, and plus, you've had soup every night for the past week. A change of pace will be good for you."

I roll my eyes. "Fine, but I'm only having two nuggets."

"Three," she says, "and corn and salad."

"Three and salad," I negotiate. "No corn."

"Okay. Three and salad—but you'd better take enough."

"Don't worry, Mom. I love vegetables."

So, after I've changed into sweats, and Jamie's finished his clarinet practice, the three of us sit down at the table to begin eating. While Mom and Jamie chat about their days, I take small bites of my nuggets and wipe olive oil off the lettuce with my napkin until it's covered in yellow stains.

Mom frowns. "Grace, what are you doing?"

"It tastes better this way," I respond. "It's not that I don't like your dressing, but it's a little too vinegary."

"You sure it doesn't have to do with the oil?"

I pretend I don't hear her. "I ate my nuggets."

She smiles weakly. "Thank you for being flexible."

"Yeah, no problem. Can you pick up the soup tomorrow?"

"I'll add it to my shopping list."

Once dinner ends, I head upstairs to finish a literary analysis on *Macbeth*. I'm halfway through the third body paragraph when my phone vibrates. I check the Caller ID and, sure enough, Lou's name flashes across the screen.

Buzz . . . buzz . . . buzz . . .

With a sigh, I turn off the ringer and continue typing my analysis. I know without even reading it that it's trash, but I'm too exhausted to care. I just want to have a rough draft ready for tomorrow so I can go to bed.

I've transitioned to the conclusion when a Gmail notification pops into the lower left corner of my screen. *Email from Ned Cooper* it says in a tiny print. Expecting another reminder CC'd to the entire team about tomorrow's game, I unenthusiastically click on it. That's when I realize that his message was sent exclusively to me.

He writes; *Hi, Grace. We'll be short a couple girls tomorrow, so I was hoping you'd be open to playing left D in Syd's place. Let me know when you get this. – Coach*

I respond immediately: *Of course, I'd love to play. Thank you so much. – Grace*

After clicking *Send*, I add a couple filler lines to my analysis to meet the minimum "four pages double-spaced requirement" and shut down my computer. The prospect of finally having a chance to prove my worth is so exciting, I feel like dancing or jumping for joy. But since I'm too tired to do either, I instead sit on my bed, close my eyes, and envision myself on the field; sprinting after the ball, defending opponents, delivering a flawless corner kick to help my team score the winning goal. It all seems so perfect, so opportunistic, and, with my bad luck and poor decision making, so easy to fuck up.

"It's great you're starting today," Mom says. She lowers the volume on the radio, where Cardi B's *Bodak Yellow* is blasting from the speakers, so I can hear her better. "You must be excited."

"And nervous," I respond. "What if I'm not good enough?"

"Oh, Grace. Don't be a pessimist."

"I'm serious, Mom. I don't want to be the reason we lose."

"One player isn't responsible for the outcome of a game. It's called a team sport for a reason."

"Yes, but—"

"Go out there, and give it your all," she interrupts. "You can't achieve if you don't believe."

"That's so corny," I say.

Mom chuckles. "I'm a mother. Corny is what we do best."

She pulls into the backlot of Northview Academy and parks her car beside a freshly-cut soccer field. I unbuckle my seatbelt, eager to join my team for pre-game warmups, when Mom grabs my arm. She hands me a lukewarm granola bar from the console.

"Uh . . . what's this?"

"You need fuel for your game," she explains, "and I didn't see you have a snack at home."

"Okay, I'll eat it later." I pocket the bar, then reach for my door handle. But Mom locks it.

"Not later, Grace. Now."

"Mom, come on," I protest. "I'm gonna be late."

"Then you'd better get started, because you're not going anywhere until you eat the bar."

I feel myself beginning to panic. "What? Why? This is so dumb."

Mom sighs. "Did you honestly think I wouldn't notice what you're doing, Grace? Your dinner last night was pathetic. I'm a forty-one-year-old woman, and I eat twice as much as you do."

"That's not true!"

"Regardless, you need to eat more. You're an athlete, for God's sake. You can't possibly have enough energy for a ninety-minute soccer game if you don't feed yourself properly."

In the rearview mirror, I watch as Laurie leads the team in aerobic stretches. This might be my only opportunity to prove to them and Coach Cooper that I deserve a permanent spot as a starter, and I won't let a damn bar stand in my way. I've worked too hard. I've sacrificed too much.

"Fine." Pulling the bar out of my pocket, I tear open the wrapper and choke it down in fifteen seconds. "Happy, Mom?"

"Yes. Here's your drink." She hands me a Vitamin Water, which I drop in my backpack, fully intending to dispose of it when I have the chance to. "Good luck."

"Whatever."

She unlocks the door, and I hurry onto the field. Laurie shoots me a disapproving look but is thankfully too busy leading the team in standing high-knees to comment on my tardiness. I position myself between Katie and Eileen and join them for the final seconds. Next, we split into two lines behind the out of bounds marker and side-shuffle to the opposite side and back.

We've just finished our second round when the referee blows his whistle. "Kick off's in five!"

"Huddle up!" Laurie orders. She waits until we've gathered around her to continue. "Okay, so the Wildcats are obviously a good team. They've won all their games, and they're, like, super big, so they'll definitely use their size to their advantage."

While she talks, I steal a glance at the Wildcats. They're finishing their warmup with walking lunges, their muscular quads bulging with every step they take. Maybe this was a bad idea. Maybe I shouldn't have agreed to play after all.

"But we're better," Laurie continues. "We're faster, more

decisive, and we have sharper ball-handling skills. So, let's go out there and kick those pussies' asses. What do you say?"

"Yeah!" the team, myself included, cheer.

"Woodpeckers on three. One . . . two . . . three—"

"Woodpeckers!"

I follow my teammates to our bench, where they grab a quick drink of their beverages before returning to the field. I take a sip of my Vitamin Water, then leave the cap slightly ajar and place it on the grass, so it will leak out while I'm playing.

Once everyone is in position, the referee flips a coin, and the Wildcats win. They choose to kick off the second half, meaning we're up first. Kaya shoots Laurie a nervous smile. In response, Laurie mouths, "Good luck."

But it'll take more than luck to defeat the Wildcats. Number Ten immediately intercepts Kaya's pass, and before either striker has a chance to react, passes to Number Sixteen, who winds up for a shot. Thankfully, Nikki blocks the ball and rolls it to me. I boot it towards Eileen, but my accuracy is off, and Number Five beats her to it. Dammit!

"Watch her!" Coach Cooper points at Number Sixteen. She's inching towards our net, very close to surpassing me altogether. When Number Five passes her the ball, I sprint forward and the referee blows his whistle.

"Offsides! Grey ball!"

Coach Cooper flashes me two thumbs up. "Good play, Grace."

But my satisfaction is short lived when once again, I'm unable to deliver a successful free kick. Number Seven intercepts the ball and passes it to Number Sixteen, who dribbles around Emma, then Laurie, then Kaya. I plant my feet and watch her advance closer . . . closer . . . closer . . . until the next thing I know, I'm lying on the ground in a dazed shock with sharp pains shooting through my ribs.

Coach Cooper rushes onto the field. He grabs my arm, demanding to know if I'm okay. I want to tell him, *No, I'm not okay. I'm exhausted because I can't sleep or eat, and I feel like my ribs were just crushed by a monster truck.* But instead, I nod weakly.

"Atta, girl," he says. "Think you can keep playing?"

"Uh-huh."

Both teams and their fans politely applaud as Coach Cooper helps me stand up. Brushing grass off my knees, I place the ball where Number Sixteen collided with me, and when the referee blows his whistle, boot it to Laurie. She passes to Kaya, who winds up for a shot. Goal.

"Way to go, Grace!" Nikki calls from the net.

And just like that, I'm back in the game.

3-2 US. That's the final score when my teammates and I limp off the field after the second overtime, tired and breathless but elated nevertheless. "Good game, good game." We shake hands with the Wildcats, who don't bother to hide their dissatisfaction.

As I'm packing up my belongings, Number Sixteen approaches me. "Listen, I'm, uh, sorry about what happened."

Her courtesy takes me by surprise. "Huh?"

"You know, in the first half? When we ran into each other? I hope I didn't hurt you."

"Oh, that." I chuckle. "Don't worry. It's nothing a little ice can't fix."

"Good." She rolls up the sleeve of her jacket, exposing a lumpy cast that I'd noticed when she was called off-sides. "I fell down the stairs a couple weeks ago and broke my radius. Too bad ice couldn't fix that."

I wince. "That sucks."

"No kidding. I'm Lana, by the way."

"Grace."

"Cool."

"Yeah." I stare at my cleats as an awkward silence develops between us. "So, uh . . . how long have you been playing?" I ask finally.

"Ten years. You?"

"Same. This is my first time on Varsity, so it's a lot more intense than JV."

"I know what you mean. Varsity's hardcore."

"No shit."

"Hey, Grace!" Katie calls. "Wanna go to Olive Garden with us?"

"I can't!" I respond. "My mom's making pizza!"

"Well, I should probably go," Lana says. "I'll see you around, Grace."

"We live on the opposite ends of town," I remind her.

"I know, but people have a funny way of reconnecting when they don't expect it. It's a small world."

I watch Lana walk away. She unlocks a black Subaru with her working arm and joins the lineup of drivers eager to leave the parking lot, blasting Eminem from her speakers while she waits.

I should have asked her for a ride, I think, since Mom had mentioned earlier that she wouldn't be able to pick me up. *Now, how am I going to get home?*

I ultimately decide to call an Uber, which arrives at Northview twelve minutes later. I've used Uber more than once, though this is the first time the driver is a man. I feel his eyes watching me in the mirror as I listlessly scroll through Instagram. I wonder what he's thinking about right now. I wonder if any of those thoughts have to do with touching me.

I ask him to drop me off at the end of my block instead of bringing me directly to my house. I pay him ten dollars, even though he only charges me eight, and thank him in a shaky voice.

He smiles politely. "Have a good evening."

Only when he's gone am I able to relax. I check the time on my phone—six-oh-seven—then insert my earbuds to listen to the new songs I downloaded the other day. With my music playing, I wander through my neighborhood until the sky becomes so dark, I can no longer see my ice-cold hands. Mom's car, which wasn't in the driveway when the Uber dropped me off, now is when I unlock the door.

"Grace!" she exclaims. "Where were you?"

"I was at Olive Garden with my team," I lie. "I meant to text you, but my phone died. Mom, we won. We're moving on to the semi-finals!"

"That's great, hon," she responds, and I can tell just by looking at her that although she wants to believe me, she's still skeptical. "Was Coach Cooper pleased with your performance?"

I nod. "He even got us cheesecake for dessert."

"He did?"

"Uh-huh. It was really good."

"I guess you forgot it was pizza night then."

"Oh, crap. Mom, it totally slipped my mind."

"Well, I'm glad you're bonding with your teammates. I know you'd struggled with that in the beginning."

"Uh-huh. So, our next game is on Saturday at two. Can you give me a ride?"

Mom frowns. "I'm sorry, hon. I have to be in the office."

"Oh. Okay."

"You know I'd come if I could," she continues. "I love seeing you play."

"It's fine. Your work is more important."

"That may be true, but it'll never be more important than you and Jamie. You know that, right?"

"Yeah." I hang my jacket in the kitchen closet and cross my arms, shivering despite the warmth of our house. "Do you mind if I take a shower? I'm super sweaty."

"As long as you're out in ten minutes. I'm trying to conserve the hot water."

"Ten minutes," I repeat. "Got it."

Upstairs, I select a pair of fleece pajamas and discard my sweaty uniform and underclothes in a pile on the bathroom floor. In the shower, I scrub dirt and sweat from my body and wash off my makeup with soap that stings my eyes.

For once, the tears trickling down my cheeks do not fall because I'm sad.

Ten minutes pass much quicker than I'd anticipated. I'm still shaving my calves when my timer dings, so I hurry up, accidentally nicking myself in the process. Once I'm dressed, I pile my damp hair into a bun and return to my room. I lie on my bed with a blanket wrapped around me and listen to music until my phone dies—for real, this time. So, I begin to hum instead.

At half-past nine, someone knocks on my door. "Come in!" I call.

"Hi, hon." Mom sits beside me, her slim-fit khakis cinching at the knees. "How are you?"

"Tired."

"You should be. You've had a busy day."

"Uh-huh." After a brief pause, I say, "I'm sorry about earlier, you know with the bar. Pre-game jitters really got to me."

"Are you sure that's all it was?"

"Yeah. Who knew high school sports would be so stressful?"

"Your coach does seem pretty intense," she says.

"He's okay," I assure her. "He just likes the sound of his voice too much."

"Well, he's not the only one. One of my patients today—a little, old lady who reminded me a lot of Mrs. Anderson—talked nonstop. She would have rambled on forever if I hadn't had someone else waiting."

"I miss Mrs. Anderson. I wonder how she's doing."

"She's well. The last time we talked, she said she was going to take her grandson to Disneyland for his sixth birthday."

"It's funny, I was thinking about Disney earlier too," I say.

"Yeah?"

"Uh-huh. For some reason, I can't get *It's a Small World* out of my head."

"That was your favorite ride. Your father and I took you on it so many times, I was sure that damn jingle would eventually drive me crazy. But it never did."

"Do you ever miss Dad?" I ask.

Mom considers this. "I miss the sound of his voice. When he sang you to bed, I swear it was like listening to a choir of angels."

"*Sweet Child O' Mine*," I say.

She smiles wistfully. "Yes. He loved Guns N' Roses."

"Do you think he's happy, wherever he is?"

"I don't know, Grace. Part of me wishes he wasn't but . . ." She sighs.

"But what?"

"But your father was a good man. He believed all people were created equal. He provided for this family in ways I never could. He loved you and Jamie so, so much. And it's for those reasons that I'm not angry anymore."

"I'm still angry," I say.

"I know." Mom gently massages my shoulders. In the reflection of my window, I see her eyes sadden as her fingers caress my protruding scapula. "I can only hope that one day, you won't be."

"Yeah. Me too."

She kisses my forehead, then rises to her feet. "Goodnight, Grace. I'll see you tomorrow."

"Are you gonna be here in the morning?"

"Yes. Do you want me to wake you up? You've had a hard time getting out of bed lately."

"If you don't mind."

"Of course not. How does six sound?"

"Six-thirty," I negotiate.

"Okay, six-thirty it is. I'll see you then."

"Could you turn off the lights?"

"Of course."

She leaves my room, shutting my door behind her. Encompassed by darkness, I close my eyes and will myself to fall asleep; to succumb to fatigue, not thoughts; to count sheep, not calories; to focus on this moment, rather than worrying about tomorrow.

One hour later, however, I'm still wide awake. I sigh. It's going to be a long night.

8

"Grace, it's six-thirty. You've gotta get up."

When I open my eyes, Mom is kneeling beside me. I notice that she's wearing a darker shade of eyeshadow than usual. Perhaps if I was more awake, I'd tell her point-blank that the color isn't remotely compatible with her pale complexion. But since I'm still groggy as hell, I say nothing.

Mom gently nudges my shoulder. "C'mon, you're going to be late."

"I'm coming, calm down," I mumble.

While she walks away, I force myself out of bed and rummage through my dresser. I pull on a long-sleeved under-shirt, a black sweater, and a fleece jacket over grey jeans, then pile my hair into a ponytail, ignoring the few loose strands that float to the floor, and rub concealer around my eyes to disguise the otherwise conspicuous bags.

"Grace!" Mom calls. "If you want a ride, you'd better be ready in five minutes!"

"One second!" I add two strokes of mascara to my lashes,

then slide the makeup into a drawer and hurry downstairs. Mom is waiting by the door. "Sorry. I lost track of time."

"It happens to the best of us," she responds.

"Yeah. So, should we go?"

Mom frowns. "Aren't you forgetting something?"

"Uh . . . I don't think so."

"Starts with a 'b.' It's the most important meal of the day."

"It's fine, Mom," I say. "I'll—I'll buy something in the cafeteria."

"I'd rather you eat in the car." She rummages through the snack cabinet, setting aside an energy bar and a bottle of juice. "I know you prefer cranberry, but we're all out, so I hope apple's okay."

"Mom, that's not nec—"

"Grace, I don't have time for games," Mom interrupts. "Take the damn food, and let's hit the road, all right?"

Too tired to argue, I reluctantly toss my makeshift breakfast into my bookbag and follow Mom outside. As she drives me to school, I take small sips of the apple juice and try not to gag at the sickeningly-sweet taste. It's a good thing I remembered to pack my peppermint gum.

Ten minutes later, Mom pulls into Chuckle's parking lot. She waits until I've finished the juice to unlock my door. "Have a good day, hon."

"Whatever."

I watch her join the lineup of parents, noshing on a sesame bagel with cream cheese while she checks her phone. Once I'm certain she's not looking, I toss my bar in a nearby trashcan and join the mob of students surging through the entrance.

As usual, the morning crawls by with each class seeming even longer than the one before. Lou texts me during third period to ask if I can help her study for a quiz at lunch. *Np*, I respond while I'm waiting for Señora Martinez to begin her lesson on written communication. *see u then.*

"*Hola, estudiantes,*" Señora Martinez greets us. "*Saque un trozo de papel y un utensilio de escritura para que podamos comenzar nuestra lección. ¿Bueno?*"

I sigh. When I thought today couldn't get any more confusing, it just did.

Forty tiresome minutes later, the bell finally rings, and I drag myself downstairs for gym. As I'm maneuvering through the crowded locker room, I bump into Bianca as she's changing into a hot pink Adidas top. She scowls.

"Watch it, freak."

"Sorry," I mumble. Grabbing my gym clothes—head-to-toe sweats and sneakers—I retreat to the stall. I hear her talking about me with Jess and Tiffany as I lean against the door to catch my breath.

"What a loser," Jess says. "I can't believe she's still after your boyfriend."

"I know, right?" Bianca agrees. "I see her eye-fucking him every day in the hall."

"I heard they used to be best friends," Tiffany says.

"I don't see why anyone would want to be friends with her," Bianca responds. "She's just so . . . weird."

"Tif, you forgot to close your locker again," Jess says. "People steal, you know."

"Whoopsie." Tiffany giggles. "I can be so forgetful."

"Well, you are blonde."

"There are plenty of smart blondes," Tiffany insists. "Like . . . like Hillary Clinton."

"Hillary Clinton?" Jess repeats. "You mean the woman who lost the election to that disgusting orange shithead? That Hillary Clinton?"

"It's not her fault the Electric College sucks."

"It's 'Electoral,' Tif."

"Yeah . . . isn't that what I said?"

I wait until they're gone, as is everyone else, to reemerge from the stall. In the gymnasium, I hear Coach Berger blow his whistle once, then again seconds later when my classmates continue to talk. I know I should join them, but I'm too paralyzed with anxiety and too overwhelmed by the cruel thoughts about how disgusting my body looks in the filthy mirror above the sink to move. I need something to make them shut up; I need something to stop this madness.

I rummage through my pockets for that "something," but all I find is my new Student ID, which Mademoiselle Rousseau handed out yesterday in advisory. I barely recognize the face of the girl plastered above the six-digit barcode. She seems so content, so hopeful, so . . . what's the opposite of weird?

Normal.

I use my teeth to tear my ID into uneven halves and hold the larger of the two against my wrist. The jagged edges aren't as sharp as a knife or razor, so it takes several tries to produce a thin line of blood. I'm about to make a second incision when I hear someone gasp. Bianca stands behind me with her hand over her mouth, her dark eyes wide with horror.

"Oh my God, Grace! What the—what are you doing?"

I hastily adjust my sleeve to hide the cut. "Nothing. Mind your own business."

"Grace, if you're hurting yourself—"

"I'm not!" I insist. "Just go away, Bianca!"

"But—"

"Go the fuck away!"

"O—okay."

She stumbles out of the locker room while I sink to the floor and clutch my burning face in my hands. I'm so humiliated, so ashamed of myself for acting on such a desperate impulse, that I wish I could just disappear completely.

I remain seated for another few minutes. The gentle breeze drifting through a semi-ajar window sends a chill racing down my spine. Even though it's abnormally warm for the middle of October, I'm freezing cold. I always am.

I leave my gym clothes by the sink and slowly, painfully, stand up. My legs are trembling as I head to the library, where I weave through shelves of nonfiction books until I've reached the "Quiet Learning" corner. I collapse onto the tattered red couch and close my eyes. In seconds, I'm asleep.

I'm woken up an hour later to Mr. Chadwick shaking my shoulders. "C'mon, Grace. The bell's about to ring."

I shy away from him. "Don't touch me."

"My apologies. I'd just hate for you to be late to class. You already slept through lunch."

"I won't." I set the pillow aside and rise to my feet too quickly. Mr. Chadwick's bushy brows furrow as I lean against the arm of the couch to regain my balance. "I'm tired," I explain. "I didn't sleep well last night."

"Well, you seem to have made up for it this period," he jokes.

I force my lips into a small smile. "Yeah. See ya tomorrow, Mr. C."

"See you, Grace."

My dizziness lingers as I drag myself to math. Lou is standing outside the classroom with her arms folded across her chest, evidently upset.

"I guess you forgot about me," she says. "Or perhaps you had better things to do."

"Lou, I'm so sorry," I apologize. "It totally slipped my mind."

"That seems to be happening a lot, doesn't it?"

"What does?"

"You avoiding me. Lately, you've been all 'I'm too busy with soccer to hang out' and 'I can't eat lunch with you 'cause I have to study.'"

"I do."

"Bullshit! You always study the night of."

"Lou—"

"I'm worried about you," she continues. "It's bad enough that you've blown me off for weeks, but this whole eating thing is starting to scare me. I mean, when was the last time you had a proper meal?"

"Uh, this morning. I eat plenty."

"Sure you do," she says sarcastically. "Face it, Grace; you're a mess. You need to get your shit together before something bad happens."

"Nothing bad is going to happen!"

"It will if you don't stop treating yourself like total crap."

"I'm fine!" I exclaim, causing passing students to momentarily glance our way. Lowering my voice, I add, "So leave me the fuck alone, Lou."

Lou's lips part in surprise. It isn't often when I lash out at her. "Sorry if I'm just trying to be a good friend," she says bitterly. "Christ, Grace. You're always so fucking full of yourself." Shaking her head, she turns around and promptly takes off down the hall.

"Lou, don't . . ." I begin to say, though by then she's already gone. I sigh. "Go."

I trudge into the math classroom and claim my usual seat in the back. Mr. Lipschitz waits until the chatter has died down to announce that we're having a pop quiz. Whereas everyone else groans, I remain quiet. I keep hearing Lou's voice in my head; *Sorry if I'm just trying to be a good friend.*

Lou isn't just a good friend; she's a great one. Without her, I wouldn't have been able to cope with Dad's absence, or tolerate Mom's flings, or get over my childhood crush on Liam, or manage my anxiety and insecurities, both of which have steadily worsened as the years progressed.

But despite the many obstacles she's helped me overcome, this is one I need to conquer on my own. She wouldn't understand. No one would.

Mr. Lipschitz has just finished passing around our quizzes when his phone rings. "Hello? This is Hubert speaking . . . Yes, she's here . . . Yes, I'll send her down right away." He hangs up, then turns to me and says, "Grace? That was Miss Dixon. She wants you to go to Guidance."

"Now?" I ask weakly.

"Yep. Here's your pass." He hands me a slip of paper with his messy signature scribbled at the bottom. "Take your stuff too. She didn't say how long you'd be there for."

So, I hoist my bookbag over my shoulder and head to Guidance with butterflies in my stomach. While I wait, I open iMessage and click on my earlier conversation with Lou. I'm about to compose an apology text when Mrs. Hawkins, the administrative assistant, says Miss Dixon is ready to see me.

"Hello, Grace. Please, sit down." Miss Dixon offers me a kind smile as I cautiously take a seat across from her tidy desk. I've met with her once before towards the end of my freshman year, but other than that brief encounter, we might as well be strangers.

"What's going on?" I ask. "Am I in trouble?"

"No, not at all." Miss Dixon adjusts a sparkly picture frame to the left of her desktop computer, where she and a handsome man are posing in front of the Lincoln Monument. Allegedly, she used to teach history before she became a guidance counselor.

"Then—then why am I here?" I hate how my voice trembles when I speak.

"A student stopped by earlier," Miss Dixon says. "They told me that you're hurting yourself."

I don't respond.

"Many adolescents self-harm," she continues. "It's not uncommon, however—"

"And it's also none of your business," I interrupt. "If I'm not being disruptive or bullying other people, then you can't punish me. It says so in the handbook."

"I'm not punishing you, Grace. I'm just trying to help."

"I don't need help!" I exclaim. "I'm fine. Why doesn't anyone understand that?"

Miss Dixon sighs. "I'm sorry, but when someone suggests that another student is at risk, I have to report it. While you were waiting, I was on the phone with your mother."

"My mother? Why?"

"I'd like her to come in, so the three of us can talk about this."

"There's no way I'm doing that," I say. "You can't make me."

"Would you prefer if I talked to her one-on-one?"

"No, I'd prefer if you didn't talk to her at all," I snap. "This isn't fair. You're violating my privacy!"

"I'm not," she responds calmly. "I'm just doing my job."

"Well, screw your job!" I jump to my feet, unintentionally bumping my knee into her desk and knocking over the picture. As I reach forward to fix it, my sleeve lifts enough to expose a glimpse of my lowermost cuts. Shit.

Miss Dixon's face remains devoid of emotion as she says, "You don't have to talk to me if you don't want to, but you should talk to someone. Our social workers are excellent. They'll help you sort out whatever it is that's making you hurt yourself."

I stare down at my moccasins, too ashamed to look her in the eye. "I don't know what's making me do it. That's the problem."

"Perhaps it's pressure. You have an ambitious schedule, and you're also on the Varsity soccer team. I imagine that's quite a commitment."

"I love soccer," I say. "Coach Cooper can be intense at times, but that's a good thing. I'll never get better if I'm not challenged."

"Do you see yourself pursuing soccer in the future?" she asks.

"Definitely. It's been my dream to play professionally since I was eight. Nothing's gonna stand in my way."

"Not even those?"

She points at my wrist, which I self-consciously tuck behind my back. "You people act like it's such a big deal, but it's really not. Everything is under control."

Before she has a chance to respond, there's a knock on her door. "Come in!" she calls.

Mom breathlessly enters Miss Dixon's office. Her crimson lipstick is slightly smudged in one corner. "Sorry I'm late. Traffic was hell."

"It's no problem, Kira. I was just talking with Grace about, uh, do you want to tell your mother what you told me, Grace?"

I gaze into Mom's hazel eyes, and in that moment, without either of us saying a word, I realize that she already knows what's going on. She's probably known it for weeks, but like me was too in denial, too convinced that things would work themselves out with time, to admit I had a problem.

But I'm done flirting with the flames, so I step into the fire and roll up my sleeves, exposing the secrets I've hidden from her and everyone else since that crucial day in the kitchen.

A soft sigh escapes her lips. "Oh, Grace."

"Please don't be angry," I whisper.

"I'm not angry, hon. I just . . . I just want to understand."

"You can't."

"Why not?"

I glance at Miss Dixon, who nods her head, prompting me to proceed. "Because I don't really understand it either."

Mom closes her eyes. "Grace, can you give us a moment?"

"Yeah, okay." Pulling down my sleeves, I hurriedly leave Miss Dixon's office. I sit in the chair beside her room, hoping to overhear their conversation, but a sound machine projecting an ocean atmosphere inhibits me from doing so.

Time moves at a snail's pace. The longer I wait, the more anxious I feel, so I find my earbuds where they're nestled in my pocket with the smaller half of my ID, insert them into my phone, and tune out my thoughts and worries with Thom Yorke's soothing falsetto.

Three Radiohead songs later, Miss Dixon's office reopens, and Mom steps out. She offers Miss Dixon a few parting words, then gestures for me to remove my buds, which I do.

"Do you know where the attendance office is?"

"I think it's next to the auditorium," I say. "Why? Are you leaving?"

"Yes, and you're coming with me."

"I am?" When she nods, I ask, "Where are we going?"

"The hospital," she responds matter-of-factly. "Grace, it's time to get you some help."

9

The last time I visited Connecticut Treatment Center's Emergency Room was in the seventh grade when I busted my chin open playing Rec Basketball. There's still a faint scar from the nine stitches Dr. Stewart sewed up the wound with. I was so proud of that scar; for weeks, I boasted about it to my classmates as if it was the coolest thing ever. Now, I just think it looks stupid.

The ER is much busier than I remember—noisier too. While Mom waits her turn to talk to the receptionist, I skim through September's *US Weekly* magazine and immerse myself in a story about the Kardashians' latest drama.

"Grace?" Mom, having reached the front of the line, beckons me to her side. "Can you tell Mr. Jenkins why you're here?"

The overweight man sitting behind the desk stares at me with his beady brown eyes. "I, uh . . ." I clear my throat uncomfortably. "I don't really know."

"Grace is cutting herself," Mom says. "Her guidance counselor and I are worried about her safety."

"What's Grace's date of birth?" Mr. Jenkins asks.

"She'll be seventeen on May 8th."

Mr. Jenkins types this into his computer. "Last name?"

"Edwards. E-D-W-A-R- D-S."

"Grace, hold out your arm."

I do, and he straps a paper admissions bracelet around my wrist, right beneath another glaring cut. When I look at Mom to see if she noticed, her eyes are averted to the floor.

"Straight through the door. A triage nurse will help you."

"Thank you."

Mr. Jenkins buzzes Mom and me into the ER, where sure enough, a slender brown-haired nurse is waiting for us. She's dressed in ugly lavender scrubs and carries a small notebook in her breast pocket.

"Hello, I'm Belle," she greets us. "You must be Mrs. Edwards."

"Ms. Sinclair," Mom corrects, "but you can call me Kira. This is my daughter, Grace."

Nurse Belle shakes Mom's hand. "Do you mind waiting here? I need to get Grace's height and weight."

"Of course not."

"Great. Come with me, Grace."

Uncertainty has my stomach twisted in knots as I struggle to keep up with Nurse Belle's quick pace. A digital scale is located to the left of the bathrooms, alongside a stadiometer. At five-foot-six, my pediatrician predicted at my last physical that I'll grow at least another inch or two before slowing down. I was not pleased.

When I was younger, I loved my height. I cherished my long legs and strong arms, attributing them to the reason I was an excellent athlete. But when puberty came, my body image took a turn for the worse. Being taller than my peers suddenly made me feel awkward and unattractive. I had neck pains from hunching over, and it was difficult to find age-appropriate shoes that fit my large feet, so I usually had to settle for women's sizes.

"Why can't I be small, like the other girls?" I once asked Mom.

"I used to wonder the same thing when I was your age," she responded. "But looking back on all the years I spent trying to be someone I wasn't, I realize I was wasting my time. There are some things in life you simply can't change."

"Grace? Did you hear me?" Nurse Belle's sharp voice snaps me back to reality.

"What?"

"I asked you if you could step on the scale. Backwards."

I follow her instructions, and she records my weight into her notebook. As she's pocketing her pencil, I quickly glance behind me at the number. A smile tugs at the corner of my lips. I'm down two pounds.

Once she's reset the scale, she invites Mom and me into a crammed room shielded by a sheer green curtain. While she wraps a blood pressure cuff around my upper left arm, she asks, "So, how come you're here today?"

"No idea."

"Grace, come on," Mom urges.

I sigh. "This girl at my school caught me cutting in the locker room, so she told my guidance counselor, and she and my mom decided I needed to be evaluated or something."

"What were you cutting with?"

"My Student ID."

"Wait, what?" Mom asks, but both the nurse and I ignore her.

"Is this the first time you've self-harmed?"

"No, I've done it before."

"More than once?"

"Uh-huh."

The BP machine beeps. Nurse Belle records the numbers displayed on the screen, then has me stick out my tongue so she can take my temperature. After she's jotted down that number as well, she pockets her notebook and pen.

"Come with me," she says.

Mom and I follow her through a crowded hall, navigating around fretful guardians, screaming children, and scrambling nurses who somehow manage to moderate the chaos.

"Where are we going?" I quietly ask Mom.

"I don't know," she responds. "I guess we'll find out."

Nurse Belle unlocks a metal door with her ID and ushers us into another unit. Unlike the central ER, the bleak corridors are quieter, aside from someone's intermittent screams. Patients lounge in stretchers, watching television or sleeping or talking with their families in hushed voices.

"Where am I?" I ask.

"The psychiatric unit," Nurse Belle responds.

"What?" I glance at Mom, waiting for her to object, and when she doesn't, my heart begins to race. "Why?"

"We'd like to monitor you for a little longer. This is Fiona." Nurse Belle gestures to a plump dark-haired woman, who nods politely. "She'll help you from here."

Nurse Fiona hands me a cloth gown and a pair of yellow socks with grippers on the bottom. "I need you to change into these. The bathroom is this way."

I stare down at the scant materials. "I don't understand. What's this for?"

"It's protocol," she responds. "All patients are required to wear them."

"But I'm not a patient," I protest. "Right, Mom?"

Mom refuses to look me in the eyes. "Just do as the nurse says, Grace. Please."

"But—but—"

Before I can finish, Nurse Fiona places her hands on my shoulders and guides me to a gender-neutral bathroom. She wedges her foot between the door while I reluctantly change into the gown and socks. Once I've finished, she stuffs my clothing and moccasins into a paper bag.

"Earrings too." I unfasten my faux-diamond studs, and she places them with the rest of my belongings. "We're in the process of transferring a patient, so until his room is available, you can wait with your mother."

"O—okay."

Mom is seated in a plastic chair outside of Room Nine. Her chipped fingernails tap against the arm as I sit beside her. "I don't belong here. If you take me home, I'll do whatever you want. I'll—I'll stop cutting and eat more, and everything will be fine."

"Grace, I—"

She's interrupted by someone's noisy ringtone. A man stands in the doorway of Room Ten as another nurse wheels a sleeping boy on a stretcher towards the exit, talking on his phone in a shaky voice.

"They're transferring him now . . . no, he's not resisting anymore . . . they sedated him, Mary . . ." The man chuckles at Mary's inaudible response. "Our son was always a biter . . . Listen, I gotta go. I'll call you soon . . . Bye."

Mom and I watch him frantically chase after the nurse. "Wow," she whispers. "That poor man."

"At least we might finally get a room," I say.

"Yeah." Her gaze returns to her lap. Since I've changed into my gown, she's blatantly avoided looking at my arms. I don't blame her. After hiding my cuts for weeks, even I'm somewhat alarmed by their naked visibility.

Ten minutes pass, followed by fifteen more. Around three o'clock, Nurse Fiona announces that Room Ten, as I'd predicted, is available. She stashes my clothing, along with my phone and Mom's car keys, into a locked cabinet while I settle onto a stretcher.

"We have games and coloring books if you need something to keep you entertained," she says. "It may be a while until the social worker can see you."

"Do you have *Scrabble*?" I ask.

"Let me check." She exits the room and returns thirty seconds later with the game tucked under her pudgy arm. "Here you go. Would you like anything to eat?"

I shake my head. "I'm good."

Mom frowns. "Grace, you should eat something. It's past your snack time."

"I'm really not in the mood right now, okay?"

"Grace, I'm just—"

"I said I'm not in the mood!" I reiterate. "Jesus Christ, Mom! Why do you always do this?"

"Do what?"

"Push me to do stuff I don't want to. I'm sixteen. I know how to feed myself."

Mom sighs. "Okay, okay. We're all set, Fiona."

Nurse Fiona nods. "Great. If you need anything else or have additional questions, I'll be in the hall."

"Thank you, Fiona." Mom nudges me.

"Thanks," I echo.

After we've set up the game on the end of my stretcher, we draw to see who starts, and Mom, who selects an E, wins. Her first word is S-K-I-N. Since it's on a double-word square, she receives sixteen points.

I jot this down on a scrap of paper with a green crayon. "Not bad."

"Your turn, Grace." She still seems flustered, though I can tell she's trying to hide it from me, so I pretend I don't notice.

The letters I have are M, D, Q, S, I, U, and N. If I go off Mom's N, I can spell M-O-U-N-D-S. "Like the candy bar," I explain.

"Ah, your favorite. Have you decided what you're going to be for Halloween this year?"

"Lou and Cassie are going as characters from *Orange is the New Black*. She wants me to match with them even though I haven't seen the show."

"That sounds fun."

"Yeah. Does Jamie need someone to take him?"

Mom nods. "I don't feel comfortable letting him trick-or-treat alone, and since he doesn't have friends to go with—"

"I'm his last resort," I finish. "That's cool. I don't mind."

"Well, he'll be happy to hear that."

"Does he know I'm here?" I ask.

"I left a message on his phone an hour ago, saying I was at the hospital and would be home as soon as I could. I also called Ms. Phelps and asked if she'd keep an eye on him in the meantime."

"Think we'll be home for dinner?"

Mom glances at her watch. "It's almost four o'clock. Hopefully, your social worker won't take much longer."

"Yeah. Wanna finish *Scrabble*?"

Mom nods. "Bring it on."

I remain ahead for most of the game until I run out of vowels. Mom's final move is Z-A; a two-letter abbreviation of "pizza." Place it on one triple-letter square, and you get thirty-one points. Pin it between another A in the same spot, and your score doubles to a staggering sixty-two.

"Dammit. That was close."

"Close but no cigar," she responds.

"What does that mean?"

Mom chuckles. "I have no idea. It's something my father used to say. He was a strange man."

"He's still alive, isn't he?"

"As far as I know," she responds with a sigh.

"It sucks not knowing stuff about your parents," I say. "I feel that way about Dad sometimes."

"Well, at least you still have little ol' me."

"Uh-huh. What time is it now?"

Mom checks her watch again. "Four forty-five."

"Where the hell is the social worker?" I wonder aloud. "Can you make her hurry up? I have to get at least eight hours of sleep if I'm gonna have energy for tomorrow's game."

"Honey, I can't control when she comes. You have to be patient."

"But—"

"Grace Edwards?" A petite Asian woman dressed in a fitted navy suit enters my room. "Hello, I'm Michelle Lee. I'm your social worker."

"It's nice to meet you, Michelle," Mom says. "I'm Kira Sinclair, Grace's mother."

Ms. Lee shakes Mom's hand. "Kira, I'd like to meet with Grace alone, and then I'll talk to you in the family waiting area."

"Sounds good." Mom places the board and tiles back in the *Scrabble* box, then plants a kiss on my cheek. "Talk to her, okay? Let her help you."

"Okay, Mom."

Once Mom is gone, Ms. Lee claims her vacant seat. "Why are you here, Grace?"

"My mom's worried about me," I respond. "This girl at school caught me cutting, and she told my GC, who called my mom, and they decided that I'm in crisis or something. But I think they're totally overreacting."

"How long have you been self-harming for?" Ms. Lee asks.

"A few weeks."

"Can you identify any triggers?"

"I dunno. I guess I didn't want to feel stuff."

"Like what?"

"Anxiety, mostly. High school's hard, and between sports and classwork and wanting to fit in but not knowing how, it was a lot. I just wanted it to go away."

"And that's when you started self-harming?"

"Yeah. Everything's so much easier when I'm numb."

"Are you currently experiencing urges to harm yourself?"

"No."

"How about urges to harm someone else?"

"What? No."

"Have you contemplated suicide over the past month?"

"I mean, it crosses my mind every now and then," I admit, "but it's not like I'm planning on actually doing anything. They're just thoughts."

"Can you describe these thoughts for me?"

"Uh, well, there are times when I think everything would be easier if I wasn't alive, and then—I think it was last week—I was getting an ibuprofen from my mom's bathroom and saw a bottle of sleeping pills. For a minute, I considered taking them."

"What made you stop?"

"I guess . . . I guess I decided it wasn't worth it. That, and I was afraid my brother would find me. I couldn't do that to Jamie."

Ms. Lee scribbles this into her notebook. "Have you experienced hallucinations or heard voices that weren't there?"

"No."

"Have you ever been physically assaulted or abused?"

"No."

"How about verbally?"

"No."

"Sexually?"

"No. Are we done yet?"

She chuckles. "Almost. Before we finish, I'd like to know if you feel that you're safe enough to go home."

"Yeah. Yeah, totally."

"Will you be able to resist urges to harm yourself?"

I hesitate a second too long. "Uh, I can try."

"Okay. Thank you for being honest." She closes her notebook, wedges the pen behind her ear, and rises to her feet. "I'm going to meet with your mom now."

"Then I can leave, right?"

"Our doctor will determine that. He'll stop by this evening, hopefully within the hour."

"Doctor?"

"Yes. He decides whether you're well enough to go home or if you require more care."

"I don't require more care."

"Well, I'm afraid that's not my call. It was nice meeting you, Grace."

"Uh-huh."

"Do you need anything before I go?"

"No, but can you turn off the light? I want to take a nap."

"Of course. Have a good rest."

My heart feels as heavy as a sack of bricks as I watch her leave, flicking off the switch on her way out. Surrounded by muddled conversations between the nurses and the occasional opening and closing of that impenetrable metal door, I close my eyes and drift into a restless sleep.

"GRACE? GRACE, CAN YOU HEAR ME?"

When I open my eyes, I'm momentarily blinded by bright lights. A short man wearing a white lab coat with *Michael Preston, MD* written in blue cursive beneath the collar hovers above me. A much taller woman in lavender scrubs stands beside him.

"Who are you?"

"Dr. Preston."

"Huh?"

"I'm your doctor. I'm going to talk to you about why you're here."

"Oh, yeah. Right." Forgetting I'm wearing makeup, I rub my eyes, vaguely annoyed when my knuckle returns covered in black smudges. "Where's my mom?"

"She left to check on your brother. She'll be back shortly."

"Be back? What time is it?"

"Six-thirty."

My jaw drops. "Are you serious? I thought I was gonna leave hours ago."

"It's a busy day," he responds matter-of-factly. "I did the best I could. So, why don't you tell me what's going on?"

"Didn't Ms. Lee already tell you that?"

"She did, however I'd like to hear it from you as well."

So, for the third time this afternoon, I recap my morning, starting with Bianca and ending when Mom and I left school to drive to CTC. Once I'm finished, he proceeds to drill me with the same procedural questions Ms. Lee had covered hours early.

Thankfully, Dr. Preston is more efficient. He concludes his evaluation within ten minutes, then says a few parting words and exits my room, leaving me alone with the tall nurse.

"Where's he going?" I ask. "He'll be back, right?"

The nurse shakes her head. "No, but he'll let one us know when he's made his decision. In the meantime, what would you like for dinner?"

"I'm not hungry."

"There has to be something you're willing to eat. At least take a look at our menu." She tries to hand me a laminated sheet of paper, but I stubbornly keep my arms crossed. "Well, that's your choice. Do you need anything before I go?"

"No, I'm good."

"Okay. I'm Kellie in case you were wondering."

I shake my head. "I really wasn't."

Once she's gone, I recline into my stiff stretcher and listlessly stare at the drab ceiling until my eyes slide shut again. I'm not sure how long I've been asleep for this time when I'm woken up by Mom and Nurse Kellie.

"Look who finally decided to show," I mumble sarcastically.

"I had to check on Jamie," she says. "He matters too, you know."

"Yeah, I know. What's the latest?"

"Dr. Preston doesn't feel comfortable discharging you right now," Nurse Kellie responds, "and therefore has decided to admit you to our psychiatric hospital. A patient is discharging tomorrow, so you'll stay here until then."

This isn't what I expected to hear. "Like—like the psych ward?"

"Yes."

I feel like I'm in a nightmare, and every time I think it's finally going to end, that I'm going to wake up in my bed to the sound of Mom preparing breakfast and Jamie's gentle snoring, it persists.

"Mom, you can't let them do this," I plead. "Please don't let them do this."

Mom closes her eyes. When she reopens them, a single tear slips down her cheek. "I'm sorry, honey. This is out of my control."

"Bullshit!" I grab Mom's blouse and clutch the silky beige fabric in my hands. "Please, Mom." She tries to pull away, but I hold on tightly. "Don't make me stay here. I wanna go home."

"Grace, stop it." Mom finally manages to break free of my grip. Drying her eyes on her sleeve, she says, "This isn't forever. You'll come home soon—I promise."

"How soon?"

"I don't know."

"Fuck."

"I really am sorry. I know this sucks."

"No, you don't. How could you?" When she doesn't respond, I sigh. "Can you just go? I want to be alone right now."

Mom nods. "Of course. I'll see you tomorrow."

Tomorrow. The mere thought of waking up in this godawful place sends a chill down my spine, complimenting the goosebumps covering my bare arms. No matter how tightly I wrap my blanket around me, they simply won't disappear.

I'm beginning to wish I'd taken those pills after all.

10

There's no winner when you play the Waiting Game. After several hours of tossing and turning in my stretcher, interwoven with nightmares about pizza and pills, I abruptly awaken to the sound of screaming. I tiptoe to my ajar door and glance down the hall, where two nurses are struggling to restrain a burly boy.

"Hey! Get back in bed!" the watch nurse, an elderly woman sitting behind a desk across from my room, hisses at me.

So, I return to my stretcher and hold a pillow to my ears to stifle the boy's screams. *This isn't fair,* I think. *I don't belong in this madhouse. I'm not crazy.*

Sometime around midnight, the hall becomes quiet again. I drift in and out of dreams until ten thirty when Nurse Fiona wakes me up for breakfast. I choke down three spoonfuls of Cheerios and a carton of cranberry juice before claiming that I'm full.

"We'll try again later," she says to my relief. "Would you like to watch TV?"

"Yeah. Do you know if my mom's here?"

She shakes her head. "Sorry. I haven't seen her."

I spend most of the morning watching *Supernatural* reruns on TNT. Shortly after eleven thirty, Nurse Kellie brings me the lunch menu. "We offer a variety of vegetarian options," she says, as if she's reading lines off of a script, "like grilled cheese, hummus wraps, mozzarella sti—"

"I ate breakfast an hour ago," I interrupt. "I'm not hungry."

"Well, if you need anything—'

"Actually, I was wondering if I could use the phone."

"Of course. I'll be right back." She leaves my room and returns one minute later with a cordless telephone. "Here you go."

"Thanks."

Nurse Kellie smiles kindly. "You're welcome, Grace."

Once she's gone, I dial Lou's number and cross my fingers, hoping she'll answer.

Ring . . . ring . . . ring . . .

"Come on, pick up," I mumble. "Pick up, pick up, pick up."

"You've reached the voicemail of Lou Jackson. Here's the beep, so I hope you know what to do with it. Later."

"At the tone, please record your message," an automated voice instructs.

Beep!

I clear my throat. "Hi, Lou. It's Grace. Uh, I wanted to apologize for the things I said at school yesterday. They weren't nice, and well, I just thought you should know I'm sorry. Uh, I don't have my phone right now, so I'll have my mom text you this number. If you could call me back, that'd be great. I'm not doing so good, and I really need to talk to you. Okay. Bye."

I press *End* with a lump in my throat. "All done," I tell Nurse

Fiona as she's passing my room with a tray of chicken nuggets and fries.

She takes the phone from me. "How was your call?"

"Fine," I lie. "It was fine."

Mom visits me around twelve o'clock. Her eyes appear suspiciously wet, like she's been crying again. "Hi, hon."

"Hi."

"Are you doing okay?"

I shake my head. "Have you seen this place? Mom, I feel like I'm in a prison."

Mom sighs. "I know, it sucks. I wish I could say something else, but that's just the reality of it for the time being."

"No kidding." After a brief hesitation, I ask, "So . . . what happens now?"

"An EMT will take you to the psychiatric hospital." Mom glances into the hall, where Nurse Fiona is chatting with a man in a black uniform. "I'm not allowed to ride in the ambulance, so I'll drive over and meet you there."

"Ambulance?"

"It's across the street," Nurse Fiona explains, "therefore we need to transfer you via ambulance. A stretcher is in the hall, if you'd come with me."

"Can't I walk?"

She shakes her head. "You have to use the ambulance. It's protocol."

"But—"

"Grace, please," Mom interrupts. "Don't make this any more difficult than it needs to be."

I'm too exhausted to argue otherwise, so I let Fiona guide me out of my room and onto another stretcher. It's even more uncomfortable than the one I slept on—smaller too. My feet dangle over the end as the EMT unlocks the wheels and begins to push me towards the exit.

"I'll see you soon, Grace!" Mom calls.

She watches me reenter the central section of the ER with her hand clutching the silver heart-shaped necklace I bought her for her fortieth birthday. I wish I could tell her a hundred things; that I'm sorry, that this isn't her fault, that she needs to remember that Jamie's haircut appointment is tomorrow, that I forgot to shut down my computer, that I think about Dad all the time, that it's not her I'm angry at; it's me.

But instead, I say nothing.

I've never ridden in an ambulance before, nor do I want to again. The EMT keeps rechecking my pulse while his female companion hums along to a catchy pop song up front.

"You all right, Grace?" he asks.

I wrap a thin green blanket tighter around me to combat the cold. "How much longer until we get there?"

"We're here right now."

The driver pulls the ambulance into a vacant garage and parks it beside an elevator. She opens the back so they can transfer me to the concrete ground, but in the process, my right arm whacks the deck. I wince.

"My apologies," the man says. "It's a bit of a squeeze."

I feel sick to my stomach as he wheels me to the elevator. Once we're on the second floor, we proceed through two sets of locked double doors until reaching a desk that's like the one Mom checked me in at yesterday.

"I'm with Grace Edwards," he informs the receptionist.

"Go ahead," she responds, and with one push of a button, I enter the psych ward.

I'm surprised at how immensely different it is from what I'd expected. After all the depictions of psych wards I've seen in movies and TV shows, I guess I assumed it'd be louder, entirely white, and bursting with chaos and commotion. But the mostly-grey hallway in front of me is even quieter than the ER. There's no screaming or cursing—in fact, the only sound I hear as the EMT helps me off my stretcher is muffled conversation coming from a nearby room.

"What do I do now?" I ask.

"Wait," he responds. "Is your mom or dad coming to check you in?"

I cross my arms. "You shouldn't assume everyone has a mom and dad. It's homophobic."

"I'm sorry. I assure you that wasn't my inten—"

"Grace!" Before he can finish speaking, Mom breathlessly rushes to my side. She adjusts the strings on the back of my gown, which have loosened over the course of the morning. "You look cold. Did they give you a blanket?"

I nod. "I forgot it in the ambulance."

"Oh. How was the ride?"

"Bumpy."

She chuckles. "I'll bet."

I sit in a plastic chair outside of an oval office while she signs paperwork, her hand trembling with each signature that places me in the care of these unfamiliar people. Through the glass window, I watch three nurses dressed in identical turquoise scrubs type into their computers. One of them, a busty blonde with eighties-style glasses, pauses to shovel a forkful of salad in her mouth. Perhaps if she'd chosen a lighter vinaigrette, her shirt wouldn't cinch around her midsection.

"Grace Edwards?" Another nurse, a smiley brunette that's even rounder than the salad woman, approaches me with a navy sweatshirt and matching sweatpants folded in her stocky arms. "Ready to ditch that gown?"

"Uh-huh."

"Great. Follow me."

She leads me to a bathroom and unlocks the door so I can change. I watch in the dusty mirror above the sink as the gown falls to my feet, revealing the top half of my body. It's the first time in days that I've allowed myself a thorough look, and I don't know if I should feel more disgusted or scared. I run my hands over my prominent ribs, then down to my stomach, which is still too pudgy for my liking. I'm beginning to worry that it will always be.

"Grace?" The nurse knocks on the door. "You all right in there?"

"Yeah. One sec."

I turn away from the mirror and shimmy into the sweats. "Is there a tie?" I ask the nurse—her nametag says Carlie—when I remerge, gripping the baggy waistband in my hands.

Nurse Carlie shakes her head. "Drawstrings aren't allowed. I can check if we have a smaller size."

"Don't bother," I say. "I won't be here for long."

Once she's relocked the bathroom, I follow her to a large yet simple room with two beds, two desks, another locked bathroom, and two dressers. A thin brown-haired girl is rummaging through the dresser on the right in a towel. A white bandage is wrapped around her left wrist.

"Therese!" Nurse Carlie exclaims. "Where are your clothes?"

"That's what I'm trying to fucking figure out," Therese snaps. "Whoever did the wash must have mixed them up with Stephanie's again."

"Well, you should have asked for help," Nurse Carlie responds, "because walking around in a towel isn't appropriate."

Mischief fills Therese's dark eyes. She drops the towel to the floor and faces Nurse Carlie and me butt-naked. "Better?"

Nurse Carlie's jaw drops. "Therese! Put that back on!"

As uncomfortable as the situation is, I cannot tear my gaze away from Therese. She'd have a nice body, I suppose, if it weren't for the numerous red marks carved into her stomach and thighs. Even her hips are marred with scars.

Therese begrudgingly rewraps the towel around herself. She sees me looking, and her lips curl into a smirk. "Grace, is it? I saw your name on the admissions board." When I nod, she says, "I'm Therese, your roommate."

I still can't shake the image of her scarred skin from my mind. "Oh, uh, nice to meet you."

"Is this your first time?" she asks.

"Uh-huh."

"Don't worry. After a while, you get used to this place."

"I'm not staying for long," I say. "Two days, max."

Therese's smirk broadens. "Who told you that?"

"Therese, that's enough," Nurse Carlie demands firmly. "Now, put something on before Liza sees you."

Therese rolls her eyes. "Fine. But tell whoever fucked up the wash that this is the third day in a row I'm wearing the same underwear."

"Will do." Nurse Carlie unlocks the bathroom, which is to the left of a window overlooking a desolate courtyard. "All yours, Therese."

"Whatever."

"She's a sweet girl," Nurse Carlie says while Therese is changing. "She just takes a little getting used to."

"How many others are there?" I ask.

"Five. You'll meet them in group therapy."

"When's that?"

"Right now. Come on, I'll show you to the Rec Room."

So, after adjusting my sweatpants, I follow her through the

hall to a larger room complete with three couches, a television, and shelves stocked with games and art supplies. Four teenagers sit around a table with the salad woman, discussing something. When they see me, their conversation abruptly stops.

"You must be Grace." The nurse—Liza, I now see—smiles kindly. "Take a seat please. We're learning about Distress Tolerance."

"Huh?"

"Coping skills," the girl I sit beside explains. Like Therese, she's slender and brown-haired, though there's a certain charisma to her that my surly roommate lacks. "Distress Tolerance is—"

"Bullshit," a Latina girl interrupts. Whereas everyone else wears baggy clothing like me, her magenta cowl neck and leopard-print leggings hug her curves.

"Ludmilla! Language!" Nurse Liza scolds.

Ludmilla rolls her eyes. "Sorry. I just don't see the point of this stupid lesson."

"Well, I assure you that others here find lessons like these quite helpful," Nurse Liza says, "so keep your comments to yourself." She returns her attention to me. "Grace, Distress Tolerance is a skill we use to replace harmful behaviors with safer alternatives. For example, is there a behavior you currently engage in that you'd like to change?"

I subtly adjust the sleeves of my sweatshirt, feeling the coarse fabric rub against the Band-Aids Nurse Fiona applied earlier to the cuts that were infected. "I don't think so."

"Okay. How 'bout anyone else?"

"I wish I wasn't so angry all the time," a muscular guy says.

"Can you elaborate, Kevin?" Nurse Liza prods.

"Little things people do piss me off. So, I lash out. I say bad words and throw shit and punch holes in walls. I don't mean to. It's just . . . an instinct, I guess." Kevin sighs. "I pushed my sister down the stairs because she called me a bitch. Her arm broke, and now she has to wear a cast for three months. And the worst thing is, I don't even feel that bad about it."

I remember a question Ms. Lee asked at my evaluation; *Have you experienced urges to harm someone else?* Even the thought of deliberately hurting another person makes my skin crawl. Why would anyone do that? *How* could anyone do that?

"Thank you for sharing, Kevin. Before we proceed, let's introduce ourselves to Grace."

"I'm Stephanie," the girl next to me says. "I'm seventeen, and I've been here for eight days."

"Ludmilla," the angsty Latina girl mumbles. "Fifteen. Two weeks."

"Anne," the final girl—a short, pale brunette—says softly. "I'm sixteen, and I've been here for almost three months."

"Three months?" I repeat.

She nods. "I'm waiting for a spot in a state residential facility, but a lot of people are, so I don't know when I'm gonna leave. It could be days or weeks or months or . . ." she abruptly trails off, gazing at the blank television screen with a distant look in her eyes.

Nurse Liza clears her throat. "Who's next?"

"Just Jonathan," Kevin responds.

"Ah. Well, you'll meet him later. Now, for our activity . . ."

While she passes around a packet titled *Adult and Adolescent Pleasurable Activities*, I whisper-ask Stephanie, "Where's Jonathan?"

"Probably napping," she responds quietly. "He does that a lot."

"Oh. How come?"

"It's his meds. He's on, like, five or something, so his sleep schedule is totally fucked."

"Are you on meds?" I ask.

"Everyone is," she says. "Being numb is better than being crazy. I mean, isn't that why you cut yourself?"

"You can tell?"

She nods. "Only cutters adjust their sleeves that much. So, vertical or horizontal?"

"Huh?"

"Girls, that's enough," Nurse Liza scolds. "As I was saying, learning to control your emotions is important when you're in a state of distress. This lesson will teach you how to regulate stress through pleasurable pastimes. An example might be —yes, Kevin?"

"Exercise," Kevin says. "At home when I was feeling shitty, I'd take walks or kick around a soccer ball with my sister. She tells me her team's doing really good."

I feel myself well-up at the mention of soccer. Soccer is everything to me. It's my passion, my talent—my future career, if all goes as planned. But all is not going as planned. Today, I missed playoffs. Next week—who knows? My fate is no longer determined by my actions but by whether those actions please the people who have the power to keep me here for as long as they want to.

I used to have all the control in the world. Now, I have none.

We spend the next twenty minutes circling activities pertaining to our interests and writing why that's the case with dull golf pencils. Afterwards, Nurse Liza delves into an explanation about something called Radical Acceptance and how "only when we're able to accept what's out of our control, can we stop fighting against what is." I zone out immediately, and judging by the apathetic expressions on their faces, so does everyone else.

Nurse Liza's lesson then subsequent demonstration drags on for another thirty minutes, and it probably would have prolonged if not for dinner. After she's collected our packets and pencils, we follow her into the cafeteria; a small room packed with a refrigerator, two microwaves, and three square folding tables with accompanying chairs.

I sit with Stephanie at the table nearest to the back. She chows down on a cheeseburger, waffle fries, and chocolate milk while I use a plastic fork to saw my mozzarella sticks into twelve pieces.

"What are you doing?" she asks as she's polishing off her final fry. It's been twenty minutes since we were given our meals, and I still haven't eaten anything other than a couple buttery green beans.

"I'm not hungry," I say. "I had a big lunch."

"Oh. Well, they don't like it when we don't eat."

"Who?"

"The nurses. I assume you're on a meal plan?"

I shake my head. "Not that I know of."

"I find that hard to believe."

"How come?"

"Because the last anorexic spent more time here than anywhere else. The poor girl was up to, like, four thousand calories at one point."

"I'm not anorexic," I say.

"Yeah, I'm sure you're just naturally stick-thin."

"Steph—"

"Grace, how's it goin'?" Nurse Carlie asks, sitting down beside me. "I see you haven't touched your dinner."

"I'm not hungry," I say.

"Well, I'm afraid you'll have to work through that. Your meal plan requires you to eat three meals and three snacks a day."

"They're coming for me!" Jonathan screams. "They're going to kill me!"

"Jonathan, if you do not lower your voice—" one of the nurses—Liza, I think—begins to say, but Jonathan doesn't let her finish.

"Get your fucking hands off me, you cunt!"

"Just stay here," Therese instructs. "It'll be over as soon as they give him booty juice."

"What's booty juice?"

"Butt injection. It's like a sedative—except it's faster and apparently more painful."

I cringe. "Yikes. Have you had one?"

"God no. I'm not actually crazy, you know."

"Then what are you?"

Therese shrugs. "Damaged, I guess. How 'bout you?"

I shake my head. "Not sure. I'm still trying to figure that out."

As Therese predicted, it isn't long before Jonathan's screams are replaced with conversations among staff and groans from the others as they're woken up for breakfast. I stand in a line behind Anne and Ludmilla to use the bathroom while our food is being prepared in the cafeteria. Whereas Anne takes her turn efficiently, Ludmilla spends forever applying her makeup. When she finally reemerges, she looks like a racoon.

As I stand before the sink, scrubbing my teeth with the toothbrush and paste Nurse Carlie gave me yesterday, I'm once again unable to tear my gaze away from the mirror. My face appears fuller than usual, and when I adjust my pants after using the toilet, I'm nearly certain that my waistband has tightened.

But no, that wouldn't make sense. I haven't eaten any more than usual since I was admitted to the hospital, at least according to their scales. Ironically, I think I might have eaten less.

Nevertheless, my insecurities persist. They exacerbate at breakfast when Nurse Liza hands me a tray consisting of a single-serving box of Cheerios, two-percent milk, an apple, and yogurt with granola.

"No way," I say. "I'll throw up."

Stephanie, who's plowing through a plate of scrambled eggs and sausage links across from me, rolls her eyes. "You're such a drama queen, Grace. It's not *that* bad."

"But—but weight gain is supposed to be gradual," I respond.

"Where'd you hear that?"

"The Internet."

"Ah, such a reliable source."

"It can be," I insist. "You just have to know the right places to look."

"And do you?"

I'm about to respond when a scrawny blonde-haired boy stumbles into the cafeteria. He's scantily dressed in a cloth gown and mismatched socks—one red and one yellow. But despite his peculiar outfit, it's his eyes I notice the most; frenzied baby-blues that drift around the room, not once settling on a certain spot.

"Is that Jonathan?" I ask Stephanie.

She nods. "That's him."

Jonathan staggers past us. He opens the refrigerator and grabs a bag of raw kale from behind a row of individual milk cartons. As he's walking back, he leans down and whispers in Stephanie's ear, "Animal killer."

Stephanie finishes chewing her second sausage link, then says, "Different strokes for different folks, Johnny."

Jonathan's eyes narrow. He's about to retaliate when Nurse

Liza clamps her hands on his bony shoulders and forcefully guides him away from us. "Nice goin', Steph."

"No prob, Liz."

"You've got some nerve," I say once both the nurse and Jonathan are out of earshot.

Stephanie shrugs. "I'm used to him. He's always saying fucked up shit."

"Like what?"

"Well, for starters, he's convinced that he can speak to God. He says if he doesn't do what God says, He'll send demons to rape him and burn him alive—or something crazy like that. Then this one time, my dad came for a family session, and he got it in his head that he was Satan."

"Really?"

"Uh-huh. He kept following my dad around, mumbling shit about some guy named Chris under his breath. My dad's name is Michael."

"Maybe he meant Christ."

"Maybe. He is pretty religious."

"But doesn't he scare you? You know, with the violence and all?"

"After what I've seen, nothing scares me anymore. Except spiders." Stephanie shudders. "How 'bout you? What are you afraid of, Grace?"

I choose the first fear that pops into my mind. "Being alone."

Stephanie nods. "Loneliness sucks."

"I think my best friend hates me," I say. "We got into a fight the morning I was admitted to the ER, and I said some really mean things. I tried calling her to apologize—I even left a message—but she hasn't responded. I'm worried it's over."

"Does she know you're here?"

"I think so."

"She's probably just freaked out. Give her time. Camille didn't visit until my sixth day."

"Camille?"

"My twin sister. She's great, but she's also normal, so it's hard for her to understand why we're like this."

"Lou's great too. She's the one person I've always been able to count on when things got bad."

"You don't belong to people forever," Stephanie says, "so when you find someone who makes you feel like you're not alone in this fucking awful world, don't let them go. 'Cause you might not get another chance."

"But what if it's too late?" I ask. "What if she's already moved on?"

"Well, if I were you—"

"Grace?" Nurse Helen approaches our table, and Stephanie trails off. "Dr. Bennett is ready to meet with you."

"Now? But I'm eating breakfast."

"Bring it with you. He won't mind."

So, with my tray in my hands, I follow Nurse Helen through the cafeteria and into a small office across the hall. Dr. Bennett is seated in one of two chairs around a rectangular table, texting on an outdated phone. He's a spitting-image of Dr. Emmett Brown who starred in the *Back to the Future* rerun I watched with Jamie last weekend; penetrating brown eyes, pale skin, wispy grey hair that's desperately in need of gel.

"Hello, Grace," he greets me in a surprisingly deep voice. "I'm Dr. Bennett."

"I know who you are." I sit across from him and open my box of Cheerios. My hands tremble as I add a splash of milk, but I carry on. I have to do this. I have to prove to him that I'm okay.

"How are you feeling?" Dr. Bennett asks.

"Fine," I respond. "I mean, I hate being here, but it's not like I have a choice."

"What do you hate the most?"

"Everything. The noise, the people, the beds. It literally feels like I'm sleeping on concrete."

"I'm sorry about that."

I shrug. "Whatever. I'm used to tossing and turning."

"What do you mean?"

"Ever since I was ten, I've had trouble staying asleep."

"Do you have nightmares?"

"Yeah."

"Are they about anything in particular?"

"I don't know. I usually can't remember them when I wake up."

He jots this down on a pad of paper. "Well, if you're open to it, I could prescribe you something to help you sleep more comfortably."

"Just for sleep, right?"

He nods. "Just for sleep. I see you're following your meal plan as well."

I choke down another spoonful of Cheerios, then push the box aside. "I actually wanted to talk to you about that."

"Oh? What about it?"

"It's too much food. Like, I'm not even *that* underweight. I don't need to be gorging myself at every meal just to gain a pound or two."

"It's more than a pound or two, Grace."

"Yeah, but if weight gain isn't gradual, I could compromise my health."

"Grace, I assure you the number of calories we've prescribed won't compromise your health," he responds.

"And what is that number exactly?" I pry. "Twenty-eight hundred? Three thousand?"

"About that, yes."

Although I'd expected this, having him confirm it triggers another wave of anxious thoughts nevertheless. "Fuck, that's a lot."

"It really isn't. You must've been eating something similar to sustain your energy for soccer."

I almost laugh aloud. "You're kidding, right?"

"How do you figure?"

"Doctor, if I ate that much, I'd be huge."

"So, roughly how many calories were you eating at home then?"

"I dunno," I lie. "It's not like I was keeping track."

"No, of course not."

"Either way, I still think it's too much. I'm not even halfway done with breakfast, and I already feel like I'm gonna throw up."

"Perhaps a Tums would help."

"I tried that yesterday."

"And?"

I shake my head. "It didn't."

"Well, how have your snacks been going?"

"My snacks?"

"Yes. You're having them, right?"

"No, but . . ." Suddenly, I have an idea. "But if I did, would you reduce my amount at meals?"

He hesitates. "Only if you promise to eat three adequate snacks three times a day."

"I can do that."

"And by 'adequate' I mean chips or cookies—not just fruit."

"I know."

Dr. Bennett's bushy brows furrow; a sign that, I hope, means he's considering my proposal. I hold my breath, nervously awaiting his decision.

"Fine," he says finally. "I'll adjust your plan."

It takes every ounce of willpower I have to refrain from grinning. "Thanks, doctor."

"You're welcome, Grace. I trust you'll comply with what we've agreed to, yes?"

"Of course. You have my word."

Dr. Bennett's lips twitch into a thin smile. "Is there anything else that you're having difficulty with?"

"Besides getting used to all these bullshit rules, not really."

"I understand being here is an adjustment, but it's for your own good. You should try mingling with the others. They're nice kids once you get to know them."

"That's what Carlie said."

"She's a smart woman. I'd listen to her."

"It seems like that's all everyone does around here, isn't it?"

"What is?"

"Listen. Follow rules. Tell the truth."

"Well, compliance and honesty are very important in recovery."

"How long will that take?"

"Recovery?" When I nod, he says, "I don't know. It depends on the individual."

"Oh."

"You'll get there, Grace. The fact that you're willing to seek treatment is one tremendous step in the right direction."

"One of how many?"

"Recovery isn't a sprint; it's a marathon. There are times when you'll feel dehydrated and exhausted, and times when you'll want to lie down and give up. But by utilizing external support and internal motivation, you *will* reach that finish line."

Even though his analogy seems rather foolish, I nod like I agree completely. "Cool."

"I'll check in with you on Monday," he says. "Depending on how your weekend goes, we will establish a more thorough plan to aid your progression. Okay?"

"Sounds good. Thanks again."

"It's my pleasure. It was nice meeting you, Grace."

"Yeah. You too."

I leave his office, closing the door behind me, and dump the contents of my tray in the trashcan before Nurse Liza realizes that I haven't finished my breakfast. Afterwards, I join Stephanie and Therese in the Rec Room. Stephanie's just begun distributing cards for Uno.

"Ooh, I love this game." I take a seat beside Therese on a blue plastic chair. "Can I play?"

"Sure," Therese responds. "Do you want snack? Liza brought them out while you were in your session."

She points at a bin on the table that's overflowing with chips, packaged cookies, and other junk food of the sort. Kevin sits next to it shoveling handfuls of Barbecue Baked Lays in his mouth.

I shake my head. "Nah, I'm not hungry."

"You sure? Looks like your skinny ass could use some carbs."

"Positive." In my periphery, I see Dr. Bennett talking to Nurse Liza. "I think I'm gonna take a nap before Group."

"What happened to Uno?" Stephanie asks.

"Uh, I'll play some other time. I got tired all of a sudden."

"Okay. Later, Grace."

"Later."

My heart is racing as I walk to my room and lie down on my cot with my face turned towards the drab grey wall. I keep waiting for them to find me; to drag me back to the Rec Room and force me to eat snack, like I'd promised I would.

Then five minutes pass, followed by ten, and I realize that nobody is coming after all. I should feel relieved—triumphant, even—but I don't, not really. Instead, I just feel lonely.

THE HOURS CRAWL BY, each one seeming longer than the one before. I pour what little energy I have into finding ways to occupy myself, so I don't succumb to boredom. I read a book, I watch several *Friends* reruns on the one decent TV channel, I play Uno with Therese and Stephanie more times than I can count, and I sleep. I sleep a lot.

But when Monday rolls around and I find myself longing to be in school, I know I've failed epically.

After eating breakfast—a box of Cheerios and cranberry juice—I sit through another mundane group, and after that, I return to my bedroom to pretend to nap, so I can skip morning snack. I've been lying down for barely ten minutes when Nurse Carlie announces that it's time for school.

"C'mon, Grace. You can sleep later."

"We have school?" I mumble.

She nods. "Yep. You gotta keep that mind of yours sharp."

Unsure of what to expect, I follow her to the cafeteria, where an elderly woman with cat-eyed glasses is pushing around a cart stocked with textbooks and worksheets. After she's distributed the materials, she sits down at the first table with a Stephen King novel.

"I expect no talking for the next two hours," she says. "You know the rules."

While everyone else begins working, I approach her. "Um, ma'am?"

"Ah, you must be Grace. I'm Ms. Crawford." She sets down her book long enough to give me a limp handshake. "I emailed your school earlier, so you should have your work by tomorrow."

"You emailed my school?"

"Yes. I don't want you to fall behind."

"I'm only going to be here for a couple days," I say. "I'll make it up when I get back."

"Grace, regardless of how long you're here, it's required that all patients do a minimum of two hours of schoolwork every weekday. I have several vocabulary sheets or if you're interested in math—"

"I'll do the vocab," I interrupt.

"Great. Did you get a pencil?"

I nod. "It's pretty dull though."

"Well, you'll have to make do. Patients aren't allowed to have sharpeners."

"Of course not," I mumble as she retrieves a worksheet and a dictionary from her cart. Once I have my materials, I sit beside Therese and spend the next twenty-five minutes filling in juvenile sentences with words I learned in middle school.

1. To the inexperienced detective, the motive of the crime was an ____.

Enigma.

2. The lack of players caused the team to ____ the game.

Forfeit.

3. It is ____ that you read the directions before beginning the quiz.

Imperative.

4. When my father decided to start his own business, he had no idea how ____ it would be.

Based on the word box, I can infer that the correct answer is "lucrative." But I don't want to give Dad that satisfaction, so I write *DEPLORABLE* in capital letters instead. That's when the tip of my pencil breaks. Dammit.

Our lunches arrive as school is ending. Today's selection is a grilled cheese sandwich with an apple on the side.

"Look, we're twinning," Stephanie says. She's right; aside from her bag of chips, our lunches are identical. "What happened to your meal plan? I thought you had to eat three thousand calories or something."

"Dr. Bennett says as long as I have my snacks, I don't have to eat as much at meals."

"But you don't have snacks," she points out. "Like, ever."

I shrug. "He doesn't know that."

Stephanie arches an eyebrow. "Damn, Grace. That's some shady shit you're pulling."

"Thanks."

She chuckles. "You know, I didn't mean it as a compliment."

Dr. Bennett, however, is full of praise when we meet for my second session this afternoon. He hears from the nurses that I'm eating my meals but doesn't question my absence at snacks. He sees Sunday's number, but neglects to realize that it's all water weight from the approximate thirty-two ounces I chugged in the shower the night before.

"How has your mood been, Grace?" he asks.

"Fine. I'm feeling much better."

"I heard your mother visited you yesterday."

"Yeah, she came in the afternoon for a couple hours."

"And how was that?"

"Okay, I guess. She told me my team won their game."

"Congratulations."

"Why are you congratulating me?" I ask. "I didn't play. I couldn't."

"And understandably so," he says. "You have more important priorities."

"Like what? All I've done this weekend is sit around and listen to everyone get all sentimental about issues that are twenty times worse than mine. I don't understand why you won't let me go home."

"Grace, the last time you were home, you were self-harming on a regular basis."

"I'm over that," I say. "Like, I know now that cutting doesn't solve anything."

"That's great, however—"

"Doctor, you're not listening to me. This isn't fair."

"I'm sorry you feel that way," he responds unsympathetically. "Our time is up, so we'll discuss this more at your family session on Wednesday. Until then, keep up the good work. You're making progress. You should be proud of yourself."

"Whatever."

I retreat to my room in a huff after seeing Nurse Liza lugging the snack bin into the Rec Room. Therese is standing at my desk, admiring a photo of Jamie and me that Mom brought yesterday, along with clothing and toiletries.

"Is this your brother?"

"Uh-huh. His name's Jamie."

"He's adorable. He almost makes me miss mine."

"You have a brother?"

"Yeah, but I haven't seen him in a year. He's serving somewhere in the Middle East, as far as we know."

"That must suck."

"I've dealt with worse. So has he." As she talks, Therese tugs at the frayed ends of the bandage on her wrist.

"Therese, can I ask you something?"

"You want to know why I did it, don't you?" When I nod,

she says, "It wasn't just one reason. There was a lot of shit going on in my life, and I felt like a burden to everyone I cared about. I was flunking school, I was getting in fights over the stupidest stuff, I was sleeping all the time because I had no motivation to do anything. I thought they'd be better off if I wasn't around, so one night, after a particularly shitty day, I stole my mom's razor, got in the bathtub, and, well, you know what happened next.

"It wasn't until I woke up in the hospital and saw my mom sitting next to me, sobbing into a handful of napkins, that I realized I'd been wrong about everything." Therese sighs. "I don't feel like a burden anymore. I just feel like an asshole."

"I know what you mean." For the umpteenth time, I replay Lou's spiteful words in my mind; *Sorry if I'm just trying to be a good friend.*

"You thinking about Lou?" Therese asks.

I nod. "I miss her a lot."

"Have you tried calling her again?"

"What's the point? It's not like she wants anything to do with me."

"Maybe she's scared."

"She doesn't get to be scared," I say. "She doesn't have to spend every day in this awful place."

"I don't know then. I guess you just gotta give it time."

"Time, huh? That's all you got?"

"What am I supposed to say, Grace? That you'll wake up one morning and everything will be peachy again? You know just as well as I do that that's bullshit. This isn't the common cold we're talking about; it's a fucking mental illness. It takes time, and the sooner you realize that, the easier getting better will be."

"Okay, okay. You don't have to yell at me."

"I'm not yelling. I'm just telling it like it is."

I collapse face-first onto my bed. "This sucks," I grumble into my pillow.

"I know." Therese sits beside me and awkwardly pats my shoulder. "It does."

"It will get better though, right?"

"My mom says everything ends eventually," she responds, "so if that's the case, then someday, somehow, yes. It will get better."

"So . . . what do we do in the meantime?"

Therese shakes her head. "I have no fucking clue. Keep on keeping on, I guess."

"Did your mom say that too?"

"No, I saw it on tumblr. It's cheesy as fuck, but also kinda true, you know?"

"Yeah," I say. "I know."

"It's your turn, Grace."

Jamie hands me the dice, so I can make my roll. I blow on my clenched fist for luck, shake it around, then release them onto the table. 2, 2, 2, 2 . . . 3.

"Bummer," he says. "You could've had a Yahtzee."

"I've still got two more tries." I pick up the fifth die and roll it again. 4. "Come on, come on, come on . . ." My third roll lands between the 2 and the 5, wobbling slightly before settling on the latter. "Dammit."

"Ha! I win!" Jamie grins. "That's twice in a row."

"You're just too good." In my periphery, I watch Stephanie and Anne walk into the Rec Room, audibly bitching about their periods.

"I've been on the rag for six fucking days," Stephanie complains. "I'm so fucking bloated, it's disgusting."

"At least you have a light flow," Anne responds. "My mom forgot to bring me Maxi pads when she visited, so I've had to double up so I won't bleed through."

"Have you tried tampons?"

"Yeah, but I've never liked them. They're super uncomfortable."

"Maybe you're doing it wrong."

"I dunno. I think my vagina's too tight."

"Sorry we couldn't hang out in my room," I say to Jamie. "It'd be a lot quieter."

"That's okay," he responds. "I'm just happy to see you."

I smile. "I'm happy to see you too."

When Dr. Bennett explained family therapy at our last session, I admit I was a little worried. I was dying to ask what information he'd share with Mom, as he'd mentioned he'd meet in private with her first, but I didn't want to give him a reason to be suspicious, so I kept quiet. Even though I'm fairly certain he's under the impression that I'm fine, I also know guzzling water and pocketing food will only work for so long before they catch onto my tricks.

That said, at least family therapy gives Jamie and me a chance to catch up after days without communication. He sits across from me, still gloating over his win, in an auburn sweater and light-wash skinny jeans that put my grey sweats to shame. Even my turquoise nail polish, which Therese applied three days ago, pales in comparison to his pristine purple.

"What color is that?" I ask, pointing at his nails.

"Not sure," he responds. "Plum or something. I borrowed it from Mom."

"Well, it looks good."

"Not too dark?"

I shake my head. "No. It's perfect."

For the first time since he and Mom arrived, we fall quiet; him playing with a loose thread in his sweater while I pick at my damaged cuticles. Finally, he asks, "Grace, when are you gonna come home?"

"That's what Mom's talking to Dr. Bennett about," I say. "I'm hoping before Halloween."

"Me too. Mom says I can't go trick-or-treating by myself, and I don't want Trevor to take me."

"Trevor?"

"Mom's boyfriend."

"Mom has a boyfriend?"

"Yeah, but it's nothing serious. They've just gone on a couple dates."

"Really? Why didn't she tell me?" When he doesn't respond, I say, "Whatever. Knowing her, he won't be around long."

"Facts."

"Grace?"

When I turn around, Mom is standing behind me. She looks different than she did earlier; she looks more flustered and, if I'm reading her correctly, vaguely pissed off.

"Yeah?"

"Dr. Bennett is ready to see you."

"Okay. Wish me luck, kiddo."

Jamie nods. "I'll keep my fingers crossed."

I follow Mom through the hall, past Ludmilla who's complaining to Nurse Liza about the side effects of her new mood stabilizer, and into Dr. Bennett' office. Like Mom, he also appears strangely perturbed in comparison to his usual impassive demeanor.

"Hello, Grace. Please sit down."

"What's going on?" I ask. "Why are you two acting so weird?"

"Well, it has come to my attention that, uh . . ." Dr. Bennett rubs his bulbous nose, unable to look Mom or me in the eyes. "It has come to my attention that you've lost weight."

"Oh? I did?" Part of me is pleased by this while another part fears the repercussions of breaking the promise I made with him.

"Grace, drop the act," Mom says. "You're a smart girl. You know what you're doing."

"No, I don't," I lie. "I have no idea what you're talking about."

"The staff has noticed several problematic behaviors you've exhibited over the past week," Dr. Bennett responds. "Carlie says you're rarely present at snacks, and Helen sees you pacing the hall between groups. Additionally, when Pete washed your clothing last night, he discovered two tater tots in the pocket of your sweatpants."

"I can't believe you're just finding this out," Mom says. "Where the hell were you when this was going on?"

"Kira, please understand that there are six other patients I must attend to as well."

"But I'm not talking about your other patients, am I? I'm talking about my daughter. Look at her, Alan. She's practically skin and bones!"

"Mom, it's okay," I say.

"Of course it's not okay, Grace. This is completely unacceptable." Mom buries her face in her hands. "I—I'm speechless. You're in a place that's supposed to know how to treat kids like you, yet five days later, you're down three pounds. How does that even happen?"

"We infrequently run into situations like Grace's," Dr. Bennett responds calmly. "When she was admitted, we were primarily focused on helping her cope with her depression and identify her triggers, so she'd be less inclined to self-harm when she discharged. She was always our priority, Kira; we just never expected that her eating would become an issue as well. That was our mistake. But as I already explained to you, we have the means to fix it."

"Fix it?" I repeat. "Can't I just promise to eat?"

"You mean before or after you lose another pound?" Mom challenges. "As much as I want to trust you, Grace, your safety is more important. That's why Alan and I have agreed that you need a revised approach."

"What type of approach?"

"Are you familiar with one-on-one?" Dr. Bennett asks. When I shake my head, he explains, "One-on-one means that a nurse is required to be with you at all times."

"All times? Like . . . even in the bathroom?"

"That's correct."

"But—but that's stupid," I say. "I'm not bulimic. I use the bathroom to pee, not to make myself sick." Tears pool in my eyes. "This is so unfair! You can't treat me like this!"

"It's only temporary," Mom reminds me. "Prove to us that you can cooperate, and you'll earn back your privacy in a week, maybe less."

"A week? But I thought I'd be out by then. Mom, I have to take Jamie trick-or-treating, and I still haven't gotten a costume for Sam's party, and I have school and PSATS and soccer. I have to be there for my team. I made a commitment."

Mom sighs. "I'm sorry, Grace. I don't know what to tell you."

"Tell me you'll take me home," I plead. "I don't need to be here. I'm better—I promise."

"I want to, honey—trust me, I'd like nothing more than for you to come home too—but I can't. Not yet." Mom reaches for my hand, but I pull away.

"Don't touch me! Don't fucking touch me!"

"Grace, please—"

I jump to my feet and storm out of Dr. Bennett's office, slamming the door so hard, Nurse Pete nearly fumbles his medication tray.

"Grace, what's going on?"

Dismissing his question, I retreat to my room, where Jamie is perched on the edge of my bed talking to Therese, who must have just woken up from her nap. Their conversation abruptly stops when they see me.

"Damn, Grace," Therese says. "Is everything all right?"

I sink to the floor with tears streaming down my cheeks. Jamie sits beside me and wraps his arms around my quivering shoulders. I sob into his soft sweater as he strokes my messy hair.

"Why are you crying, Grace?"

"It's complicated," I whisper. "There's a lot of stuff going on right now, and it's just a lot to process."

"Oh, okay." After a brief pause, he asks, "Do you at least know when you're coming home?"

I shake my head. "I'm sorry, kid. I'm doing my best."

"Yes, you are," Mom says. When I glance up, she's standing in my doorway with a crumpled tissue in her hand. "I thought you could use this."

"Leave," I say.

"Grace—"

"I said leave! I don't want to talk to you right now. I hate you."

"Easy there, tiger," Therese says, whereas Mom merely nods.

"Okay. Okay, I'll respect that. Come on, Jamie. It's time to go."

Jamie hugs me once more. "Bye, Gracie. I hope you feel better."

I don't bother to correct him. "See ya, Jamie."

"See ya."

"Yikes," Therese remarks once they're gone. "You must've had a really bad session."

"What do you know about one-on-one?" I ask.

"Not much. Why? You on it?"

"Uh-huh."

"Jeez, that sucks. Sorry."

"I'm so fucked," I mumble. "Therese, what am I gonna do?"

"Cooperate, I guess. I mean, that's your only option now, right?"

I nod. "Unfortunately."

"You know, my friend had anorexia when she was your age. She's better now, but for a while, it was a fucking nightmare. They even had to tube her."

"I'm not anorexic," I say.

Therese stands up. She rummages through the top drawer of her dresser and tosses me a panty liner. "Dry your eyes, Twiggy. And stop living in denial too. It's not doing you much good."

"Where are you going?" I ask.

"To see Dr. Bennett. I've got my own family shit to deal with."

Seconds after she's left, Nurse Pete enters my room with a bag of potato chips. "Your snack," he explains. He tosses me the chips, then takes a seat at Therese's desk.

"So, this is what one-on-one is like, huh?"

Nurse Pete nods. "Just pretend I'm not here. I won't bother you as long as you eat your chips."

"I don't like Salt & Vinegar," I say.

"We have Sour Cream & Onion, if you'd prefer that."

"Don't bother." I reluctantly tear open the bag and stuff a couple broken pieces in my mouth. "This sucks."

"It's only temporary."

"Yeah, but it still sucks having all your freedom taken away over some stupid number. I'm not even *that* thin. If I was, they would've put me in cardiac."

"Would you have preferred cardiac?" he asks.

"Yes," I respond impulsively. "I mean, no. I don't know! Why are you asking me? You said you'd leave me alone."

"I'm sorry."

"No, it's fine. It's not your fault that things are this way."

Nurse Pete stares at his clogs while I fiddle with the bracelet around my wrist. The fine print has begun to fade, as has my name and DOB. I wonder if there will come a day when I cannot see them at all.

I finish my chips ten minutes later and wipe my salty fingers on my bedspread. "Pete? Can you unlock the bathroom? I need to go."

"Would you prefer if Helen supervised?" he asks.

His question makes my skin crawl. "Are you serious?"

"I am."

"Fuck. Fine, get Nurse Helen."

Nurse Pete pulls a walkie-talkie out of his pocket. Pressing the red button with his thumb, he barks into the transceiver, "Helen? Room Two."

"I didn't know those things still existed," I say. "It would've been easier to text her."

Nurse Pete chuckles. "You sound just like my daughter. I tried to explain rotary phones to her, and she looked at me like I had three heads."

"You have a daughter?"

He nods. "Two. They're my world."

"I wish my dad felt that way about Jamie and me. Maybe then he wouldn't have left."

"You shouldn't blame yourself, Grace."

"I don't. I blame my mom. Every time I think things are bad enough, she always finds a way to make them worse."

"I know you're angry," he says, "however, if there's something I've learned from working here for seven years, it's that anger never resolves anything."

"So, what does then?"

"Acceptance. Learning how to accept the past and move on is a skill we like to teach you guys before you discharge. I believe it would help you a lot."

"I mean, I guess it might," I respond. "It's just—it's just that I think a lot about my past; I think about the mistakes I made and the things I could've done but didn't to correct them. And I learn from those mistakes too. I grow from them. Basically what I'm trying to say is that we are who we are because of our pasts, and no amount of therapy or forgetting or even accepting will change that."

"Change what?" Nurse Helen asks.

"The past," I say.

"There's an expression my mother used to tell my brother and me when we were younger. She'd tell us; 'life is like underwear; change is good.'" Nurse Helen chuckles. "Now, what can I help you with?"

"Grace needs to use the bathroom," Nurse Pete responds.

"Alrighty." She unlocks the bathroom door with her key, then holds it open for me. "Whenever you're ready, Grace."

"Do you have to look?" I ask as Nurse Pete leaves my room with my empty bag of chips.

"I do."

"You know I'm sixteen, right?"

"Age is irrelevant when it comes to your safety," she responds. "I promise it isn't so bad."

"Easy for you to say."

As I pull down my pants, I realize something. I'm not sixteen; I'm two, and Nurse Helen is my mother making sure I've mastered potty training. I have no privacy, I have no freedom, and I have no voice—at least not one they'll listen to. I'm completely vulnerable, and it's a terrifying feeling.

Lunch isn't any better. The second Nurse Liza presents me with my meal, which comprises of another grilled cheese, vanilla yogurt, an orange, and a Styrofoam cup brimming with chocolate milk, butterflies swarm my stomach.

"No, no, no. I can't." I push the tray away, repulsed by the mere sight. "It's too much."

"Grace, I understand you're upset—"

"Don't talk to me like I'm a fucking child!" I yell, causing the lively conversations between the others to immediately die down. "This is unfair! You can't do this!"

"You're right," she responds calmly. "We cannot force you to eat. However, if you refuse to comply with your meal plan, we'll have to use alternative methods to feed you. Are you familiar with a nasogastric tube?"

The butterflies intensify. "You'll tube me?" I whisper.

"No, but we'll send you somewhere that's authorized to. There's a hospital in Manhattan that uses NG tubes for refeeding purposes. I'm sure they'd have no problem admitting you if you're unable to stay here."

Suddenly, my lunch no longer seems so unappealing. I dip my spoon into the yogurt and force a bite through my lips, then another, and then another. Once I've finished the serving, I move onto the chocolate milk. But there's something not right; it's too rich and thick, so much so that I almost spit it out.

"I think my milk is spoiled."

"Oh, that's not milk," she responds. "It's a protein shake. I would've offered you vanilla or strawberry, but chocolate is the only flavor we have in stock."

I remember reading about these kind of protein shakes on a myproana thread a few weeks ago, where users were complaining about drinking them when they were refeeding. Not only did they taste awful, they said; they were also loaded with calories. I can't recall the exact number now; I just remember that it was scarily high.

"Can I have regular milk instead?" I ask.

Nurse Liza shakes her head. "Regular milk doesn't have the amount of protein you need. What past patients have done is plugged their noses and chugged. Just think, Grace; in ten seconds, you could be finished."

"And puking all over the place."

"Is it really that bad?"

"Have *you* tried one?" When she shakes her head again, I exclaim, "Then you can't understand! Hell, nobody in this stupid place understands! It's such bullshit!"

For the second time since lunch began, the room falls completely silent. Nurse Liza clears her throat. "Perhaps you should eat somewhere else."

"Why?"

"Because you're not the only one who's struggling, Grace." She swoops my tray off the table and stands up, gesturing for me to do the same. "C'mon, let's go."

I follow her through the hall and into Dr. Bennett's vacant office. We sit across from each other separated by my barely-touched lunch and the palpable tension that plagues the room with its ugly presence.

"Begin whenever you're ready," she says.

"What if I'm not?"

"Then we'll wait."

The minutes crawl by. I pick at a hole in my sweatpants while she twists an exquisite diamond ring around her fourth finger.

"Are you married?" I ask.

"Engaged. Our wedding is in April."

"What's your fiancé like?"

Nurse Liza smiles. "Kyle's wonderful. He teaches US History at UConn. All the students love him."

"Do you?"

"Very much."

"My parents used to love each other. Then my mom had to screw up everything."

"Everyone makes mistakes, Grace," she reminds me.

"I know. I'm still angry though."

"There's nothing wrong with feeling that way."

"Uh-huh." I pick up half of my lukewarm grilled cheese and take small nibbles, starting with the crust, until it's gone. As I'm washing down the taste with a sip of the disgusting shake, I say, "The problem is, I'm beginning to think I'll always be."

13

"Christ, Grace! You fucking reek!"

I glance up from my AP Euro textbook, where I'm reading about the Hundred Years War, and roll my eyes at my roommate's blunt assertion. "Gee thanks, Therese."

"I'm serious. When was the last time you showered?"

"Uh . . . five days ago."

"For real? Girl, that's a long-ass time."

"I'm waiting until I get off one-on-one," I say. "Peeing in front of the nurses is bad enough, but cleaning myself while they watch? That's just disgusting."

"No, what's disgusting is your stench," she responds. "It's not like this is the first they've seen a naked body. Right, Carls?"

Nurse Carlie, who's typing into an outdated Mac at Therese's desk, nods. "That's right."

"See? I don't understand what the problem is."

"I'm modest," I say. "I've always been."

"Well, get over it. I don't want to hang around someone who smells like they just crawled out of a fucking sewer."

"Screw you."

"You know, breakfast doesn't start for twenty minutes," she continues. "You could totally take a shower in that amount of time."

"But—"

"Just saying. Now, if you'll excuse me, I'm going to the Rec Room to be with people who give a damn about their hygiene."

"She's a handful, that one," Nurse Carlie remarks once Therese is gone.

"No kidding." I sniff my armpit and, to my dismay, Therese wasn't overexaggerating; I smell awful. "Do you mind?"

"If you shower?" When I nod, she says, "Of course not. C'mon, I'll get you shampoo."

I follow her into the hall, where she unlocks the cabinet next to the teeth-brushing station and removes a bottle of Pantene. She squirts a couple globs into a small paper cup and hands it to me.

"Enough?"

"Uh-huh."

In the bathroom, she sits on the closed toilet seat with her Mac while I wait for the water to warm up. "Leave the curtain open."

"Okay."

I hesitantly remove my clothes with my back turned towards her and step into the shower. My stomach, I notice, is more bloated than usual, and I can no longer see my lowest ribs unless I suck in. As much as I hate one-on-one, I also know that if Nurse Carlie weren't here, I'd be on the floor frantically performing crunches and pushups to pacify my frenzied thoughts.

Except now, there's nothing I can do but try to block them out. I close my eyes and pretend the shower water is waves lapping over my golden skin. The dim ceiling light becomes a radiant sun, and Nurse Carlie's expeditious typing evolves into a gentle breeze rapping against swaying palm trees.

For eight minutes, I'm at peace . . . until she asks, "Are you almost done in there? I don't want you to be late to breakfast."

"Yeah. Hand me the towel."

She does, and I wrap it around my body before I reemerge into the chilly bathroom. I throw on my clean clothing—black leggings and a grey sweatshirt—and pile my hair into a messy bun.

"Was that so bad?" she asks as she's relocking the door.

"Let's just go to breakfast," I respond.

In the cafeteria, Ludmilla and Kevin argue about politics at the first table while Anne picks at a stack of pancakes at the second. Beside her, Jonathan chows down on a hamburger. He pays no attention to the ketchup stains that are smeared across his raggedy grey t-shirt.

I sit next to Stephanie at the third table and whisper, "I thought Jonathan was a vegan."

When she sees Jonathan's breakfast, Stephanie's eyes grow wide. "He isn't anymore."

"That can't be good for his body."

She nods. "Yeah, he's definitely gonna have a stomachache later. Have you seen Therese? Her underwear got mixed up with mine again."

"I haven't. She's probably with Dr. Bennett."

"Probably. Oh, guess what? I'm discharging tomorrow!"

"Really? Steph, I'm so happy for you."

"Thanks," she responds graciously. "Do you know when you're leaving yet?"

I shake my head. "Not soon enough. Jamie's gonna be pissed I can't take him trick-or-treating."

"I'm sure he understands that you have more important things to do."

"He's twelve years old. I don't think he even understands why I'm here."

"Has your friend visited you yet?"

"No, and she's not going to. She's made that crystal clear."

"Sucks."

"Whatever. It's not like I can do anything about it now."

I finish my breakfast—Cheerios, two-percent milk, a banana, and yogurt with granola—in thirty-seven minutes, after spending the first twenty unsuccessfully trying to convince Nurse Carlie that it's too much. Once she's checked my pockets for "one-hundred-percent completion," I return to my room to retrieve my textbook for school, and I'm surprised to find Therese lying on her bed, sobbing into her pillow.

"What's wrong?" I ask.

Therese wipes her nose on the sleeve of her sweatshirt. "My insurance won't cover any more days. I'm leaving this afternoon."

"They can do that?"

She nods. "I've seen it happen before. I just didn't expect it to happen to *me*."

"I'm so sorry, Therese."

"Don't be. You didn't do anything wrong. It's all my insurer's fucking fault!" She throws her pillow across the room, then breaks down again. In the brief time I've known her, I've never seen her so vulnerable, so . . . weak.

She's just human, I realize. *We all are.*

"Oh, Therese." Nurse Carlie sits beside her and gently massages her shoulders. "It'll be okay."

"But I'm not ready," Therese mumbles. "I'm so scared, Carls. I feel like I want to die."

"Why don't you go to school, Grace?" Nurse Carlie suggests, upon seeing the alarmed look on my face. "I'll stay here with Therese."

"O—okay. You've got this, Therese."

"Thanks, Grace," she whispers. "So do you."

I'm still in shock as I follow Nurse Helen back to the cafeteria to rejoin Stephanie. Her brown eyes are filled with a mix of concern and confusion.

"Is she all right?"

"I don't know," I respond. "I think she's scared."

"Therese? Scared?" Stephanie shakes her head. "I never thought I'd see the day."

"Me neither."

Ms. Crawford pushes her cart around the cafeteria, so we can gather our school supplies. Once again, Mr. Lipschitz's algebra assignment confuses the hell out of me. Keeping up with math inside the classroom is challenging enough; keeping up outside is next to impossible.

"Where are the pencils?" I ask.

"Temporarily unavailable. Here." Ms. Crawford hands me a stubby blue crayon. "You can use this."

"How do you expect me to do my schoolwork with a crayon?"

"I'm sure you'll figure it out." She offers me a strained smile, then hobbles over to Anne, who's raising her hand.

"What the hell?" I wonder aloud. "This is so dumb."

Stephanie, who's using her thumbnail to sharpen the tip of her red crayon, nods in agreement. "It's such bullshit. I mean, why should everyone be punished because some idiot went mental?"

"What are you talking about?"

Stephanie mimics dragging her crayon across her wrist.

"You mean someone cut themselves with a pencil?"

"Do you have a better explanation?"

I shake my head. "That's just so lame."

"And a School ID isn't?" she challenges. "We've all done stupid things, Grace. If we hadn't, we wouldn't be here."

"How do you know about the ID?" I ask.

"Therese told me."

"Ladies, that's enough!" Ms. Crawford hisses. "You're being disruptive!"

Stephanie rolls her eyes. "I'll tell ya one thing; my teacher's gonna hate grading this."

I run my finger over the smooth wax of my crayon, then gaze at the tiny algebraic equations in dismay. "No kidding."

I finish two barely-legible worksheets in the remaining eighty minutes of school. When I return to my room with Nurse Helen to relax before lunch, both Therese and her belongings are gone. A skinny bleach-blonde boy is unpacking clothing from a duffle bag. I watch as he folds his shirts, pants, and underwear into three orderly piles, which he then places on his desk.

"Who are you?"

The boy sets down a white sweatshirt and turns around. "Ryan. Are you my roommate?"

I nod. "I'm Grace."

"Nice to meet you, Grace." He glances at Nurse Liza, who smiles politely. "Let me guess; one-on-one?"

"How'd you know?"

"Been there. It sucks, doesn't it?"

"Sucks is an understatement," I say. "So, when'd you get here?"

"I was in cardiac for a couple days. I came this morning when a spot opened up."

"Therese's. Her insurance wouldn't cover her anymore."

"Shit."

"Been there too?" I ask.

Ryan shakes his head. "No, but at my last hospital, it happened to my roommate. The sad thing was, I knew she'd be back. Recovering takes time. It's not something you can do in just days or weeks or even months or years."

"Ryan?" Nurse Carlie pokes her head into our room. "Come with me please."

"Sure." Ryan finishes folding his sweatshirt and fixes his hair in the reflection of the window, so his dark roots aren't showing. "See ya, Grace."

"See ya," I echo.

"He seems nice," Nurse Helen says. "Don't you think?"

"I guess so," I respond. "I'm worried about Therese."

"Not everyone relapses when they discharge. Hopefully, her parents will find her an outpatient program that'll give her the support she needs."

"I hope so. She deserves it after everything she's been through."

"That she does. Are you ready for lunch?"

"No."

"Yes, you are. You've got this, Grace."

"You think?"

"I do," she says. "And who knows? Maybe this time won't be so bad."

"Yeah. Maybe."

Ten minutes later, however, as I stare down at a thick slice of vegetarian lasagna with an apple and a dinner roll on the side, what little optimism I had vanishes into thin air.

"I'm not eating this," I say. "It's too much. I'm gonna be sick."

"You'll be fine," Nurse Helen responds. "Just take it one bite at a time."

Across from me, Ryan swirls a strand of buttery linguine around his plastic fork. "She's right, you know," he says. "It's all in your head. Don't overthink it."

"How do you do it?" I ask.

"Eat?"

"Yeah."

"Because I don't have another choice. Feeding tubes fucking suck. And to be honest, the food here isn't so bad—at least compared to Mistlyn."

"Mistlyn?"

"My last hospital. Six months ago, I was transferred there because the waiting list for CTC was too long. It's in Manhattan."

"I've never been to Manhattan," I say. "Is it nice?"

"I don't know. Most of what I saw was the backs of buildings and alleys."

"Bummer." I finish my apple and reluctantly move on to the lasagna. "You don't have to stay," I tell Ryan as the others clear their trays. It's twelve-thirty, meaning everyone who's eaten lunch is allowed to leave.

"You sure? I can if you want me to."

"No, I'll be fine."

"Okay. How's the lasagna?"

"Gross. It's way too cheesy."

"I know it sucks," he says, "but from one anorexic to another, it does get better. I promise."

Anorexic. The word leaves a bitter taste in my mouth. "You think I'm anorexic?"

"Grace, you just spent thirty minutes eating a lunch most people would've finished in ten. And you're still not done."

I glance at my lasagna, which I've subconsciously divided into eight pieces with my fork. Six remain untouched. "I'm not anorexic."

"I used to be in denial too," he says. "I thought I wasn't skinny enough or sick enough to need treatment, but then I realized that by pretending nothing was wrong, I was fucking up my future. I can't go to college if I'm battling anorexia, so I had to accept that this was my reality and deal with it."

"Then why are you here?" I ask.

"Just because recovery's possible doesn't mean it's easy. Shit happens."

"No kidding." After a brief pause, I add, "Lately, it seems like everything's gone to shit."

"Mmm. Mental illness does that."

I stuff a piece of lasagna in my mouth and chew, feeling the gooey cheese stick to the roof of my mouth, like gum adhering to the bottom of a brand-new shoe. "It sure does."

"Is it true?"

Dr. Bennett glances up from his pad of paper, where he's scribbling illegible notes about my uneventful weekend, and asks, "Is what true, Grace?"

"What Ryan said. Am I . . ." I take a deep breath. "Anorexic."

He nods. "Yes. Your behaviors and symptoms clearly indicate that you are suffering from an eating disorder."

"Oh."

"How do you feel, hearing me say that?"

His question stumps me. Of course, I'd had some suspicions;

I mean, what else would explain my crippling fear of food and my constant need to burn calories and my obsession with the thinspo sites and videos? Yet as Ryan said yesterday, part of me was under the impression that I wasn't thin enough to have a diagnosable illness. In every book I've read or Lifetime movie I've watched, the emaciated protagonist starved herself to the point where an IV was the only thing keeping her alive. But I'm not like that. Ten days ago, I was conditioning for a soccer tournament, and I felt fine. I still do.

"Grace? Did you hear my question?"

"Indifferent," I respond truthfully. "I'm on one-on-one, so it's not like I can do anything; you know, restrict or whatever."

"Just because you're unable to engage in disordered behaviors doesn't mean your feelings are invalid."

"What do you want me to say; that I'm scared? I know the statistics, doctor. I know anorexia has the highest mortality rate of any mental illness. But I'm not afraid of death."

Dr. Bennett jots this down. "Have you been experiencing suicidal thoughts lately?"

"Would it matter if I was?"

"Of course it matters, Grace."

"Well, I'm not, so you don't have to worry."

"Speaking of worry, your mother called me this morning. She says you're still angry at her."

"Well, yeah. If she hadn't freaked out, I wouldn't have to be watched twenty-four seven because I lost a few pounds."

"It's more than just that."

"Maybe, but I still don't want to forgive her. At least not until I get out of here."

"You do realize that your mother needs to be involved in establishing an aftercare plan for you, yes?"

I groan. "I know, I know. But that doesn't mean I like it."

"Nobody does, Grace. That said, there are some things you simply must do. Like eating."

"Eating also sucks," I say. "I feel bloated all the time. Sometimes nauseous too."

"Well, I commend you for persevering. You're a strong girl."

"I mean, I guess so. It just seems so unfair."

"What does?"

"Tomorrow's Halloween. I'm supposed to take Jamie trick-or-treating and go to a party with my friend and watch scary movies, like a normal teen. But instead, I'm stuck here with complete strangers and adults who treat me like I'm four and all these things in my head that just don't make sense."

"Are these things voices?"

"No. They're more like thoughts, I guess, but they're not my thoughts. It's like they belong to someone else, someone I barely know." I shake my head. "I sound crazy, don't I?"

"You don't sound crazy, Grace. You sound conflicted and possibly trapped, if I'm reading you correctly."

"You're right," I say. "About everything. But what I want to know, doctor, is if it's this place that's making me feel trapped . . . or if it's me."

14

The morning of October 31st begins in the same mundane fashion as every other morning this week with a six o'clock weigh-in and breakfast of Cheerios, milk, fruit, and yogurt with granola. The nurses have hung Halloween decorations in the cafeteria and the Rec Room, and our usual groups have been replaced with the same juvenile activities my elementary school teachers organized to keep us entertained when we were children, like coloring pages, cross-word puzzles, and a round of Consequences themed "Halloween Party" as the grand finale.

Once Avi, who arrived shortly after Stephanie discharged yesterday, has taken his turn, we go around the table reading our nonsensical stories aloud.

Mine is; *The sinister Freddy Kruger met the frightening Samara Morgan at a Halloween Party. He gave her a severed head and said to her, "Let's have intercorpse." She said to him, "I love this Rob Zombie song," and the consequence was they drank the poisonous punch and died. The world said, "Heeeeeeere's Johnny!"*

Jonathan, who's sitting on the floor shading in a pumpkin mandala with a black crayon, glances up when he hears this last part. "I don't like that nickname."

"We're not talking about you," Ludmilla says. "Haven't you seen *The Shining*? You know, 'all work and no play makes Jack a dull boy?'"

"I don't watch movies like that."

"Movies like what?"

"Movies that glorify insanity. Movies where innocent people get hurt."

"So, what you do you watch then; *My Little Pony*?"

Jonathan scrunches his mandala into a ball and hurls it at Ludmilla. "Fuck this bullshit!"

"Jonathan, where are you going?" Nurse Helen asks as he storms out of the Rec Room. When Jonathan ignores her, she calls to her colleague, "Pete! Some help please!"

The six of us listen as Nurse Pete unsuccessfully tries to calm Jonathan down; with every attempt, he becomes even more hysterical, so that before long, his ear-piercing screams consume the entire ward.

As more backup is called, this time in the form of two brawny security guards, Anne leans over and whispers, "I used to be afraid of horror movies, like pee-in-my-pants type afraid. Then I came here and realized that real life is much scarier than the stuff we see in films."

"No kidding," I say. "You know, I never imagined this would be how I spent Halloween."

Anne snorts. "Like any of us did."

After Jonathan's outburst, nobody is in the mood to celebrate. We spend the rest of the morning killing time by playing board games and watching *Coraline* on DVD until lunch.

"Does he do that often?" Ryan asks. He tears open a pack of

ketchup, accidently spilling a blob on his white *Love is Love* sweatshirt. "Shit."

"He's getting better," I respond. "He's not napping as much as he used to."

"He's been here for a while, hasn't he?"

I nod. "Almost eight weeks. He missed his seventeenth birthday."

"I was in Mistlyn for my seventeenth last February. It wasn't one of my better birthdays to say the least."

"I'll bet."

"My boyfriend visited me though, and that was nice. He's actually driving here now so we can catch up. I hope you don't mind if I use our room."

"No, that's fine. I was going to hang out in the Rec Room anyway. Anne beat Avi and me in *Clue*, and I want a rematch."

"Ah. Nothing says spooky like a game of murder."

"Except it sucks that we have to use marker caps as our weapon tokens," I say. "I'm so sick of being treated like a little kid."

Ryan glances at Nurse Carlie, who's watching us out of her periphery from table two. "Do you know when you're getting off one-on-one?"

"No idea. After what happened, I doubt Dr. Bennett's eager to take any chances."

"So, how'd you do it anyway?"

"Lose weight?" When he nods, I say, "It was easy. I just told him what he wanted to hear."

"I used to do that too."

"Lie?"

He shakes his head. "Manipulate. There's a difference."

"Yeah?"

"Uh-huh. And for a while, it was entertaining to see how

much shit I could get away with, but then people began to catch on, and it stopped being fun, because I realized if I kept it up, I'd die. So, I stopped manipulating and started telling the truth. And it worked—at least in the beginning."

"What went wrong?" I ask.

"Nothing. That's the problem. One moment, I was goofing off at the Six Flags Fright Fest with my friends; the next, I was skipping meals and lying about food again."

"You relapsed."

"Yes, but it didn't make sense. I mean, I'd gone through intensive outpatient treatment. I had a therapist, a nutritionist, a 504 plan at school. Everything was going so well."

"None of this makes sense," I say. "It's scientifically proven that humans need food to survive, so why is it that whenever I eat, I feel like I'm committing a crime? How do you explain that? Or Ludmilla feeling so happy one moment and so depressed the next? Or Jonathan thinking that God is trying to kill him?"

"You don't," Ryan responds. "You accept it for what it is, and you deal with it, because there's really only one other option."

"Death?"

He nods. "Exactly. So, that's why we listen to science. That's why we—"

"Eat." I swallow the last bite of my quesadilla, licking guacamole off my fingertips. "It's kinda funny when you think about it."

"What is?"

"That for once, I actually understand science."

Keeping to his word, after lunch Ryan and his boyfriend disappear into our room. Every time I pass, I hear them laughing, and every time I peek inside, Ryan's face is lit up with a smile. I know I should feel happy for him, but at the same time,

I'm envious of what he has; a dependable social life, clear-cut future goals, and people he can turn to in times of sadness and despair.

As for me; my best friend still hasn't responded to the three voicemails I've left her, my mother and I barely talk anymore, the boy I like is dating the girl who's indirectly the reason I'm stuck in the psych ward on one of my favorite days of the year, and my brother can't go trick-or-treating tonight because I'm not around to take him. The last time I felt this lonely was when Dad left, and at least then I had Lou to help me cope with the guilt and pain.

But now, I have no one.

"Hey, are you all right?" Anne touches my shoulder, and I flinch. Lost in my thoughts, I hadn't realized that she had joined me in the Rec Room. "You don't look so good."

"I'm thinking about last Halloween," I say, "and how things were so much better than they are now."

"Yeah? What'd you do?"

"Lou and I took my brother trick-or-treating, and then we hung out at her house eating candy and watching cheesy horror flicks and talking about . . . I don't even remember what we talked about. It doesn't matter anyway. The point is that I had a great time. I was so happy."

Anne smiles sadly. "I wish I was as lucky as you are."

"You think I'm lucky?"

"I do. I know things with Lou aren't good right now, but at least you had a chance to know what friendship was like before it all went to shit. That's more than I ever got."

"Grace!" Nurse Pete calls. "Phone!"

I groan. "Great. That's probably my mom calling to wish me a Happy Halloween."

"My mom did that this morning," Anne says. "She tried to

pretend like she wasn't crying, but I knew she was. These phones pick up everything."

"My mom doesn't cry when she's upset," I respond. "She just gets real quiet. She didn't speak to anyone for two weeks straight after my dad left."

"Grace!"

With a sigh, I force myself to stand up and trudge into the hall. Nurse Pete hands me the cordless phone. "Twenty minutes, okay?"

"Okay." I wait until he's some distance away to hold the phone to my ear. "Hey, Mom. What's going on?"

"Grace? It's Lou."

"Lou?" I repeat in disbelief. My knees feel weak, as if the shock of hearing her voice is enough to make them give out. "I—I didn't think you'd call."

"Yeah, well, here I am." She chuckles nervously. "I hope you're not upset."

My shock quickly becomes outrage. "Not upset? Not upset! You're kidding, right?"

"I, uh, I didn't mean—"

"Lou, do you know what it's like to always be surrounded by people and still feel like you're all alone?" I ask. "I do. Every morning, I wake up in the same place to the same faces, but the face I want to see more than anyone else's is too busy making out with her girlfriend and stuffing her cheeks with Halloween candy to give a damn about her best friend. I'm miserable here, Lou. I'm sad, and I'm lonely, and I'm confused, and sometimes, I just want to fall asleep and never wake up. I know I said things I shouldn't have, and I know I treated you unfairly, but you're the only person who hasn't given up on me. So, why now? Why did you give up on me now?"

"Because I was scared."

"And you think I'm not? Lou—"

"Let me explain. For the past year, I've watched my mom battle an illness that she might not beat. I've seen heartbroken families, adults surviving off ventilators, and kids our age who are so sick, they can barely stand. That shit does something to your brain, man. Something that no amount of time or therapy can ever erase.

"When your mom told me you were in the hospital, that fear took over. I replayed our stupid fight in my head again and again, and with every time, I believed a little more that it was my fault; that I was the reason you were sick. After that, I didn't know how I could possibly face you."

"You could've at least called," I say.

"I know."

"So, why didn't you?"

"Because . . ." Lou sighs. "I guess because I didn't know what to say."

"Even just 'hi' or 'how are you' would've worked. I hated not knowing if you were still angry at me."

"You thought I was angry at you?"

"Well, what else was I supposed to think?"

"I don't know. I don't fucking know." She sighs again. "I get it. I fucked up, and I hurt you for reasons that were stupid and selfish. But I can fix it."

"How?"

"I'm not going to that party tonight. Cass is sick, and I'm not in the mood to go by myself."

"Okay. So, what?"

"So, tomorrow after school, Ma and I are driving to CTC. I think it's time I saw my best friend again."

"What changed?" I ask.

"I did. I remembered something you told me a while ago

when Cass' brother was getting out of juvie. 'Being there for her is enough,' you said. 'She needs to know she isn't alone.'"

"Words to live by, huh?"

"Damn right. I just—I just hope it isn't too late."

I don't respond.

"Grace? You there?"

"I'm here, Lou. I'm just thinking."

"About what?"

"About how angry I was at you, and how for days, I wanted nothing to do with you ever again. But if being in this place has taught me anything, it's that life is too short to hold grudges. So, if you're willing to try again, then I am too."

"Oh my god. You're the best."

"Grace?" Nurse Pete taps his watch, indicating that my twenty minutes are up.

"I gotta go," I say. "See you tomorrow?"

"Totally. I can't wait."

"Me neither." I'm about to hang up when suddenly an idea dawns on me. "Hey, Lou? You said you're staying in tonight, right?"

"Uh-huh."

"I know it's last minute, but can you take Jamie trick-or-treating? He doesn't have friends, and with me here—"

"Yeah, sounds great," she interrupts. "I'll tell him you say hi."

"Thanks. That'll mean a lot to him."

"You're a good sister, you know?" When I don't respond, she says, "Well, you should. Happy Halloween, Grace."

"Happy Halloween, Lou."

Click.

"Good call?" Nurse Pete asks when I return the phone to him.

"My best friend doesn't hate me," I respond.

"I'll take that as a yes. Listen, Liza's setting up *Harry Potter and the Sorcerer's Stone* in the Rec Room if you'd like to watch."

"Damn. I haven't seen that movie since I was, like, nine years old."

"Sometimes, it's good to revisit our childhood," he says.

"Where's a Time Turner when you need it?" I joke.

"Time Turner?"

"It's a reference to—" I shake my head. "Never mind. Yeah, I'd love to watch."

"Oh, one more thing," he says. "Everyone else had snack while you were on the phone. We're offering candy in lieu of trick-or-treating. I believe we have Hershey's bars, M&Ms, Snickers—"

"Got any Mounds?" I ask.

Nurse Pete shakes his head. "I'm afraid not."

"That's okay. I'll, uh, I'll have Hershey's."

"Milk Chocolate or Cookies 'N Cream?"

"Milk."

"You sure? I hear the Cookies 'N Cream is mighty delicious."

"Yeah, I'm sure."

"Then Milk it is. You coming?"

I nod. "I'm right behind you."

I'M a mess when I wake up the morning after Halloween; lethargic, irritable, and exhausted from spending another night tossing and turning, unable to shut off my active mind. As I follow Nurse Carlie to the Weigh-In Room, I complain about the poor heating and the stiff cots and Jonathan's bothersome habit of pacing the hall until his sleeping meds kick in.

Then after she's recorded my number, I continue to whine about how ludicrous it is that Dr. Bennett hasn't reduced my meal plan, even though I'm complying with everything he's asked me to.

"Grace, you know I don't have that answer," she says finally. "You can talk to him about it at your next session. Now, please stay here with Nurse Helen while I get Ryan's weight."

"How'd you sleep, Grace?" Nurse Helen asks while her colleague guides a drowsy Ryan into the hall.

"Fan-fucking-tastic," I respond sarcastically. "I've never slept better."

Five minutes of uncomfortable silence later, Ryan returns. He swaps his sleeping shirt with a flannel button-down, then tosses the former into a paper bag designated for his dirty clothing. He's even skinnier shirtless; his stomach is concave, and his ribs protrude from his skin. It's no wonder his boyfriend looked so sad when he hugged him goodbye; I bet he could feel all of Ryan's bones.

Ryan catches me looking and blushes. "Sorry."

"No, it's fine," I lie. "The first time I saw Therese, she was butt-naked."

"I wish I'd met that girl. She sounds super cool."

"She was," I say. "I mean, *is*. She is cool."

The morning crawls by; first breakfast, then group, then snack, then school, then a brief break that I spend relieving myself while Nurse Liza watches. At lunch, I finish my macaroni and cheese on time thanks to Ryan's support, but when everyone follows Nurse Pete to the Rec Room for Art Therapy, I head to my room with Nurse Helen to take a much-needed nap. The second my head hits my pillow, I'm asleep.

An hour or so later, I awaken to someone shaking my shoulders. "Rise and shine, sleepyhead," a familiar voice says.

When I open my eyes, Lou hovers over me with a silly grin on her face. "Oh. You came."

Her smile wavers. "Why do you sound disappointed? Are you still angry at me, because if you are, I'll do anything? I'll—I'll say I'm sorry a hundred times or, uh . . . how does twenty bucks sound?"

I laugh. "Lou, I'm not angry. I'm just tired."

"Phew."

"I really had you there for a minute, didn't I?"

She rolls her eyes. "You little bitch, I missed you so much."

"I missed you too," I say.

"Look what I brought." Lou sits next to me and pulls a fun-sized Mounds out of the pocket of her electric-blue jeans. "It was the only thing that blonde lady didn't confiscate when she checked me in."

"Thanks." I hold the candy in my palm and think about last night when I asked Nurse Pete if I could have one for snack. It's funny how something I wanted less than twenty-four hours ago now seems so undesirable.

"Aren't you gonna eat it?"

"What? Yeah." I tear open the wrapper with my teeth and pop the candy in my mouth. "Mmm. That's good."

"Right? We had a crapload of leftovers, so I figured I'd bring you one. You seem like you need a little sweetness in your life."

"Lou, there's something I have to tell you," I say.

"I know, Grace."

"You do?"

She nods. "Your mom already told me."

"Oh." After a brief pause, I ask, "So, how do you feel about it? Are you, like, freaked out?"

"Of course not. Grace, I love you. In sickness and in health."

"You make it sound like we're getting married," I joke.

Lou laughs. "I mean, there are enough people here for a ceremony, and that blonde guy with the mismatched socks seems pretty religious so . . ."

"Ah, Jonathan," I say. "He's a handful."

"No kidding. But in all seriousness, I'm not freaked out. Like, I could tell kinda something was up when you stopped eating lunch at school."

"Then what are you?" I ask.

"Hopeful," she says.

"Hopeful? How come?"

"Because I know you, Grace, and I know that when you want something, nothing will stand in your way."

I laugh. "My mom said the same thing the other day."

"How're things with your mom?"

"They've been better. She visits me every afternoon between shifts, and we play cards and talk about TV shows and other trivial stuff like that until we run out of things to say. Then she leaves."

"That doesn't sound so bad."

"I think the bad part is how fake everything has become. I've tried not to be mad, because I'm trying not to hold grudges anymore, but after what she did, it's not easy."

"What'd she do?"

"She overreacted when I lost a few pounds and made my doctor put me on one-on-one, which basically means that I have to be supervised twenty-four seven. That's why there's a nurse sitting outside my room."

"Supervised . . . even when you use the bathroom?"

"Yep. And when I shower too."

Lou's dark eyes grow wide. "You must hate that, Miss Modesty."

"Yeah, it's pretty shitty."

"Well, as long as you're safe . . ."

"I am."

". . . and eating enough . . ."

"Three thousand calories a day."

". . . then I guess it's not for nothing. You don't have to be happy or love life if that's not where you're at; you just have to be okay. When Ma was getting chemo for the first time, her doctor told me and Pa something. He said; 'If one day seems like too much, take it one hour at a time. And if one hour seems like too much, take it one minute at a time.' Think you can do that?"

"One minute at a time," I repeat. "Yeah, I like that. What are we gonna do in this minute?"

"In this minute . . ." Lou strokes her chin thoughtfully. "In this minute, I will tell you about Mr. Dipshit's reaction to the NSFW costumes half the girls wore to school yesterday."

I grin. "Okay."

While Lou animatedly recaps our dorky math teacher's "appropriate attire" spiel, I glance at the analog clock overlooking Ryan's tidy desk. The big hand is on the seven while the small hand hovers between the two and the three. In twenty-five minutes, one of the nurses will bring me my afternoon snack; in an hour, Lou will have to leave so I can meet with Dr. Bennett.

But I won't worry about either right now. Instead, I'll do as she suggests and take things—take life—one minute at a time until my days aren't so long and exhausting and my nights are no longer spent tossing and turning but are filled with peaceful, uninterrupted sleep.

"Has taking melatonin before bed improved your sleep?"

In response to Dr. Bennett's question, I nod. "I don't wake up at night anymore, and the bad dreams are mostly gone."

"So, this dosage feels sufficient?"

"I mean, I actually have energy again, so yeah. It does."

He smiles. "I'm glad to hear that. And how's your mood been?"

"My mood's been okay. Since Lou visited last week and I started the medication, things have seemed a little more . . ."

"Stable?"

"Yes, but also hopeful. I think that's improved my mood too."

"I bet you're right. While we're talking about improvement, there's something else I'd like to discuss with you today."

"What's that?"

"Your nurses and I have noticed you're making progress, therefore we've agreed to limit one-to-one exclusively to meals and snacks."

"Does that mean I can shower in private?"

"Yes, it does."

"Finally! You don't know how long I've been waiting to hear you say that."

"There's another thing. Because you're progressing so well, we can begin exploring next steps for when you're no longer with us."

"You mean like when I discharge?"

"Exactly."

"Oh," I respond uncertainly. "Cool."

When I was admitted to CTC twelve days ago, discharging was all I thought about. But as time passed, I developed a sickening comfort for being, well, sick. There isn't judgement or pressure or an overwhelming amount of responsibility in the hospital. Even the rules are simple; eat your food, take your medication, and cooperate with your treatment team, so when you eventually leave, you won't have to come back.

Real life is much more complicated. Here, I am a caterpillar swaddled inside the safety of my cocoon; out there, I am a butterfly hopelessly drifting from place to place without ever finding her footing—or wings, in this analogy. What if I'm not ready? What if I relapse, like Ryan did when he left Mistlyn?

"Grace? Did you hear me?" Dr. Bennett's voice snaps me back to reality.

"Sorry, what?"

"I was saying; with your mother's input, we've drafted a plan moving forward. Have you heard of PHP?"

I shake my head.

"PHP stands for Partial Hospital Program. There's a facility in Manhattan that offers an eight-week stepdown program. This will give you a clearer overview."

He hands me a pamphlet titled *Welcome to The Center for Adolescents with Disordered Eating*, and I turn to the second page, where a detailed synopsis states:

At CADE, we strive to assist adolescents ages eleven to eighteen who suffer from eating disorders through our DBT approach. DBT, short for Dialectical Behavioral Therapy, combines cognitive and behavioral therapies to provide an individual with healthier methods of coping with painful emotions, often through acceptance and change.

Our Partial Hospital Program runs from noon to six forty-five Monday through Saturday with a provided lunch upon arrival and a premade dinner at six o'clock. CADE encourages family members of the adolescents to attend Multi-Family Therapy on Wednesday. Additional groups will be provided for parents/caretakers on Monday and Friday.

We invite new clients to join by signing up on our website or scheduling an appointment in person. All contact information is listed below.

It then proceeds to explain the history of CADE and

provides blurbs from past clients who'd had "an intense, eye-opening experience" and were given "an opportunity to redefine myself and my future."

"I don't want to do a program," I say. "I just want to go back to my old life."

"That's what CADE does," Dr. Bennett responds. "The staff there are experts; they know how to help mentally ill teens successfully readjust to their lives outside of a hospital setting. Give them a chance, Grace. I promise it will be worthwhile."

"But what if my mother can't drive me?" I challenge. "Manhattan is almost an hour away from our house, you know."

"Perhaps you can take a bus."

"Yeah, because sending her 'mentally ill teen' on a bus to another state is a fantastic idea," I respond sarcastically. "Get real, doctor. This will never work."

"We need to establish a plan before you leave. Without one, there's a much greater chance that you'll relapse."

"Well, figure something else out. I'm not going, and that's final."

"Grace, be rational about this," he pleads as I abruptly stand up. "You just got off one-on-one. Don't give me a reason to put you back on."

"See you in family therapy," I snap. Then before he can say another word, I indignantly leave his office, slamming the door behind me, and head in the direction of my room.

"Grace?" a vaguely familiar voice asks. "Is that you?"

When I turn around, Lana, the fierce Wildcat's striker who I collided with at our soccer match nearly two weeks ago, stands behind me snacking from a bag of pretzels.

"Lana? What are you doing here?"

"I'm visiting Kevin," she responds. "He's my brother. What are *you* doing here?"

"I, uh . . ." I stare down at my socks, suddenly self-conscious. "Uh, how's your arm?"

"It's all right. I got my cast changed yesterday. Wanna sign it?"

"Sure." She hands me a blue Sharpie, and I scribble *3-2* between *i told you humans couldn't fly* and *need a hand?*

Lana laughs. "Are you coming back for the end of the season?"

"I don't think so. I'm taking a little break from sports so I can sort some stuff out. Is your team still in the tournament?"

"Final four, baby."

"And mine?"

She nods. "Rematch is next week."

"Wildcats versus Woodpeckers," I say. "That should be an exciting game."

"Well, hopefully I'll see you on the sidelines," she responds, "even though as far as high school competition goes, I'm supposed to hate your guts."

"Screw competition. Friends are better than enemies."

"Damn straight." After a brief hesitation, Lana throws her arms around me in an awkward, yet surprisingly sweet hug. "I knew we'd see each other again."

"It's a small world," I joke.

She smiles. "But it's full of big opportunity. Don't let yours go to waste."

I watch her walk away, headed towards Kevin and Avi's shared room, with a nagging feeling in my stomach that I cannot dismiss. Ever since Dr. Bennett authorized one-on-one, I've been too preoccupied with bad body image and too full of resentment to remember the things I miss about my regular life; things I'll only be able to reattain in recovery.

I miss soccer. I miss the thrill of victory. I miss the satisfaction of improvement. I miss the way my quads burn when I sprint up and down the field. I even miss my teammates, despite how awful they can be. I miss being able to participate in sports or join a club or hang out with Lou without twenty-four seven supervision. I miss my freedom.

So, ignoring the parts of me that insist I'm not sick enough to require aftercare, I return to Dr. Bennet's office, where he's texting someone. "Um, doctor?"

When he sees me, he slips his phone into the pocket of his baggy khakis. "How can I help you, Grace?"

I sit across from him and tuck my legs beneath me, anxiously toying with my bracelet. "I was, uh, I was hoping you could tell me more about CADE."

Dr. Bennett smiles. "Of course. What would you like to know?"

15

I discharge from CTC's psych ward on November 11th, two days after Dad's forty-third birthday. Mom helps me transfer my belongings from the hospital to her car, where Jamie is waiting in the backseat. He greets me with a hug, and I cradle his head against my chest, stroking his overgrown hair. I guess Mom hadn't managed to get him to the barbershop after all.

As we drive home, listening to "Nineties at Noon" on Light 100.5, I gaze out my window at the affluent neighborhood we're passing through. Potch Lane, nicknamed "Posh Lane" for owning the most expensive houses in town, is no longer boasting beautiful fall foliage and extravagant Halloween decorations, but bare trees and rotten Jack-O-Lanterns that squirrels hungrily feast on.

Lou said Jamie looked adorable in the Dustin Henderson costume Mom bought him at Savers. She also said she would have taken pictures for me if Mrs. Jackson hadn't temporarily confiscated her phone when she saw Lou's Quarter One report card. It turns out flash cards aren't as effective with algebra as they are with chemistry.

My house is the same as I remember it, aside from a few small differences due to the rapidly changing weather. I kick off my moccasins next to Mom's heels and breathe a sigh of relief. The familiar smells of coffee grinds and citrus air freshener embrace me like a warm hug.

"Welcome home, Grace," Mom says. "Here you go." She hands me a duffel bag, then begins huffing the second upstairs. "I didn't realize I'd brought you so much clothing."

"I didn't wear most of it," I respond. "I mainly stuck to sweats."

"Comfort before cool, huh?"

"Yeah, except they made me take the strings off. Isn't that dumb?"

"Rules are rules."

"I know, but I still think it's dumb." I walk into my room and toss the bag on my floor with an audible *thunk*. "Everything about CTC was."

"At least you're home now," Jamie says. "I missed you so much."

"Not as much as I missed you, kiddo."

Jamie cracks a small smile. "You wanna bet?"

"All right, that's enough," Mom says. "Save the competition for another time. I imagine you're pretty tired, Grace."

"Exhausted."

"Then we'll give you some space until dinner. How does pasta sound?"

"Pasta's fine."

"Okay. Just—just let me know if you need anything."

"I will."

"You know I'm always here for you, right?"

"Yeah, Mom. I know."

"Good." Mom kisses my forehead. "When was the last time things were this quiet?"

"I can't remember," I respond. "God, it feels so freakin' amazing."

"You never realize how much you miss something until it's gone. Here, I bet you missed this too." She takes my phone out of the pocket of her jeans and hands it to me. "I thought you'd want to let Lou know you're home."

"Sweet. Thanks, Mom."

"You're welcome. Tell her I say hi."

"Okay, I will."

Once she's gone, however, I toss my phone aside and collapse onto my bed. I'm too tired to text and too disinterested to bother with social media or worse, my school email, which is probably overflowing with dozens of unread messages. I don't know what will happen with school moving forward—or most of my future, for that matter—and that worries me. As much as I've tried living minute by minute, I cannot dismiss the anxiety I feel simply imagining everything that could go wrong now that I'm no longer bound to clear-cut rules, like I was in the hospital.

While Mom was signing my discharge papers with Dr. Bennett, Ryan sat beside me on my cot. "Will you be all right?"

"I hope so," I responded. "How 'bout you?"

Ryan shrugged. "Right now, hope's all I've got too."

"This all feels so surreal," I said. "Is it bad to be scared?"

"Nah, I think that's normal. I was pretty scared too when I discharged from Mistlyn."

"Yeah?"

"Big time." Ryan was quiet for a moment or two, gazing out the window with a distant look in his blue eyes. Finally, he said, "I'd wish you luck, but I know you'll kick ass."

I grinned. "Thanks."

That's when Mom announced that it was time for us to leave. Ryan and I hugged, and I thanked him one more time. When I walked through the door, this time without a stretcher and an EMT, I didn't look back. I knew if I did, I'd cry.

Now that I'm home, the tears I've suppressed all afternoon stream down my cheeks. I'm scared, and I'm conflicted, and I'm more confused than I was before—if that's even possible. So, I grab my phone, insert my earbuds, and drown out my troubling thoughts with the Goo Goo Dolls until I've drifted into a soundless sleep.

I awaken a short while later to Mom calling my name. "Grace? Are you up?"

"Shit," I mumble. I yank my earbuds out as they're blasting *Iris* and toss them aside. My phone says it's six thirty-six, which in addition to the garlicky aroma wafting through the house can only mean one thing; dinnertime.

After I've used the bathroom, splashing water on my face to snub my lingering drowsiness, I head downstairs, where Mom is tending to a bubbling pot of marinara sauce. She's already placed three plates of linguine at our seats. I have the largest serving.

"Uh, Mom? Isn't that too much?"

"It's not," she responds. "I measured out one cup to be sure."

"But that's three hundred calories!"

"And?" When she sees the distraught look on my face, Mom sighs. "Hon, you still have a long way to go before you're in your target weight range. I know this isn't easy, but it's what's best for you and your health."

I'm sick of hearing other people claim that they know what's best for me, but since I'm not in the mood to argue with her, I say, "Okay, whatever. Is there anything I can do to help?"

"Because I love you, and I'm going to let that—that damn thing boss you around anymore. Got it?"

I scowl. "Fine. If it makes you so happy, I'll eat."

"Thank you." Returning her attention to Jamie, she says, "Tell me about the songs Mr. Gangi selected."

"Well, for the first one . . ."

While Jamie animatedly recaps the four pieces he'll be playing, including a 1920s rhythm and blues and a premature *Walking in a Winter Wonderland*, I wind a couple strands of saucy linguine around my fork and force them through my lips. I should be used to this—after all, I've been eating these portions, if not more, for the past week—yet it's still incredibly challenging. I'm beginning to think that it'll always be.

Ten minutes later, as I'm polishing off my final bite of pasta, the door opens, and an unfamiliar man walks through. He discards his black leather jacket on the counter and kicks off his Oxfords, revealing ugly argyle socks. Then he sees me.

"Who's this?"

"My daughter, Grace," Mom responds. "Grace, this is my boyfriend, Trevor."

"Ah, so this is the famous Grace. It's a pleasure to meet you."

"You too." I extend my hand, expecting a shake, but he surprises me by kissing it instead. The second his scruff touches my skin, I quickly retract. "So, uh, how do you know my mom?"

"From work."

"Oh. Are you her boss?"

Mom chuckles, as if I've made a joke. "No, honey. We're in different departments."

"What's for dinner?" Trevor asks. "I'm fucking starving."

"Please, Trevor. Watch your language around Grace and Jamie."

"Oh, come on, Kira. It's nothing they haven't heard before."

Mom sighs. "There's pasta on the stove. Would you like something to drink?"

"Yeah. Got any beer?"

"First shelf in the fridge."

"Thanks." Trevor spoons a heaping pile of pasta and sauce into a bowl, grabs a Budweiser, and sits down beside Jamie. "What's shakin', my man?"

"Not much. Are you coming to my Jazz Band show on Friday?"

"Wouldn't miss it for the world."

"Do you mind driving him, Trevor?" Mom asks. "I have to be in Manhattan with Grace."

"Of course not," he says. "I'll bring the Bentley. You like that one, don't you, Jamester?"

"Yeah, it's all right."

"Just all right?"

Jamie shrugs. "I mean, I don't know much about cars."

Trevor shoots him an incredulous look. "What kind of guy doesn't know his cars? When I was your age, my father would let me ride his Chevy around our neighborhood. Best fucking thing he ever did for me."

"What happened to your father?" I ask.

"We grew apart. After I graduated high school, he stayed in Nevada, and I moved here to start a new life. We haven't spoken much since."

"Oh."

"We don't speak to our father either," Jamie says.

"Uh, maybe we shouldn't have this conversation," Mom begins to say, but Jamie ignores her.

"It's okay though," he continues. "I never knew him, not really. But Grace did."

"Do you miss him, Grace?" Trevor asks.

"What?"

"Your father? Do you miss him?"

"Yeah, of course. He was . . ." I clear my throat. "Never mind. Uh, Mom? Can I be excused? I finished my dinner."

Mom frowns. "Are you sure you're all right, Grace? You seem on edge."

"I'm fine. I'm still a little tired, I guess."

"Well, okay. If you need someone to talk to—"

"I know, Mom," I interrupt. "I will."

Upstairs on my dresser, three texts from Lou light up the lockscreen of my phone. When I open iMessage, I'm surprised to find that our conversation from the morning of my admission to the ER is still there. I guess with everything that had happened, I never had the chance to delete it.

Lou: hey girl. whats up?

Grace: not much. just sitting in spanish bored af.

Lou: i feel u. im so not in the mood for another euro lecture.

Grace: yeah mr duffy is super dull.

Lou: ikr? talk about a snooze fest.

Grace: lol so true.

Lou: oh btw could u help me study for my math quiz at lunch? im so fucked if I fail again!

Grace: np. see u then.

Lou: thnx ur the best <3

Even though less than three weeks have passed since then, to me it feels more like months—years even. Time is endless in the hospital. I remember spending many groups staring at the clock, willing the hands to move faster. Between them and my three meals and snacks, I'd do anything I could to distract myself from the boredom. More often than not, that "anything" was sleeping.

I should feel more awake now that I'm home, but I don't. I keep thinking that this is a dream, and I'll wake up soon in my cot surrounded by squeaky clogs and the sound of Jonathan screaming in the hall. Perhaps a part of me hopes it is. Perhaps that's the part Dr. Bennett warned me about; the part that will make my recovery a marathon and not a sprint.

I spend the rest of the evening catching up on my YouTube subscriptions and listening to more music. Around eleven o'clock, as my battery hits one-percent, I realize I've forgotten to take my melatonin. I tiptoe into Mom's room to see if she's still awake, but she's already asleep in her bed with Trevor. Casual slacks and a button-up shirt are folded neatly on his nightstand to the right of his phone. As I watch, the screen silently lights up with a text from someone named Heather.

She could be anyone, I tell myself. *A colleague, a relative . . . or a love interest.*

I don't like Trevor. From the moment I met him, I had a gut feeling that he was no good. Maybe it's the condescending way he talks to my brother. Maybe it's because he kissed my hand when he should have shaken it. Or maybe it's because he reminds me too much of my father just before he left.

With a sigh, I trudge back to my room, where I lie beneath my tangled covers and gaze out my window at the starless sky.

It's going to be a long night.

I DON'T HAVE high expectations for my first day at CADE. To make matters worse, the highway is backed up pretty badly, making an already lengthy fifty-minute drive twenty minutes longer. The traffic station reports a head-on collision with multiple injuries and one possible death. But all I see is a bunch of dirty men in hats repairing a pothole.

"So, this is New York City," Mom says as she passes a *Welcome to Manhattan* sign. The car on our right—a silver Volkswagen with a *Black Lives Matter* bumper sticker—takes a sharp turn into her lane, and she honks. "What do you think?"

"It's loud," I say.

"Yes, it is."

"And polluted."

"Another reason why you shouldn't smoke."

"And the traffic fucking sucks."

"Grace, language!" she scolds. "Could you at least try to look on the bright side?"

"And what would that be?" I ask. "Like, I know CADE has a good reputation or whatever, but it's just so inconvenient. What are you going to do when you have to work a double shift? Or Jamie has a show? Or something else comes up, and you can't drive me? Trevor won't always be around to cover for you, you know. He's got a life too."

"We'll figure it out," she insists.

"Uh-huh. That's what you always say."

"Grace, I'm—" Mom shakes her head. "Never mind. Just don't be argumentative, okay? We're almost there."

"Fine," I say.

"Fine." After a brief pause, she asks, "Would you like to listen to some music?"

"No, I'm not in the mood."

I spend the remaining ten minutes gazing out my window at the mammoth skyscrapers we're driving by. They loom hundreds of feet above us, casting shadows onto the bustling streets. Never in my life have I felt so small.

The Center for Adolescents with Disordered Eating is an ugly brick building that's sandwiched between a crappy hotel and an elementary school. It's only four stories tall, yet its width expands triple the length of most of the skyscrapers. Mom parks her car in an underground parking garage, and then we take an elevator to the third floor.

The inside of CADE is surprisingly welcoming compared to its mundane exterior. An eclectic array of Christmas decorations is plastered along the turquoise walls, and a gingerbread house the size of our television sits on top of a desk containing pamphlets ranging from ADHD to STDs to why parents shouldn't micromanage their children. Mom would benefit from reading the latter.

The Adolescence Services Department is located at the end of the hall next to a gender-neutral bathroom. In the waiting room, one girl has already arrived and is sitting three seats away from us, quietly talking to her mother. She's so thin, I bet if I wrapped my hands around one of her thighs, my fingers would overlap.

I wonder if Mom has made the same observation or if she's too immersed in an article in *The New Yorker* to notice anything or anyone else. I wish I had my phone to keep me entertained until PHP begins, but it died while I was texting Lou on the ride over.

Teens and their families arrive at different intervals, so by the time the clock strikes twelve, all twenty-two seats are occupied. The counselors who run the program are Brooklyn Smith and Brett Ryder. They split us into two groups—adolescents and family members—and Brooklyn leads the former, myself included, into a casual dining room while the families follow Brett elsewhere.

"You must be Grace," she says. "Your therapist, Emilia, will meet with you shortly to give you a run-through of our program. In the meantime, let me get your weight."

I follow her into a smallish office jam-packed with two desks and a printer. She pulls a digital scale out from under the desk closest to the door, then has me remove my sweatshirt and step on backwards. Once she's recorded my weight, she asks, "Are you familiar with Exchanges?"

I shake my head.

"Well lucky for you, I have your sheet right here."

She hands me a piece of paper that was conveniently lying on the desk. I flip it over and peer at a chart that's divided into six horizonal sections—starch, protein, veg, fruit, dairy, and fat—and six vertical; breakfast, AM snack, lunch, PM snack, dinner, and night snack.

"Uh . . . what do I do with this?"

"One second." Brooklyn rummages through the top-right drawer until she finds a booklet titled CADE Exchanges. "All the food groups and their equivalent Exchanges are in here. For example, let's say you wanted a cup of Cheerios and a cup of milk for breakfast. That would equal one starch and one dairy out of the ten starches and two dairies we've recommended for somebody with your height and weight."

"I'm so confused."

"You'll catch on. We've already recorded your Exchanges for lunch, so you can use those as a model."

I find the section labeled "Lunch," where she's written *PB+J (two starches, one protein) potato chips (one starch) carrots (one veg) ranch dressing (one fat)* onto the four provided parallel lines.

"So, how many calories is that?" I ask.

"We don't do calories."

"But the hospital did calories."

"We don't do calories," she reiterates. "We believe that Exchanges are a better approach at this stage in your recovery."

"But—"

"Grace?" a middle-aged Asian woman calls. She stands

outside the office, waving her hand in a *Single Ladies*-esque fashion.

"Emilia?"

She nods. "Come with me, please."

I follow Emilia through a large room equipped with a long rectangular folding table, two faux-leather couches, and a television and into another office. Mom is sitting on an ugly leopard-print sofa, studying the same booklet Brooklyn had given me.

"Do you get it?" I ask her.

"I'm starting to."

"Good, then maybe you can explain it to me."

"I will later. I believe Emilia wanted to meet with you privately."

"That's correct," Emilia says. "Brett is with the other parents in the Group Room, if you'd like to join him."

"Yes, of course. Thank you."

"It's my pleasure."

Once she's gone, Emilia hands me a tray with my lunch. "I hope you don't mind eating in here. Your mother told me what's been going on, but I'd like to hear it from your perspective as well."

"What do you want to know?"

"Let's start at the beginning."

"Okay." So, while I nibble on my peanut butter sandwich, Emilia proceeds to drill me with the routine questions I'd grown accustomed to answering in the ER and psych ward;

"How long have you been restricting?"

"A couple months."

"Can you identify any triggers?"

"Sadness, loneliness, bad body image. Stuff like that."

"When was the last time you self-harmed?"

"Three weeks ago."

"Are you currently having urges to harm yourself?"

"No."

"How about urges to harm someone else?"

"No."

"Have you ever been physically, verbally, or sexually abused?"

"No, no, and no."

This prolongs for another thirty minutes. After she's finished recording my responses, and after I've chugged two cups of water to wash the repugnant taste of full-fat ranch out of my mouth, I join seven teens in another room for a group led by a petite woman named Teagan. They begin by introducing themselves.

Seventeen-year-old Aria has been battling anorexia since she was raped in eighth grade, more than four years ago. Chloe, the skinny girl I saw in the waiting room, Miguel, a Puerto Rican native who moved to the states after Hurricane Maria struck his hometown, and gothic Miriam also have anorexia. Pink-haired Faith suffers from bulimia while overweight Mandy turned to junk food after a messy break up and hasn't been able to find a healthy balance since.

The final person is twelve-year-old Eva, who was diagnosed with a rare eating disorder known as Avoidant/Restrictive Food Intake Disorder when she was eight. After Teagan's transitioned us to something called Process Group, she raises her hand.

"Can I share something?"

"Is it a Process Statement?" Teagan asks.

"No, but it's important."

Teagan nods. "Go ahead."

"Okay, so you know how I always have Cheerios for breakfast? Well, yesterday we were out, so Mama made me Cream of Wheat instead. And get this," Eva's childlike face breaks into a broad grin, "I ate almost the entire bowl!"

Aria gives her a high-five. "Way to go, kid. You should be super proud of yourself."

"I don't like Cream of Wheat," Faith says.

"No one asked you," Aria retorts.

"What? Don't I get an opinion too? That shit's nasty."

Eva scowls. "At least I don't eat doughnuts for breakfast every morning!"

"Brat! I do not!"

"Girls, that's enough!" Teagan exclaims. "I understand you two have different tastes, but that doesn't warrant an argument. We're here to support each other—not to fight. Got it?"

"Yes, T," Faith and Eva mumble.

"Great. Now, does anyone else have something to share?"

"I do," Mandy says. "It's about something that happened last night."

"With Emmy?" Aria asks.

Mandy nods. "Yeah. It started when I got home . . ."

While Mandy gripes about an argument with her younger sister, I tug at a hole in my sweatshirt and pretend to pay attention, even though my thoughts are elsewhere. I keep glancing at Chloe; at her tiny limbs, at her baggy clothing. In fact, everyone aside from Mandy and maybe Aria is thinner than me, so therefore they must be sicker. From the moment Dr. Bennett mentioned it, I knew PHP was a waste of my time. I knew I wouldn't belong.

"And then Emmy called me a cunt, so I called her a bitch, but my mom heard and got upset at me," Mandy continues. "She totally babies Emmy. It's so unfair."

A soft sigh escapes my lips. I just wish they knew it too.

16

"So, how was your program."

In response to my brother's question, I groan. "Awful. It sucked."

"How come?" Jamie reaches across the table and snags one of the thirty M&Ms I'm eating for my night snack, which according to the booklet is one starch.

"I dunno. Everyone's just so annoying and cliché, and I hate this Exchange thing. Isn't it stupid, Mom?"

"Uh . . ." Mom hesitates. "It's certainly an adjustment."

"A stupid adjustment," I say. "Counting calories was so much easier."

"Counting calories was also disordered," she points out.

"What are Exchanges?" Jamie asks.

I show him my sheet. With Brooklyn's help, I've recorded my three meals and three snacks—including the M&Ms—onto it. "You know the food groups, right?"

Jamie nods. "I learned about them in health. Starches, fruits, fats, proteins, dairy, and, uh . . ."

"Vegetables. Your favorite."

"Yeah, right."

"Anyway, Exchanges requires me to eat a certain amount of foods from those groups each day. Ten starches, six proteins, three fruits, two vegetables, two dairies, and eight fats, to be exact."

"How do you know what a starch or protein or fat is?"

I toss him the booklet. "Everything I need to know is in there. Knock yourself out."

While he flips through it and Mom responds to a text, I sneak three M&Ms into the pocket of my sweatshirt.

Mom clears her throat. "Grace, what are you doing?"

"Nothing."

"Okay, then let me see your pockets."

With a sigh, I reluctantly place the M&Ms back on the table. "Sorry."

"Don't apologize," she says. "Just don't do it again."

"Why does this have to be so difficult?" I wonder aloud.

"Because life is difficult. Learning how to cope with that difficulty is what builds strength and character. It's what teaches you who you are."

"I already know that," I say.

She arches an eyebrow. "You do?"

"Uh, yeah. Don't you believe me?"

"Grace, it's not that I don't believe you. I just think that every person, no matter how old they are or what they've been through, has room to change their ways."

"What if I don't want to change?" I ask. "What if I want things to stay the way they are?"

"You mean like having to be supervised while you eat?"

"Well, not exac—"

"Or how 'bout having to drive to and from Manhattan every

day? Do you want that too?"

"Okay, okay," I begrudgingly agree. "Some things can change."

"And they will. While you were finishing dinner, I talked to Emilia. She'd like to create a plan that'll help you stay on track with your schoolwork until you can return to the classroom."

"What kind of plan?"

"Emilia recommended tutoring. I'll call Miss Dixon tomorrow to see if she knows anyone who lives locally."

"I don't need a tutor," I say. "I've been doing fine on my own."

"Is that why there's a pile of untouched worksheets on your desk?" When I don't respond, she says, "Grace, please be open-minded. We're just trying to help."

"By bossing me around? Shouldn't I know what's best for me better than anyone else?"

Jamie, who's skimming through the fruits category in the Exchanges book, glances up when I raise my voice. "Why are you screaming, Gracie?"

"It's Grace," I snap. "My name is Grace!"

His eyes grow wide with surprise. "I—I'm sorry."

"No, forget it," I say. "It's not your fault. I'm tired. I'm gonna go to bed."

"Grace, be rational about this," Mom begins to say, but by the time she's finished, I'm already storming upstairs.

"Is she okay?" I hear Jamie ask.

"She's had a hard day," Mom responds, "but she'll pull through. She just needs some time."

"She's not going back to the hospital, right?"

Mom sighs. "That's the hope."

Alone in Mom's bedroom, I stand in front of her full-length mirror in my underwear and bra and struggle to withhold tears. I know how I feel about my body is illogical, yet whenever I remind myself of this, the cruel thoughts return. They tell me I'm ugly and selfish, and that I don't deserve to recover.

According to the handbook on Mom's dresser, not only is anorexia the deadliest mental illness; it's also very challenging to recover from. *With* treatment, just sixty percent will fully recover. The remaining forty percent is split between partial recovery and continual relapse.

I don't want that to be me—at least I think I don't. And although I know Mom is right about difficulty building character, at times the simplicity and comfort I'd felt when I was in the hospital seems much more ideal than the complicated outside world I'm existing in now.

———

"MOM, THIS DOESN'T MAKE SENSE." I stare at my math worksheet in dismay, defeated once again by Mr. Lipschitz's assignment. "I can't do factoring."

"Well, Marilyn will be here soon," Mom responds from the kitchen, where she's baking a batch of chocolate chip cookies. "I'm sure she'll help you work through it."

"How soon?"

"Five minutes, ten at most. Finish your snack, okay? It'll get cold if you don't hurry."

I gulp down the last few sips of my lukewarm hot chocolate; two starches plus one fat with the dollop of whipped cream I added on top. On this bleak November morning, comfort food is even more of an incentive to curl up beneath my cozy blankets and rest until it's time for Mom to drive me to my fourth day at CADE.

So far, adjusting to Program hasn't been easy; I find the rules confusing, and coexisting with so many strong personalities can be incredibly frustrating. At least at CTC, the kids knew when to shut the hell up. With this group, however, it's endless chatter that neither Teagan nor anyone else has figured out how to put an end to.

The only person who isn't as boisterous is Miriam. We've bonded over our shared interests in alternative music and psychological thrillers, as well as being the same age with our birthdays only three days apart. But Miriam is also very sick; her disordered comments and the constant increase in her Exchanges makes me wonder why she was discharged from her residential in Massachusetts when she obviously wasn't ready. Maybe she was dropped by her insurance, like Therese. That, or she's just really good at faking it.

As I'm rinsing out my Mickey Mouse-shaped mug a couple minutes later, the doorbell rings. I glance out the window at the middle-aged woman with short, whiteish hair standing on our front porch. A stack of manila envelopes is tucked beneath her arm. "Looks like Satan's here."

"Grace, please."

"Sorry. Tutor."

"That's better. Now stop gawking, and let her in."

"Fine." Placing my mug in the dishwasher, I walk into the hallway and open the door to invite her into our house.

"You must be Grace," she says.

"You must be Ms. Parker."

"Call me Marilyn." She kicks off her brown boots next to my moccasins and removes her parka to reveal a pink paisley blouse. "Where should I put this?"

"I'll take it." Mom, wearing her *Don't Mess with the Chef* apron, snatches Marilyn's coat. "Are you hungry? I'm making chocolate chip cookies."

"Well, how could I say no to that?" Marilyn jokes. "It's a pleasure to meet you, Kira."

Mom smiles politely. "You too."

"I've compiled these folders for your classes, Grace." Marilyn places the manila envelopes in an orderly stack on the table. Each one is labeled *English*, *Spanish*, *Science*, *History*, and *Math* in red Sharpie. The latter is especially thick. "In them, you'll find the work your teachers have asked you to complete."

"That's a lot of work," I say.

"Actually, it's been modified. Our intention isn't to overwhelm you but rather to help you pass this school year. Your mother tells me you have the most difficulty in math, yes?"

"Uh-huh. I was trying to do a factoring worksheet before you came, but I'm honestly super confused."

"Let me see if I can help." She takes the sheet and skims through the problems, periodically mumbling "mm-hmm" and "how interesting" under her breath. Finally, she says, "You were using an incorrect formula to solve one through six. Here, this is what you should have been doing."

I watch her sketch an intricate formula at the bottom of the sheet. "Oh, I remember that. It's called . . . wait, I know this; the quadratic formula."

"Very good. Now, see if you can apply it to the equations."

I spend the next fifteen minutes redoing the problems with the quadratic formula to the best of my (admittedly limited) ability. "Done."

While Marilyn checks my answers, I tap my fingernails against the table. They're too long for my liking; perhaps later, I'll ask Mom if I can have the clippers to trim them. Although I've been clean for almost a month, she still keeps all the sharps in a lockbox under her bed.

"That's correct."

"Huh?"

"Your answers," Marilyn clarifies. "You showed your work too."

"Well, isn't that a first?" Mom asks. She places a platter of cookies on the table and sits down beside me. "How's it going?"

"Pretty well," Marilyn responds. "Are you feeling comfortable with the material, Grace?"

"Uh-huh. Guess what, Mom?"

"What's that?"

"I did factoring!"

Mom high-fives me. "Good work, hon. What's next?"

"Um . . ." I glance at Marilyn, who hands me the envelope titled *History*.

"Your class began learning about the Scientific Revolution last week. Mr. Duffy has asked you to answer questions two through five on page three sixty-seven in your textbook. Do you have that with you?"

I shake my head. "I left it at the hospital by accident."

"Emphasis on accident," Mom says.

"It really was an accident," I insist. "I think there's a link to an online textbook on Mr. Duffy's site. Can you check, Marilyn?"

"Sure. What's your password?"

"Huh?"

"Your password. Your computer's on sleep mode, so I need it to log in."

"Oh, right. It's Illmatic02."

"Illmatic?"

"Yeah. Uppercase I-l-l-m-a-t-i-c. It's the title of an album from the rapper Nas."

"I take it you like rap then," she says.

I chuckle. "Me? No, not really. My friend set that a couple months ago, and I haven't changed it yet. I think it's funny."

"Well, I'll have to ask my son if he's heard of . . . what was the name again?"

"Nas."

"Nas," she repeats. "Yes, that does sound familiar. My son's a producer for up and coming rap artists in Boston."

"That's cool," I say.

"I mean, it doesn't pay well," she responds, "but he likes it, so I'm happy for him. But enough about me. Are you ready to get started?"

I groan. "Okay, fine. What do I need to know?"

"One-half cup of granola. One-third cup of yogurt. One banana with—what's soy butter?"

"It's similar to peanut butter, only better," I say. "I think you'd like it."

"Thanks, but I'll stick with the real stuff." Lou hands me my Exchanges sheet, which is covered in orange spots from her Dorito-stained fingertips, and flops onto my bed with a sigh. "Jeez, Grace. I thought the purpose of this program was to normalize eating."

"It is."

"Then why is there so much rigidity?"

"It's a process," I explain. "You can't expect someone like me to get good at eating intuitively in days or even weeks or months. What happened to one step at a time?"

"One minute," she corrects.

"Same thing. Emilia says I have to accept that there's gonna be a lot of ups and downs."

"Emilia?"

"My therapist. She's nice but . . ."

"But what?"

"But she, like everyone at CADE, is just another reminder that I'm not normal."

"Normal's overrated. Come here." Lou spreads her arms, and I melt into her embrace, feeling the silky fabric of her emerald sweater rub against my cheek. "I'm sorry you feel shitty. I wish I could understand better."

I chuckle softly. "Me too."

We're quiet for a minute or two; her responding to a text, while I pick at my damaged cuticles. "Tell me something good," she says finally, pocking her phone. "Tell me . . . tell me about the kids in your program. I imagine they're pretty interesting."

"They are. This one girl, Chloe, was a cheerleader before she got sick, and now it's all she ever talks about. She even wore her old uniform last week."

"Were your counselors pissed?"

"Very. Her mother had to bring her a change of clothes when she came for Multi-Family."

"What's Multi-Family?"

"It's hell. Basically every Wednesday, all the families meet to talk about anything that's going on outside of CADE. Or they don't. Sometimes, there will be minutes of silence before someone starts talking."

"That sounds super awkward."

"It is. Oh, and then there's this other girl, Aria, who can perfectly rap every NWA song. I don't know how she memorized all those lyrics, but it's impressive."

"That's my kind of girl!" Lou exclaims. "*Fuck tha Police*, man!"

I can't help but laugh at her enthusiasm. "Isn't your uncle a cop?"

Lou groans. "Ugh, don't mention uncles."

"Why not?"

"Because I'm trying not to think about how fucking crazy Thursday will be when my massive extended family flies in for Thanksgiving."

"I'm not sure what I'm doing for Thanksgiving," I say. "Mom hasn't mentioned anything yet."

"You should come," she suggests.

"Your parents won't mind?"

"Of course not. The more the merrier. I'll have Ma send you the details later."

"Sweet."

"So, how do you like the city?"

"Huh?"

"Manhattan," she clarifies. "Isn't that where your program's at."

"Oh, yeah. It's okay, I guess."

"Have you driven down Fifth Avenue? My cousin Imani, who lives on Lexington, says it's ah-mazing."

"It's super busy," I say, "and anyway, it's not like I have time for shopping. Mom's night shift starts at eight, so we try to get home as fast as possible when Program ends. That, and she doesn't like to leave Trevor in charge of Jamie for too long. They don't exactly get along."

"Ah, the boyfriend of the month. How's he been?"

"Lou, don't be like that. Without Trevor, Mom wouldn't be able to drive me to Program. He's kind of her saving grace."

Lou chuckles. "Saving grace. That's funny."

"It's no better than when your mom used to call me 'Amazing Grace,'" I retort.

"Oh, that's nothing. At least your parents didn't name you after a fucking state."

"Good point."

"But whatever," she continues. "I'm just glad you're better—or at least stable."

"For now," I remind her.

She nudges me. "Quit being such a Scrooge. It's your favorite time of the year, for God's sake! You should be celebrating!"

"It isn't easy to celebrate when every day is so damn hard," I say. "Lou, you don't know what it's like to be me."

"And you don't know what it's like to have a sick mom," she responds. "Or how fucking awful it is to practice a religion that condemns you for who you love. That's not easy either."

She has a good point. "Sorry. I shouldn't have said that."

"It's cool. Just promise me you'll bring you're A-Game for Thursday. I can't have you moping around my house on the third-best day of the year."

"I will," I assure her. "Do you want me to make anything?"

"Nah, we're already gonna have too much food as it is. My family loves to cook."

"Just remember that I sometimes get anxious around food, so if I'm acting weird—"

"You don't have to explain," she interrupts. "I'm just happy you're coming."

Even though uncertainty has my stomach twisted in knots, I smile. "As long as there are plenty of vegetarian options, I'm happy too."

Lou bites her lip, suddenly less enthused. "Maybe you should make something after all."

17

Thanksgiving has never been a big deal for my family. When we lived in California, instead of hosting an extravagant feast with as many guests as we could fit around our dining room table, we'd usually get together with several family friends for a small celebration. We'd eat store-bought tofurkey—ham for the meat-eaters—and the adults would watch football while Jamie and I played outside. After the game was over, we'd gorge on an abundance of dessert, say good-bye, and walk home in the setting sun talking about what we were grateful for. The consensus was the same every year; family.

I liked it that way; I liked the simplicity, I liked the reliability, and I loved the food. My personal favorite was always Mom's pumpkin bread. I could eat an entire loaf and still have room for more.

Standing outside of the Jackson's house, warily staring at the lengthy lineup of cars parked up and down their street, I know this Thanksgiving will be anything but simple.

As though she can read my thoughts, Mom, who's carrying a

dish of roasted butternut squash, nudges my shoulder. "Grace, if at any point you feel overwhelmed—"

"I'll let you know," I finish. "I got it, Mom."

"Okay, okay. I just wanted to make sure."

"Think they'll have green bean casserole?" Jamie asks.

"What kid likes green bean casserole?" I mumble to Mom.

She ignores me. "I don't know, hon. We'll find out shortly."

We follow an elderly couple up the Jackson's icy driveway. My heart is beating so fast, it feels like it's about to leap out of my chest.

Time to put on your A-Game, I tell myself. *That's it; smile. You'll be fine. You'll be—*

"Hey, girl!" Lou exclaims. She throws her arms around me while Mom greets Mrs. Jackson and Jamie sneaks a marshmallow off a dish of sugar-glazed sweet potatoes. "You came!"

"Yeah. Thanks again for inviting me."

"Are you kidding? I need someone around who won't ask me a bazillion questions about my girlfriend. I swear, it's like they all forgot it's the twenty-first century." She notices the Exchanges book tucked beneath my arm, and her excitement dwindles. "I see that came too."

"My therapist thinks it's good to always have it with me."

"And what do *you* think?"

"I think . . ." I hesitate. "I think for now, she's right. Things can get out of control really fast if I'm not careful."

"As long as you have fun tonight, anything goes. C'mon, I'll introduce you to my cousins."

I follow Lou into her TV room where four teenagers—one girl and three identical boys—are lounging on the couch, glued to their phones.

"Hey, guys?" When she doesn't receive a response, she

stomps the heel of her black ankle boot twice against the ground. "Yo! Eye's up here!"

"What do you want?" the girl grumbles, reluctantly pocketing her phone. "And who's she?"

"My best friend, Grace. Remember? I told you this morning she was coming."

"Oh, right. The white chick down the block."

Lou rolls her eyes. "Grace, this is Aliyah and her younger brothers, Deshawn, Desmond, and Devin. They're triplets."

"Hey," one of the triplets says. He's wearing a salmon-colored shirt and distressed jeans that are so tight, it's a miracle he managed to squeeze his muscular frame into them.

"Hi. Uh, where'd you fly in from?"

"Chicago," a second triplet, this one with turkey-patterned socks, responds.

"I think my dad went there on a business trip once," I say. "Nice city."

Aliyah snorts. "Of course *you'd* think that."

"Aliyah, shut the fuck up!" Lou snaps. "If you're not gonna be nice to my friend, maybe you should leave."

"Great to see you too, cousin," Aliyah mumbles sarcastically, but she stays put, her arms folded across her chest.

Skinny Jeans clears his throat. "Lou said you're from California, Grace."

"I am."

"Was it anything like *90210*?"

"Not quite," I say, "though it was pretty. I miss it a lot. Especially during the winter."

"Winter sucks," the third triplet agrees. As he talks, he fiddles with a silver cross dangling from a chain around his neck. "Why'd you leave?"

"Because—because Connecticut's more affordable. And there are more job opportunities."

"I thought your dad is a businessman," Aliyah says. "Don't businessmen, like, make a ton of money."

"Well, uh—"

"Oh, don't be nosy," Cross Necklace scolds his sister.

"I'm not. It's a fucking question, Devin."

"Kids?" Mr. Jackson pokes his head into the living room. "We're serving the food now if you'd like to join us."

"Hell yeah! I'm starving!" Turkey Socks and his brothers charge into the kitchen with Aliyah, glued to her phone once again, trailing behind them.

"Sorry 'bout Aliyah," Lou says. "She's a bitch to everyone."

"How long do you have to put up with her?"

"Just the next two days. You ready to eat?"

"Ready as I'll ever be."

She pats my shoulder reassuringly. "You got this, girl. Easy peasy."

But despite Lou's contagious optimism, as I'm standing in line behind her Uncle Caleb minutes later, butterflies swarm my stomach. My anxiety has intensified now that all the dishes are out on display, as have the conflicting thoughts racing through my mind.

. . . remember you're A-Game . . . it's just one meal . . . resist temptation . . . aim for three-fifty . . . but it smells so good . . . four hundred max . . . fat failure . . . you'll never be good enough . . .

I scan the crowded room for Mom, and when I can't spot her, I duck into the hall to catch my breath. The bitter taste of bile in my throat sends me racing to the bathroom—the one upstairs, as the one on this level is currently occupied—where I lock the door and sit on the closed toilet seat with my head in my hands. Why is everything that's so easy for them so damn hard for me?

. . . in . . . out . . . in . . . out . . . I practice the deep breathing techniques I learned at CADE last week, and they work—at least initially. But then the Jackson's scale, which is tucked beneath the sink in its usual spot, catches my eye, and I'm overcome with intrigue and temptation.

Moving like I'm under hypnosis, I drag the scale to the center of the bathroom and strip down to my underwear. Before I step on, I turn to the mirror above the sink and stare at my reflection in spite. I don't need a scale to know I've gained weight—how could I not after the intense restoration diet I've followed for the past month? My stomach has expanded, whereas the gap between my thighs has shrunken to a sliver. I can no longer count my ribs without sucking in, and my face is noticeably fuller than before.

The only part of my appearance that hasn't changed is my eyes; they're still so sad, filled with the anguish of someone who's fallen into a deep, dark abyss and doesn't know how to climb back out.

Well, now they're filled with tears too.

"Grace?" Lou raps twice on the door. "You all right in there?"

I hastily shove the scale under the sink, then yank on my blouse and dress pants, fumbling with the zipper. "Yeah. I'll be out in a sec."

When I leave the bathroom, Lou is casually leaning against her parents' armoire. "You know you can talk to me whenever, right?"

"I know."

"So . . . is there anything you'd like to talk about?"

"No."

"Not even why you're crying?"

"I'm not. I got something in my eye—that's all. Can we please go back downstairs?"

Lou sighs. "Why'd you come if you knew you weren't going to have fun?"

"What?"

"I don't mean to be a bitch," she continues. "I just want to understand."

"You can't."

"Why not?"

"Because I don't understand it either," I say. "I don't need a therapist, Lou; I need a friend. I need someone who will listen without pitying me or judging me or telling me I should do this and that to get to here or there. If that's too much to ask, you might as well back off before things get bad again. I don't mind. I'm used to being alone." I try to move past her, but she grabs my arm.

"Stop that."

"Stop what?"

"Saying stupid shit. Do you really think I'll back off?"

"I—"

"Grace, I love you," she interrupts, "and that's never going to change. However confusing or hard these next months are and however bad things get, I want you to remember one thing."

"What's that?"

Grasping my shoulders, Lou stares me straight in the eyes and says, "I want you to remember that you are not alone."

"You mean it?"

"Absolutely. Now, get your Exchanges book or whatever the hell it's called, 'cause this night's not over until you've tried Ma's pumpkin bread."

"I do like pumpkin bread," I admit.

"Damn right. So, what do you say we go have a piece?"

I dry my eyes on the sleeve of my blouse and don't even care when my smudged makeup stains the silky ivory fabric. "Okay."

"Okay?"

Forcing my lips into a crooked smile, I nod. "Yeah. Let's go."

"THANKSGIVING WAS . . ." I listlessly play with a loose string on Emilia's leopard-print sofa until it comes undone. Then I move onto another one. "Thanksgiving was interesting."

"Can you elaborate?" Emilia asks. "For instance, how did you feel around the food?"

"Okay, I guess. I even had a slice of pumpkin bread."

She smiles. "Was it good?"

"Yes. Mrs. Jackson's an excellent cook."

"You said Lou's extended family was there?"

"Twenty-nine guests, not including Mom, Jamie, and me."

"I imagine that must have been overwhelming. How'd you cope?"

I envision the look in my eyes when I stared at my body in the mirror; how disbelieving they were, like none of this was real, like I was still skinny and sick—only a couple skipped meals away from obtaining that perfect weight.

Then I hear Lou's voice saying, *"You are not alone."* Four simple words that remarkably had the ability to turn a miserable evening around. I see her in the kitchen serving our bread, laughing as she flicked bits of whipped cream at my nose.

"You got something on your face, Edwards."

I wrangled the can from her and aimed at her scarlet blouse. "Oops. It slipped."

"What the fuck? This cost fifty bucks!"

"Well this," I gestured to my face, "is priceless."

"Grace?" Emilia peers at me from behind her rectangular glasses. "Did you hear me?"

"Yeah, uh, I did some deep breathing, and I talked to Lou. That helped a lot."

"I'm proud of you," she says. "Your ability to successfully execute the skills we've taught you demonstrates tremendous growth."

"Thanks."

"I talked to Brooklyn yesterday," she continues, "and we came to the consensus that if you did well on Thanksgiving, we'd consider stepping you down to our Intensive Outpatient Program next week."

"Really?"

She nods. "Yes. This also means we can begin discussing your return to school as a part-time student."

"I have to go back to school?" I ask nervously. "But—but isn't that why Mom hired Marilyn?"

"Marilyn can still work with you if you need extra support, however we agreed that it's more beneficial both socially and academically for you to learn in the classroom with your peers."

"But what if I'm not ready?"

"Then we'll cross that bridge when we come to it. I wouldn't worry though. Our intention isn't to overwhelm you but to make this transition as smooth and painless as possible."

"Good luck with that."

"Why don't you talk to Miguel, Aria, or Chloe?" she suggests. "They've all gone through this process, and they've done very well. Aria's even begun looking into college."

"I thought she was taking a gap year."

"It's never too early to plan ahead."

"So much for living in The Now," I grumble.

Emilia ignores my sarcasm. "Like I said; you don't need to worry. You're in excellent hands. Trust me, okay?"

I sigh. "Fine, I trust you. Can I go to Group now?"

"You may."

In the dining room, everyone is seated around the table coloring in mandalas. I sit beside Faith, and Teagan presents the two remaining options to me; a snowflake and a dreidel.

"Snowflake, I guess." Beneath my breath, I mumble, "This is so fucking pointless."

Faith, having overhead my remark, elbows me. "What's up with you?"

"Emilia wants me to go back to school," I respond.

"I remember having that conversation with her," Aria says. "It didn't end well."

"You were crying so hard, your mascara was running down your face," Eva pipes in. "I legit thought you were Miriam."

Miriam glowers at her. "At least I don't look like an eight-year-old boy."

"I do not!"

"But once I started going," Aria continues, ignoring their banter, "it wasn't that bad. I was able to reconnect with my friends and work with my GC to figure out a plan for my future. I don't know if Emilia told you, but I've recently started looking at colleges."

I nod. "She did."

"I used to think I'd never be ready for college, because being able to eat on my own seemed impossible. Of course it's still super daunting, but it's also exciting to imagine a life where I'm not chained to this disorder.

"Basically what I'm saying is that it's okay to be scared, and it's okay to fail on your first try—trust me, I know this better than anyone here. But you shouldn't let that fear stop you from stepping outside your comfort zone. It's a crazy world we live in, but it can be good too if you know where to look."

"Do you?"

"I don't know. I think I'm beginning to."

I'm about to respond when Brett and a skinny blonde-haired boy approach us. "Guys, I'd like to introduce you to our newest client, Isaac Nielsen. Isaac, why don't you tell us about yourself?"

"Okay." Isaac's voice is higher than I'd expected, almost singsongy. "Uh, I'm seventeen, I live in Fairfield, and this is my first time in PHP or any treatment facility—except for the hospital."

"Mistlyn or CTC?" Mandy asks.

"CTC."

"Oh, cool. I'm Mandy. Eighteen years old, from Greenwich, second admission."

"It's nice to meet you, Mandy."

Following Mandy's lead, we go around the table introducing ourselves. Isaac nods along, intermittently contributing comments like, "I hear that's a great town" and to Faith, "dope hairdo." Afterwards, he claims the empty chair beside me, and Teagan hands him a mandala.

"This is art therapy," she explains. "Would you prefer colored pencils or markers?"

"Colored pencils."

Miguel passes him his used twelve-pack. "I'm finished, so you can have mine."

"Sweet. Thanks, bro."

"No problem. You're hot."

Isaac blushes. "Uh . . . thank you?"

"Do you guys want to listen to music?" Teagan asks. When her question is met with nods, she finds a holiday playlist on

Spotify and the instrumental intro of *Carol of the Bells* by the Trans-Siberian Orchestra blasts through her phone's speakers.

"I love this song," Isaac says. He flips his mandala over and uses a black pencil to outline a remarkably realistic eye in the top-left corner.

"Me too," I say. "Have you heard the Pentatonix cover?"

Isaac nods. "So good."

"Yeah. What's your favorite holiday song?"

"Jeez, that's tough. There are way too many to choose from. How 'bout you?"

"Mine's this Scottish song called *Fairytale of New York*," I say. "You probably haven't heard of it though. They never play it on the radio."

"Irish, actually."

"Huh?"

"The Pogues, they're an Irish band—not Scottish," he clarifies. "And I love that song."

"Really?"

He nods. "Oh yeah."

"You know, you're the first person I've ever met who knows what I'm talking about," I say.

"Likewise," he responds.

Once we've finished our mandalas—or, in Isaac's case, an intricate abstract sketch—Teagan announces that we're going for a walk. "Bundle up," she says. "It's chilly out there."

So, after dressing warmly in coats, mittens, hats, and scarves, we take the elevator to the ground floor and follow Teagan out onto the busy streets of Manhattan.

"I used to live in the city with my aunt and uncle," Isaac says as we head towards Central Park. "My parents were getting divorced, and they didn't want me involved. I didn't care, not really. At that point, I was so over their drama, they could send me to North Korea, and I'd be happy just to be away from home."

"Seriously?"

"No, but it felt like that then. The entire situation was just so fucked up."

"I know what you mean," I say.

"Are your parents divorced too?"

"Separated," I correct. "When they were together, we lived in California. I miss it a lot. I mean, Connecticut's fine and all, but it was so much nicer there. Warmer too."

"That's cool. I've always wanted to visit the West Coast."

"I've always wanted to visit New York City. Just not like this."

"Were you at Mistlyn?" he asks.

"CTC."

"Me too. What'd you think of that Liza lady?"

I groan. "Don't even get me started on the staff. Is Anne still there?"

"No. She left two days before I did."

"Good for her."

"Yeah. She seemed relieved, but also freaked out."

"Change is scary."

He nods. "You got that right. So, what other types of music do you listen to?"

"I'm really into alternative rock. You know, artists like Radiohead, Foo Fighters, Red Hot Chili Peppers—"

"Weezer?"

"Who?"

"You're never heard of Weezer? *Say It Ain't So?*"

I shake my head. "Sorry."

"Damn, you're missing out. Okay, uh . . . how 'bout the Counting Crows?"

"Yeah, they're great. *Long December*'s one of my favorite songs. It's so relatable—especially now."

"I think that's what I like about music," he says. "It speaks to you in ways nobody else can. It makes you feel less alone."

"When I was in the hospital, everybody thought the things I missed the most were my family and my privacy and sports and stuff like that," I respond. "And yeah, I missed those too, but what I missed more than anything else was—and I know it sounds shitty—my iPod."

Isaac laughs. "I missed my dog."

Now I'm laughing as well. "What's wrong with us?"

"Do you really want me to answer that?" he asks jokingly.

"*It's the most wonderful time of the year!*" A group of carolers, snuggled together in a horse-drawn carriage, sing as they trot by us. "*With the kids jingle belling and everyone telling you be of good cheer! It's the most wonderful time of the year.*"

"*The most wonderful time of the year,*" I repeat. "Isn't that ironic?"

"I don't know . . ." Isaac hesitates. "I've got a feeling this holiday season won't be so bad."

"Yeah?"

"Yeah. I mean, obviously it's too early to know for sure, but I have hope."

"Mind passing some along to me?" I ask. "I could use a little hope right now."

"Sorry, it's non-transferable."

I roll my eyes. "Jerk."

He laughs. "Kidding, kidding. I'm sure with time, you'll find some of your own."

"How much time?"

"Not much. You and me; we have our entire lives ahead of us

to do whatever the fuck we want with them. This is just a small bump in the road, you know?"

"Seems like a pretty big bump to me," I say.

"You really are a pessimist, aren't you?"

I chuckle. "You can tell? No, but really, I'm trying to be more positive. It's just hard when, for my entire life, whenever I thought things were finally going well, they only got worse."

"You'll get there," he says. "Just take it one day at a time."

"One minute at a time."

Isaac nods. "Yeah. One minute at a time."

18

"You know what really annoys me?" Lou asks.

"Uh . . . slow Wi-Fi?" I guess. "Pop quizzes? Screaming kids? Politics?"

"Well, yeah, all that, but it also really pisses me off when I get super invested in a TV show, and then the stupid writers kill off my favorite character!" Lou sets down her bag of potato chips and melodramatically clutches her hand to her heart. "Rest in peace, Poussey."

"Does that mean you're gonna stop watching?"

"Hell no. I'm already halfway through the fifth season."

"Of course you are."

Lou stuffs a handful of chips in her mouth. "So, when are you gonna check it out?"

"When I have time," I respond. "I've been crazy busy with schoolwork and Program . . . though I did step down to IOP on Tuesday."

"That's great! Why didn't you tell me?"

"I meant to but . . ."

"But what?"

"But I'm not sure if I'm ready for that transition," I admit.

"Bullshit. You obviously are. I mean, you're kicking ass with your Exchanges, and your mom trusts you to go out with Cass and I tonight."

"That's true . . ."

"It is, so stop second guessing yourself. You've got this."

"Thanks." After a brief pause, I say, "There's another thing."

"Yeah? What's that?"

"This new guy at Program. He joined last week, and I feel like we have a, uh—"

"Special connection?"

"Exactly."

"Is he cute?"

"Very. His name's Isaac."

"I think Aliyah's boyfriend's name is Isaac," Lou says. "Or maybe it's Isaiah. No, Isaiah's her ex. I tell ya', Grace, that girl gets around. She's dated, like, six or sev—"

"Lou, can you focus?" I interrupt. "Help me. I don't know what to do."

She shrugs. "Easy. Ask him if he wants to get food."

"We're being treated for eating disorders," I remind her.

"Okay, good point. Then—then take him to the movies. I hear the new romcom they're playing in the Center is totally dope."

"Don't you think that's a little forward? I mean, we've only known each other for a week."

"So? I only knew Cass for four days when we hooked up."

"That's different. You'd already been kissed by—what was his name?"

"Benji. We were at Matt's thirteenth birthday, playing Truth or Dare. Our braces got stuck, remember? Mrs. Durham had to practically pry us apart." Lou chuckles at the memory. "That was some kiss."

"Well, I've never kissed anyone."

"What about Liam?"

"Liam doesn't count. That was more of a diss than a kiss."

"It's really not that big of a deal. People picture their first kiss as some crazy surreal experience that makes you discover life's true meaning or whatever, but it's actually pretty simple. You just do it."

"Thanks. That's real helpful."

"I'm serious, Grace. You're stressing out for no reason."

"You know, not everyone has the audacity to hook up with complete strangers," I snap. "Just because you—"

Without warning, Lou grabs my face and presses her lips against mine. I'm so taken aback, I immediately push her off me.

"What the hell are you doing?"

"Helping you," she responds casually. "Isn't that what you wanted?"

"I'm not kissing you, Lou."

"Why not? What are you so afraid of?"

"I'm not afraid. It's just weird."

"Grace, it's not like I'm asking you to have sex with me. It's just a kiss—that's all. What's the worst that can happen?"

"I don't know . . ."

"Then you've got nothing to lose."

I sigh. "Fine—but this is a one-time thing. And nobody's gonna hear about it, because you're not gonna tell."

"Deal," she agrees. "Now breathe. The more relaxed you are, the better it'll be."

Once again, she leans in towards me, but instead of pushing her away again, I reciprocate. Her lips are softer than I'd expected, almost like silk. She rests one hand on the small of my back while the other gently caresses my cheek. I don't know what to do with mine, so I leave them by my side and focus on the kiss; on which direction to tilt my head, on whether I should keep my eyes open or closed, on how to react if she tries to use tongue (thankfully, she doesn't).

Ten or so seconds later, she retracts her hands to respond to a text. "See? That wasn't too bad, was it?"

"My heart's pounding," I admit.

"Well, the first time's always the hardest. But I gotta say, Edwards; you're pretty all right."

"I can't believe you're my first," I say. "That's crazy. *You're* crazy, Lou."

"It takes one to know one. C'mon, Cass is here. I call shotgun."

"Where'd you say we're going again?"

"Some teen hangout that's having a karaoke night. Cass is really into that shit."

"Cool. Just remember that I have to be——"

"Home by nine," she finishes. "I know. We've been through this, like, twenty times. Grab your coat, okay? It's freezing out there!"

Lou's right; the weather is even colder than usual with the temperature dipping into the low twenties. While she chats with Cassie up front, I insert my earbuds and listen to *Say It Ain't So* on YouTube.

Lou nudges my knee. "What'cha listening to?"

"Just a song by this band called Weezer."

"Weezer. Ha, that's a funny name."

"I think my brother went to one of their concerts a couple years ago," Cassie says. "He had to sneak out, because my parents had grounded him a week earlier."

"Did they catch him?"

"Yep. I've never seen my dad so pissed."

"Worse than the time you were a sexy schoolgirl for Halloween?" Lou asks.

Cassie nods. "That was his fault. If he didn't like my costume, he should have said something before I left the house."

"But he's still the principal," she points out. "He, like, makes the dress code."

"You mean the one no one ever follows?"

"Yeah, that one."

Shaking my head in amusement, I adjust the volume, drowning out their conversation with the catchy chorus of the song. And when the final notes fade to silence, I click the replay button. And then I click it again.

I'm halfway through my fourth listen when Cassie comes to a stop beside a funky ranch-style house. Lou and I follow her around the back, down a concrete staircase, and through a door with a string of bells that jingle when we enter. Two adults and twenty or so teenagers mingle and play arcade games in a sizable room that's been festively decorated for the holidays.

Cassie's friends, Becca and Sam, are chatting at a circular table near the stage, where two boys are rapping *Drop It Like It's Hot.*

"Hey, girls!" Cassie says, taking a seat beside Sam. "Hope it's cool I brought company."

"Yeah, totally," Becca responds. "Sup, Lou? How's your mother?"

"Kicking cancer's ass. Scoot over." She squeezes onto Cassie's chair and grabs a candy cane from a heart-shaped bowl in the center of the table. "Sup with you?"

"I got into UConn! Early decision."

"For real? Bec, that's awesome!"

"Yeah, that's really great," I say. "You must be super excited."

"Oh, I am." She takes a sip of her soda and belches loudly. "So, how're you holding up, Grace? I hear you've had quite the fall."

"Yeah, you could say that."

"But are you, like, okay now?"

I shrug. "On some days."

"Some is better than never," Cassie says. "When Derrick's manic, it's impossible to know how good or bad things are gonna be that day. You just have to take it one minute at a time."

"That's what I told you, Grace," Lou says. "It's a good thing I'm so smart, isn't it?"

I roll my eyes. "Keep telling yourself that."

"Oh, look—the mic's free," Sam observes. "Anyone wanna go up there?"

"Grace, you should give it a try," Cassie suggests.

I shake my head. "No, no, no. That's really not my thing."

"C'mon, live a little," Lou says. "You're always so uptight. Isn't one of your goals to try things outside your comfort zone?"

"That's only for food."

"Well, it isn't anymore."

"Grace! Grace! Grace!" Cassie and her friends chant as Lou guides me onto the stage.

"Lou, I don't know about this," I say. "You know I can't sing."

"So? You think anyone here can?" Lou hands me the microphone. "Pretend you're alone; that it's you and the music and nobody else."

"But—"

"You and the music," she repeats. "That's all it is. Just you and the music."

"Me and the music."

"Exactly. Cass, hit it!"

Setting down her soda, Cassie presses PLAY on the karaoke

machine, and the familiar intro to Florence & the Machine's *Shake It Out* blasts through The Hideout.

"I love this song!" a girl playing pool exclaims.

"Turn it up!" her opponent calls.

Lou flashes me two thumbs up. "You got this," she mouths.

I begin timidly, whispering the lyrics into the mic, but as the first verse progresses, and I realize that no one is mocking me, my confidence builds. I swallow my fear, straighten my spine, and let the beautiful words flow freely out of my mouth.

"Woohoo!" Lou cheers.

I return her silly grin, thinking *this isn't so bad*. On the contrary, it's actually pretty fun.

I'm halfway through the first verse when the bells on the door jingle again. Bianca and Liam, dressed warmly in puffy jackets and oversized hats, enter the Hideout holding hands. When Bianca sees me singing, she whispers something in Liam's ear. I don't need to be an expert lip reader to know she's talking about me.

Suddenly, all my confidence disappears into thin air as a wave of anxious thoughts invade my mind. *They're going to laugh at me. They're going to laugh at how stupid I look standing here all frazzled and tongue-tied. I knew this was a bad idea.*

Just as I'm about to cowardly duck offstage, Lou comes to my rescue. She takes the mic from me and belts out the next line in her southern drawl.

"Thank you," I whisper as the song transitions to the chorus.

Lou pats my shoulder reassuringly. "No problem."

"*Shake it out, shake it out,*" we sing together. "*Shake it out, shake it out, ooh whoa.*"

"*Shake it out, shake it out,*" Cassie, Sam, and Becca echo. They must not care that they're off-key, because they carry onward, finishing the rest of the chorus with Lou and me. By the time we begin the second verse, everyone in the Hideout, including Bianca and Liam, is singing along.

Lou slings her arm around my shoulder. Her magenta sweater smells like the pumpkin pie Mrs. Jackson was baking when I came over earlier. Maybe, just maybe, I'll let myself have a slice when we return to her house. I did promise Mom I'd eat my evening snack while I was out.

When the song ends, the crowd politely applauds. My legs are trembling so furiously, Lou has to practically carry me off the stage.

"Girl, that was dope! I told you you could do it, didn't I?"

"You were right," I admit.

She grins smugly. "I'm always right."

"Sure, Lou. Whatever you say."

"I'm gonna try to convince Cass to sing *Baby, It's Cold Outside* with me. You in?"

"No, you go ahead. There's something I have to take care of first."

So, while she rejoins Cassie, Becca, and Sam, who are snacking on peppermint bark, I approach Bianca. She's sitting alone at a booth near the back scrolling through Instagram.

"Where's your boyfriend?" I ask.

"Outside," she responds without looking up. "His mom called or something. Cool song by the way. I didn't know you sing."

"I don't. Can I sit?"

"Um, okay." Slipping her phone into the pocket of her grey parka, she clears her throat. "Listen, I know you probably hate me—"

"I don't hate you," I interrupt. "I actually want to thank you."

"So . . . you're not upset that I told Miss Dixon?"

"For a while, I was," I say, "but when I was in the hospital feeling like nobody cared about me, I thought about what you did, and it made me feel less alone. You could've walked away and not said a word to anyone. But you didn't. You reached out. I just have one question."

"What's that?"

"Why did you? I mean, it's not like we're friends."

Bianca closes her eyes. When she reopens them, a single tear slips down her cheek. "My sister committed suicide six years ago. She slit her wrists and bled out. I was the one who found her."

"Bianca, I'm sorry."

"I think about Sofía every day," she continues, "so when I saw you cutting in the locker room, I had to do something. I know we haven't gotten along well in the past, and I know I can be kinda cold sometimes, but I never meant to hurt you. I was just worried that Liam still had feelings for you."

"Still? He never had feelings for me, Bianca. *I* had feelings for him."

"Well, I guess I just assumed that since you guys used to be so close—"

"Liam and I were just friends," I say. "At least we were until I fucked it up. But you don't have to worry about us anymore. I'm totally over him."

"Oh? Is there another guy?"

"Maybe. I just don't know if he feels the same way I feel about him."

"Ask him."

"Seriously?"

She shrugs. "What's the worst that can happen?"

"He could say no."

"Well, you won't know 'til you try. Boys are tricky. Just look at the one I'm dating."

The second the words have left her lips, Liam bustles through the door. "Hey, Grace."

"Hey."

"I haven't seen you around. Where've you been?"

"I, uh . . . I had, uh, this thing——"

"She had the flu," Bianca interrupts. "Careful, Liam. I wouldn't get too close to her. She could still be contagious."

"Oh, quit giving her a hard time," Liam scolds Bianca. To me, he says, "I hope you're feeling better."

I nod. "I am."

"Good. Listen, I'd love to stay and chat, but I have to go. Do you need a ride, B?"

"How else am I supposed to get home?" she snaps. "God, Liam. You're so dense sometimes."

Liam scowls. "I'll wait in the car. Feel free to join me whenever you're ready, Princess." He storms out of The Hideout, slamming the door behind him.

"Thanks, Bianca," I say as she's adjusting the ivory scarf around her neck.

"It's no problem," she responds. "So, do you know when you're coming back to school?"

"Next Monday."

"Sweet. I'll see you then."

"See ya."

"What was that about?" Lou plops down beside me. She unpeels another candy cane and pops it in her mouth, noisily chewing as she speaks. "I swear, if that bitch was harassing you, I'll——"

"She's not a bitch," I interrupt, "and anyway, we were just talking. Did you ask Cass to sing?"

"Yeah, but she has a sore throat. I hope she's not coming down with mono."

"Mono?" I repeat. "Lou, if she has mono, then she would've given it to you, and then I'd have it too."

"Chillax, Grace. It's probably just a common cold. You'll be fine."

"Well, if I do get mono, it's all your fault," I say. "I still can't believe you kissed me."

"Excuse me? If I remember correctly, *you* kissed me back."

I sigh. "Whatever happened just—just let's forget about it, okay?"

Lou chuckles. "In your dreams, Edwards. In your dreams."

On the ride home, while Lou and Cassie sing along to popular holiday songs, I text Mom to let her know I'm headed back to Lou's. She responds immediately.

Mom: did u have a good time?

Grace: yes it was great. thnx for letting me go.

Mom: np. u earned it.

Pocketing my phone, I turn to the window and gaze at the festively decorated farmhouses we're driving past. Twelve golden reindeer frolic on someone's frost-covered lawn. A six-foot-tall Santa Clause waves to the four-feet-tall gingerbread family across the street. One house has illuminated advent candles in their windows. They remind me of those my former neighbors, Mr. and Mrs. Anderson, used to commemorate their Christmas Pageant.

Every year, the Andersons hosted an "exclusive viewing" of their grandchildren performing the nativity scene in their back-yard. My family never went. We'd much rather stay at home binge-watching Christmas movies and devouring the iced-pumpkin cookies my father made from scratch. Those were always our favorite holiday treat.

We haven't had them since he left—not that I'm surprised. Although Mom claims she's moved on, I also know that no amount of time will erase the pain and guilt he caused her. She made one mistake, and now she's forced to live with it for the rest of her life. And that really sucks.

There are a lot of things that suck lately—Dad included. I love him, and I hate him, and I miss him, and I want to put a gun to his head and pull the trigger all at the same time. But more than anything else, I wish I could have one more minute with him to ask him the burning question I've suppressed inside me for the past six years.

Why?

19

In the one month and six days that I've been absent from school, I'd forgotten how overwhelmingly crowded the halls are. Walking through them again, modestly dressed in dark-denim jeans and a navy sweatshirt, I feel like that one unlucky fish who, somehow along the way, got turned around and now swims against the shoal rather than with them. An energetic sophomore boy from my math class maneuvers around me to catch up to his friends. Another familiar face—this time a girl from American Lit—steps on my foot with the heel of her combat boot as she's hurrying to her next period. I limp into the nearest bathroom to catch my breath, but to my dismay, a group of girls are standing at the sink indiscreetly passing around a Juul.

"Can I help you?" one of them asks rudely.

"N—no," I stutter. "Sorry."

Blushing furiously, I turn around and reenter the hall. My heart is pounding, and my palms are slick with sweat. I can't do this. One more minute in this hell, and I will lose my mind.

"Can I help you?" Mrs. Hawkins asks when I breathlessly burst into Guidance.

"I need to see Miss Dixon," I say. "It's urgent."

"One sec." She dials Miss Dixon's extension into a landline telephone and holds it to her ear, tapping her manicured fingernails against her desk while she waits. "Dixie? I have a student who's requesting to meet with you." She pauses momentarily, and the tapping resumes. "Uh-huh . . . I'll send her in."

"Thanks," I say.

"No problem. Next!"

While Mrs. Hawkins helps a boy who's sifting through college pamphlets, I enter Miss Dixon's room. She's typing into her computer while she simultaneously noshes on a blueberry muffin.

"Hi."

Miss Dixon holds up her finger as she finishes chewing. "Sorry about that. I didn't have time to eat breakfast at home this morning."

"It's cool."

"It's nice to see you again," she says.

"Yeah. You too."

"How are you doing?"

"Fine," I respond instinctively. "I mean, I'm kinda anxious right now, but most of the time I'm fine . . . I think."

"Is something troubling you?"

"It's probably just nerves. I'd forgotten how intense this place is."

"Well, you made the right choice to come here," she says. "I was planning on meeting with you sometime this week anyway."

"Oh, yeah?"

"Mm-hmm. Your mother called yesterday and caught me up on what's been going on, but I'd like to hear it from you as well."

"Do you want the short version or the long version?"

"Whatever feels most comfortable to you."

I chuckle dryly. "After the stuff I've seen, nothing makes me uncomfortable anymore."

"Then let's go with the long version, shall we?"

"Yeah, okay."

So, for the next thirty minutes I elaborately recap the past month, beginning with my admission to the ER and ending when I transitioned to IOP last week. I gripe about one-on-one and explain Exchanges and describe the troubled, yet still kind and cool people I met along the way, like Ryan and Therese and Stephanie and even Anne and Kevin.

"It's weird," I say, "because when I first went into the psych ward, I wanted nothing to do with them. I thought we had nothing in common; that they were all crazy and messed up, and yeah, that was true, but they also got me, you know? They understood me in ways no one out here does. They helped me realize that being mentally ill isn't something to be ashamed of, and until I could accept that this was real, that I was sick, I'd never get better. I thought it was bullshit at the time, but now I know they were right."

"Do you miss them, Grace?"

I consider this. "I don't miss them, not really. I just sometimes think about them and wonder how they're doing, if they're getting better. They deserve it after everything they've been through."

"So do you, you know."

"Thanks, Miss Dixon."

"No, thank *you*. I'm proud of you, Grace. I can already tell that you've changed."

"I'm not cutting anymore," I say. "I still have urges, but I don't act on them like I used to."

She smiles. "That makes me very happy to hear."

I return her kind smile. "Me too."

"And what are you—" Before she can finish her sentence, the bell rings. "Darn."

"Stupid bell," I say.

"It's okay, we can talk more later. Are you ready for Spanish? Señora Martinez, like all of your teachers, has been informed of your 504 Plan, so if you feel overwhelmed again, let her know, and she'll contact me."

"504 Plan?"

"Accommodations tailored to your specific needs."

"Like special ed?"

"No, they're different. We've put a 504 Plan in place to ensure that you're safe and successful while you're at Everett. These accommodations are only there if you need them."

"Still sounds like special ed."

Miss Dixon sighs. "Would you like to go to Spanish or not?"

"Yeah, sorry. Can I have a pass?"

"Sure." She scribbles her name and the time on a green slip of paper, then hands it to me. "Best of luck, Grace."

"Thanks. Oh, and one more thing?"

"What's that?"

"Where should I have my snack? Most of my teachers don't let us eat in the classroom."

"I believe your mother wants you to eat with Nurse Belinda. You can stop by her office at the beginning of your study hall. Do you know where it is?"

"Uh-huh. Thanks again."

"It's my pleasure."

Walking to Spanish, the halls are much quieter, as second period has already begun. A couple students glance up from their

¡Saludos! worksheets when I enter the classroom. I hand Señora my pass, who responds with a polite nod.

"*Qué bueno verte, Gracia.*"

I pretend I know exactly what she's saying. "*Gracias, Señora.*"

"*Toma asiento, por favor.*"

"Uh . . . *sí?*" I try, but by the look on her face, I know I'm nowhere close. "Sorry."

She sighs. "Please take your seat. You'll find the worksheet in the yellow bin behind your desk. *Bueno?*"

"*Bueno.*"

Although Marilyn can be a total pain in my ass, I know I wouldn't have been able to understand Señora's assignment if she hadn't spent two hours last week guiding me through the material. But it's because she did, it's because she didn't call quits when I couldn't remember verb-conjugation or lose her cool when I repeatedly made the same careless errors, that I can.

My other classes are comfortingly easy as well. I breeze through an acids and bases WebQuest in chemistry and score a satisfying eighty-five on a pop quiz about Absolutism after eating my Clif Bar with Nurse Belinda. She says Chocolate Brownie is her favorite flavor too.

When history ends, I meet Mom at the front office, and we drive home in silence, neither of us in a talking mood. While I head upstairs to change my clothes, she prepares vegetarian BLTS, as well as a banana smoothie for me that tastes suspiciously creamier than usual.

"Is this the regular ice cream?" I ask.

She nods. "It's just a different brand. They were out of Breyers when I went to the store."

"Oh, okay."

"So, how was school?" she asks.

I finish nibbling the crust off one half of my sandwich, then move onto the other. "Fine."

"Really? Miss Dixon seemed to have a different impression when she called to tell me that you didn't go to your first period."

"I didn't feel like it. It's my first day back, Mom. Give me a break."

"Okay, okay." After a brief pause, she asks, "Did you eat your snack with the nurse?"

"Yeah."

"Are you telling the truth?"

"Jesus Christ, Mom!" I exclaim. "If you think I'm such a liar, then call her too. I mean, you're already talking to everyone else behind my back. Why not add another name to the list?"

Mom sighs. "I'm simply keeping them informed of your unique situation."

"My special ed?"

"504 Plan," she corrects. "Miss Dixon and I arranged a PPT meeting next week, so if you have additional concerns or would like to address this further, we'll discuss it then."

"PPT?"

"Planning and Placement Team. We're required to have them twice a year so long as you're a partial-day student."

"Fantastic."

"Are you sure you're all right, Grace? If there's anything you'd like to talk about, I'm here."

"I know, I know, and I really am fine—I swear. It's just that being around so many people again is super draining."

"It'll get easier," she assures me. "Now that you're in IOP, you'll have the entire weekend to relax. Isn't that exciting?"

"I guess so."

"You know what's even more exciting?" When I shake my

head, she exclaims, "Christmas! I can't believe it's less than a month away."

"Yeah. I'm glad I get to spend it at home with you and Jamie."

Mom smiles. "Me too. Christmas definitely wouldn't be the same without you."

"You don't think I'll have to go back, right? To the hospital, I mean."

"I don't. You're working hard, and it shows. I'm proud of you, hon."

"Thanks."

"You're welcome. How's your sandwich?"

I polish off the last bite, then wash it down with my smoothie. "Pretty good. Is it cool if I take a nap before IOP? I'm exhausted."

"Of course. I'll wake you up when it's time to go."

I place my dishes in the sink and walk upstairs with my lunch sloshing around in my stomach. Two carbs, one protein, one fat, one dairy, and one veg. Emilia should be impressed.

After struggling to get comfortable, I finally drift into a soundless sleep. It seems like I've been out for mere seconds when Mom shakes my shoulders.

"Five more minutes," I mumble into my pillow.

"Hon, it's almost two o'clock. I don't want you to be late."

With a sigh, I reluctantly raise my head. "Fine, I'll get up."

"Thank you. I'll meet you outside in ten minutes, okay?"

"Okay."

In the bathroom, I splash water on my face and touch up my smudged makeup. I'm still groggy as hell as I trudge downstairs to join Mom in her car. Fifty minutes later, most of which we spend listening to holiday music, she pulls into CADE's crowded parking garage.

"Now if only I could find a spot . . ."

"Right there." I point at an empty space between a FedEx and a Mini Cooper.

"Thanks." She claims the spot, then quiets her engine. "Do you have your dinner?"

I shake my head. "It's Order-In Night. We're having Chinese."

"Nice. Your favorite."

"*Was* my favorite," I correct. "Do you know how much salt is in Wonton Soup?"

"It's tastier that way. And anyway, it's not like you eat Chinese all the time. It's okay to treat yourself every now and then, you know."

"Uh-huh. So, I'll see you at seven?"

She nods. "I'll wait in the parking lot."

"Sounds good. Later, Mom."

"Enjoy your Chinese!" she calls after me.

"I'll try," I respond as enthusiastically as I can.

As I'm waiting for the elevator, I take my phone out of the back pocket of my jeans and google the menu for Green Dragon Café. The calories are listed in microscopic print next to each dish. Of the eight vegetarian options, the Veggie Spring Rolls have the fewest.

When I arrive at the Adolescent Services Department, Brooklyn hands me a modified version of the menu. Unfortunately, Veggie Spring Rolls aren't on her list, so I select Steamed Vegetable Dumplings instead.

"Good choice," she says. "Would you prefer broccoli or mixed vegetables on the side?"

"Broccoli."

In the kitchen, everyone else—minus Chloe, who's MIA— has already prepared their snacks. I place precisely three-fourths of an ounce of pretzels and two tablespoons of hummus (one starch, one fat) on a plastic plate and sit next to Faith. She's picking at a massive pile of tortilla chips and guacamole, looking utterly repulsed.

"I'm so pissed that my fucking Exchanges went up again," she grumbles. "I'm not, like, trying to lose weight on purpose. I just have a fast metabolism."

"What's your starch number?" Isaac asks. He shovels a spoonful of vanilla yogurt in his mouth, somehow managing to look cute even when a drop falls onto his grey FIFA shirt.

"Twelve."

"Mine's fifteen. That's why I love these things." He shows her the strawberry-banana smoothie he's drinking with his yogurt. "Two starches, two proteins, and two fats. Fucking brilliant."

"Cool. I'll ask my dad to pick up a couple when he goes shopping."

"Go with him."

She shakes her head. "Nah. Grocery stores freak me out. There's too many triggers."

"I know the feeling," Aria says. "It's literally an anorexic's worst nightmare."

Isaac uses his sleeve to wipe a light-pink stain from his upper lip. "I hate that word. It makes me feel dirty, like I have some disgusting disease."

"I hate it too," Miguel says. "No, I think I just hate labels in general. The amount of times I've heard me and my sister called 'foreigners' is sick. It makes me feel like an outcast in a country that promised us protection."

"I hate the word emo," Miriam chips in. "I'm not emo; I'm scene. Learn the difference."

"Mine's slut," Aria says. "I know I've made a lot of mistakes in my past, but that doesn't mean they should define who I am now."

"Bitch," Faith says.

"Pig." That's Mandy's.

A tear trickles down Eva's cheek. "Freak," she whispers. "I hate being called a freak."

"What about you, Grace?" Isaac asks. "You got a label you hate?"

I choose the first word that pops into my mind. "Victim."

"That's a good one," Aria says. "In a way, we're all victims."

"Of what?" Eva asks.

Aria shrugs nonchalantly. "Of life."

After snack, I approach Isaac as he's washing his hands in the sink. "I liked that thing you said about labels. It was really cool."

"Thanks," he responds. "You're sweet."

I remember Bianca's words from the other night; *What's the worst that can happen?*

"There's a new movie playing at my local theater," I say. "It's supposed to be pretty good, and I was wondering if you'd, you know, want to go see it with me?"

"Technically, we're not supposed to hang out outside of Program," he says.

"Oh. Right."

"But fuck that," he continues. "I'm free Sunday afternoon. What time is it playing?"

"Four o'clock."

"Sounds great. What's your number?"

I tell him, and he adds me to his contacts. "Text me the details, okay?"

"Okay," I respond, struggling to refrain from grinning gleefully.

Stay cool, Grace, I instruct myself. *No one likes a desperate person.*

"Hey, guys!" Teagan calls. "Who's ready to learn about Interpersonal Effectiveness?"

"Not me," Isaac grumbles. "I'm so over these dumb groups."

"Same," I say. "I wish we could go on more walks. I actually don't mind those."

"Me neither."

Nevertheless, we follow Teagan into the Art Room. She passes around worksheets titled *DBT Handout #3: D-E-A-R M-A-N* and explains, "We use skills like Dear Man to learn how to express our wants and needs. Without communication, relationships can foster resentment or hurt feelings. Does anyone know why this is the case?"

"Because depression is an isolating illness," Miriam says softly.

"Very good, Miriam. Can you elaborate?"

"I dunno. I guess . . . I guess because when you're depressed, you feel like you're drowning while everyone around you is breathing. Then that makes you wonder what's wrong with you, and when you begin to think something is wrong, you assume they can see it too. And that makes you want to crawl under your covers and never come out again."

"Wow," Aria says. "That's so true."

"Yes, it is," Teagan agrees, "which is why skills like Dear Man are important in recovery. They teach us how to find the motivation to throw off our covers and face the day or hour or even—"

"Minute," Isaac interjects. He winks at me, and I shyly smile in return.

Teagan nods. "Exactly."

Minute by minute, Teagan's lesson crawls by. She provides us with a few examples, then asks us to fill out our worksheets, then opens the floor for "unfiltered discussion." As Faith is recapping an argument she had with her father last night, our food arrives. We watch Brett help the delivery boy carry four bulky Green Dragon bags into the kitchen. Besides Mandy, who eyes them hungrily, the nervous energy among us is palpable.

Teagan tries to reclaim our focus but surrenders when she realizes it's a lost cause. "You have permission to use your phones until dinner is ready," she says, "but if I see more dick pics, Mandy and Faith, they will be confiscated."

"When did that happen?" Isaac asks me.

"Two weeks ago," I respond. "It's a long story. If you want, I'll text you about it later."

He flashes his adorable smile again. "I can't wait."

Several minutes later as Brett invites Isaac and Eva into the kitchen to plate their food, Chloe finally emerges from Emilia's office. "Guess what, bitches? I'm outta here!"

"You're discharging?" Aria asks. When Chloe nods, she fist-bumps her and says, "That's great, Chlo. Those cheerleaders won't know what hit them."

"Damn right." Chloe sniffs the air with her button nose. "Smell that?"

"Sesame seeds and soy sauce?" Faith tries.

"Freedom. It's, like, the best thing ever."

"I thought that was Justin Bieber."

"Okay, well, he's a close second."

While they continue chatting, I approach Miriam. She's sitting by herself on one of the couches looking even thinner than usual—sadder too. I can see it in her empty, brown eyes.

"Hey. You all right?"

She shrugs. "Yes. I mean, no. I mean, I dunno. Chinese food makes me nauseous."

"What'd you order?"

"Sweet and Sour Chicken. With a protein shake, because I lost weight again."

"If it makes you feel better, I'm anxious too," I say.

"Rough day?"

"Yeah. It was my first day back at school."

"I remember my first day back after I got sick in tenth grade," she says. "It was awful."

"How come?"

"Nobody understood what I was going through, so when my GC found out I had pocketed my snack, she was pissed. She yelled at me for, like, ten minutes."

"You pocketed your snack?"

She nods. "It was easy. The nurse was too busy helping kids with stomach aches and broken arms and stuff like that to make sure I ate."

"It's so unfair," I gripe. "People can see a broken arm but they can't see a broken mind."

"It really does suck," she agrees.

"Miriam? Grace?" Brett calls. "Come plate your food!"

"Ready?" I ask Miriam.

A sigh escapes her pale lips. "As ready as I'll ever be."

Once Miriam and I have prepared our meals, we join everyone else in the dining room to begin eating. Mandy devours her Steamed Jumbo Shrimp while Faith and Miguel tentatively nibble on their General Tso's Chicken, and Chloe saws her Sesame Chicken into dozens of minuscule pieces. Eva picks at a small bowl of white rice—the only option on the menu she felt comfortable with—and sips a cup of apple juice. Across the table, Miriam stares down at her Sweet and Sour Chicken. She has yet to take a bite.

Two minutes later, Brooklyn comes to her side. "Miriam, you need to try something."

Miriam shakes her head. "No."

"How 'bout you begin with the vegetables?" Brooklyn

suggests.

"No."

"Miriam, you know the rules. You have to eat." When Miriam still refuses to comply, she asks, "Would you like to go somewhere private?"

"Uh-huh."

Whisking her plate off the table, Brooklyn guides Miriam into her office and closes the door behind them. The chitchat that had subsided during their exchange resumes. Chloe and Aria gush about their celebrity OTPs. Teagan encourages Eva to eat more rice. Miguel tells Faith about a boy he's interested in. Beside me, the boy I'm interested in swallows his final forkful of Beef Lo Mein and moves onto his broccoli.

"How're your dumplings, Grace?"

"Okay, I guess. They're very filling."

"Well, at least you're almost done."

"Uh-huh." I glance at Chloe. We've been at the table for nearly twenty minutes, yet she's only halfway through her chicken. "Is it just me or—"

"It's not. She definitely doesn't seem ready to leave. Then again, who does?"

"I guess there's no such thing as too much treatment," I say.

He shudders. "First frightening thought of the evening."

"Sorry."

"It's cool. So, what's that movie we're seeing called?"

"The title?"

"Uh-huh."

"Um . . . I honestly have no idea." I chuckle nervously. "My friend recommended it."

Now Isaac is laughing as well. "Good to see you're on top of things."

"Oh, shut up." I make a mental note to look up the movie's

premise when I get home. It could be about pedophilia or incest or something else equally as cringy, and I'd have no idea.

Fifteen minutes later, once Eva has finished her final grain of rice, Teagan announces that it's time for Chloe's Goodbye Group. The seven of us—aside from Miriam, who's still with Brooklyn—clear our dishes and gather in the Group Room. Chloe sits cross-legged on a beige ottoman that's usually reserved for Teagan or Brooklyn while we settle onto the surrounding couches.

"Whenever you're ready, Chloe," Teagan says.

"I didn't, like, prepare a speech or anything like that," Chloe begins, "so I guess I'll just, like, start by saying thanks for always having my back. You're all, like, super cool people, and I know you'll all kick ass. Don't have too much fun without me."

Teagan laughs. "It was a pleasure knowing you, Chloe. We'll miss you."

"Thanks, T. I'll miss you too."

"Have you thought about your Goodbye Song?"

Chloe nods. *"Scars to Your Beautiful."*

While Teagan searches Spotify for Chloe's selection, I nudge Aria. "What's a Goodbye Song?"

"A song that's significant to your recovery," she explains. "It's one that speaks to you or makes you feel like everything hasn't gone to shit."

I wonder what song I'll choose when I discharge. The thought of not needing treatment—aside from the outpatient therapist and nutritionist Mom and Emilia have started to seek out—seems strange, unfamiliar, and not that I'd ever admit it, scary. Since the middle of October when I was admitted to the ER, I've grown comfortable with the abnormal norm of a hospital setting. Even attending school for four hours was unreasonably challenging.

But everyone says things will improve, and I have to trust them, because what other choice do I have? For too long, I shut the people closest to me out of my life. I knew if they got involved, if they knew my secrets, they'd do whatever they could to rescue me from the dangerous path I was headed down. And that scared me. Getting better scared me.

I finally understand what Dr. Bennett meant when he said I had disordered thinking.

Two seats to my right, Isaac reaches around Faith to tap my arm. He waits until I'm looking to mouth something that I cannot make out.

"Huh?"

He tries again, and this time, I know what he's saying; "You are beautiful."

"Grace, I don't know if this is a good idea."

"Of course it's a good idea," I respond. "You're the one who's always saying I need to be more social, Mom."

"But with someone from Program? Isn't that risky? You could trigger each other or—"

"Nobody's getting triggered," I interrupt. "We're going to the movies—that's all. I've already had snack so you don't have to worry about food, and anyway, Isaac's super nice. You'll like him."

Mom finishes pressing a dressy indigo blouse and hands it to me, which I slip over my white camisole. "When'd you say he'd be here?"

I check my phone. "Any minute. You won't embarrass me, right?"

"No. However, I would like to establish ground rules . . ."

"I know."

". . . and ask him a couple questions . . ."

"Yeah, yeah. I know that too."

". . . to make sure he's good enough for my daughter."

I roll my eyes. "That's so pretentious."

"I have every right to be concerned, Grace. You're finally doing better, and I don't want some guy to ruin that."

"He's not just some guy, Mom. He's my friend."

"Well, let's hope it stays—" she begins to say when the doorbell rings. "Are you going to get that?"

"Yeah. How do I look?"

Mom smooths down my hair with her hand, then adjusts my blouse so the tag isn't sticking out the back. "Wonderful. You're beautiful, Grace."

I blush. "Thanks."

While she returns the ironing board to the hall closet, I open the door to invite Isaac inside. His light-blonde hair is unkept as usual, but everything else about him—from his straight-legged jeans to the olive fleece he's layered over a blue button-down—screams "presentable."

"Hey, Grace."

"Hey. Come on in."

"Thanks. It's freezing out here."

"Did your mom drop you off?"

He shakes his head. "I drove. That's my car." He points at a small black Kia that's haphazardly parked beside our house.

"I didn't know you drove."

"Yeah, but I'm not allowed to drive you. I just got my license a month ago."

"That's cool. My mom can take us to the theater."

"Good."

"She can be pretty intense," I continue, "so be prepared."

"My mom's an attorney." He kicks off his dirty sneakers beside my Converse, revealing black taco-patterned socks. "I'm used to intense."

"Yeah, well, so am I."

But to my surprise, Mom is uncharacteristically chill. She doesn't drill Isaac with questions or rattle off numerous "dos" and "don'ts." Instead, she asks him about his interests, jokes about their shared dislike for Shakespeare, and even offers him advise on how to pass his upcoming anatomy test.

"So, how do you like CADE?" she asks.

Isaac shrugs. "It's okay. It's my first PHP, so I didn't know what to expect, but I guess it's not that bad."

"Grace says you were also at CTC."

"I was. I must have come right after she left."

"So, I assume you live locally?"

"Yeah. I live in Fairfield with my mom. My parents are divorced."

"I'm sorry."

"It's fine," he says. "It's better that way."

While they're talking, I check the time again; three thirty-six. "Uh, Mom? I don't mean to rush you or anything, but the movie starts in twenty-five minutes so . . ."

"So, then we should get going," she finishes.

"Really?"

"Yes, really. What'd you think I would say?"

"I dunno. That you wanted to—ah, never mind. Thanks, Mom."

"No problem," she responds. "C'mon, you two. You don't want to be late."

Isaac and I chat in the backseat for the entire ride while Mom listens to a podcast on the latest presidential drama up front. When we arrive at the theater, she says to me, "I'll pick you up at five, okay? No later."

"Five. Got it."

"Do you have money, Grace?"

"I'm paying," Isaac interjects. "If that's all right, of course."

"It's fine with me," I say. "I'm nearly broke, so the less I spend the better."

"She's saving her money for Christmas gifts," Mom says. "Right, Grace?"

"Uh-huh. Bye, Mom."

"Bye, hon. I'll see you at five."

"Okay."

Isaac follows me up a concrete staircase to the theater's main entrance. "Have you been here before?"

I nod. "It's pretty nice. They have comfortable seats at least."

"Sweet. Is that the movie we're seeing?" He points at the third title down on the marquee.

"Yeah, that's the one."

"*When the Angels Cry,*" he reads aloud. "Where'd they come up with that; tumblr?"

I laugh. "Probably. Oh, I checked out *Say It Ain't So* the other day."

"And? What'd you think?"

"Good."

"Just good?"

"Okay, very good."

He grins. "That's what I thought."

A billboard for an upcoming FIFA documentary is plastered on the wall as we wait in line to buy tickets.

"God, I miss soccer," Isaac says.

"You played?"

He nods. "For ten years. You should've seen my room; it was insane. Even my bedspread was decorated with soccer balls."

"Same—except for me, it was my lampshade. Do you think you'll ever play again?"

"I can't."

I roll my eyes. "Don't say that. I'm sure when you're better, you'll be kicking ass on the field."

"No, I literally can't," he insists. "I have osteoporosis in my spine. If I were to get hurt, I could be paralyzed for the rest of my life."

"Are you serious?"

"Yep. I made a choice to stop eating, and now I'm paying the price." Isaac hands the cashier two twenties, politely declining when she asks us if we want snacks. "And it's pretty damn heavy."

Once the cashier has deposited Isaac's money, she hands him two tickets and directs us to Theater Ten.

"That was my room number in the ER," I say. "My mom and I had to wait for, like, almost an hour to get in. She tried to pretend that she was okay, but I could tell she didn't want to be there."

"Your mom's nice," Isaac says.

"Not too intense?"

He shakes his head. "Just wait until you meet mine. When I introduced her to Holly, she spent thirty minutes rattling off statistics about teen pregnancies and STDS."

"Holly?"

"My ex."

"Oh. How long were you two together?"

"Seven months. We broke up last April, but I don't want to talk about it if that's okay."

"Yeah, sure. Where do you want to sit?"

Isaac scans the crowded theater. "How 'bout there?" he asks, pointing to the fourth row.

"Works for me."

We settle in behind two boys who are scrolling through Instagram and audibly debating which of the girls in the pictures are "DTF."

"Sorry," Isaac mouths.

"It's fine," I assure him. "I mean, you've heard some of the things Faith and Mandy say."

"And Miguel. The dude's always hitting on me."

"He does that to everyone. Siblings, friends—he even flirted with Eva's dad."

Isaac wrinkles his nose. "Mr. O'Reilly? Gross."

"I think he just wants to feel connected to people. Most of his family's still in Puerto Rico, so he's lonely at home."

"That sucks."

"Yeah. Even though my mom is super annoying, I don't know where I'd be without her."

"Me neither."

"Shh!" One of the boys holds his finger to his lip. "It's starting."

Rolling his eyes, Isaac reclines into his seat as the lights dim. He places his arm on the armrest between us at the same time that I do, but he doesn't retract it. So neither do I.

When the Angels Cry, which follows a young woman who's struggling to cope with the death of her fiancé, is surprisingly good for a romcom. Lou, a slasher-flick diehard, said so too when she and Cassie went to see it on Friday to celebrate Cassie's eighteenth birthday.

"Seven stars, because the female lead is kind of stale, and there's no sex. Just some kissing."

"You don't think that'll be awkward, right?" I asked.

Lou scoffed. "Of course not. Thanks to me, now you're an above-the-waist pro."

"Lou! You promised we wouldn't talk about it!"

"Wait, you were serious about that?"

After ninety minutes of suspense, drama, and as Lou had warned, plenty of "above-the-waist" action, the screen darkens on the main character's face, who's finally smiling after spending most of the film in tears. Isaac and I follow the crowd back into the central theater as *I Remember You* accompanies the ending credits.

"My dad loved Skid Row," I say. "When he drove me to elementary school, eighties hair metal was all he ever played."

Isaac frowns. "Did your dad die?"

"Sort of."

"Sort of?"

"I mean, he isn't physically dead, I don't think," I say, "but parts of him definitely are."

While we wait outside for Mom, humming along to *All I Want for Christmas is You,* which is being projected from a nearby loudspeaker, snowflakes begin to fall from the sky. They adhere to our eyelashes and our headwear—Isaac's backwards baseball cap and my grey beanie.

"I remember the first time I saw snow," I say. "We'd been in Connecticut for three months, so it was a pretty big shock. Some days, I still look at it and long for the palm trees and sixty-degrees winters I grew up with."

"Holly also hated snow," Isaac says. "She thought the flakes were angels who'd been rejected from Heaven, and she was worried that would happen to her; that she would fall too if God decided she wasn't worthy."

"Seriously?"

He nods. "Dating Holly was sad and confusing and even

scary at times. She was so trapped in her own little world that anything outside of her comfort zone terrified her."

"Was she sick?"

"Very. I used to think if I was devoted enough, she'd get better. But at one point, I realized the only person standing in her way was herself, and that nobody could help her if she didn't want to be helped. I think that's true for most mental illnesses, you know?"

"I do. I feel that conflict every day."

"Me too."

We fall quiet for a couple minutes, listening to the music as snowflakes continue to fall. Every so often, our eyes briefly meet, but it isn't until the third time that I gather the courage to ask, "Can I kiss you?"

To my relief, Isaac grins. "You don't have to ask."

He gently cups my face in his ice-cold hands and leans towards me until our lips touch. I inhale his subtle scent of Axe body spray and cherry chapstick as his fingers travel from my chin to my forehead. He brushes tiny flakes off the stands of my hair that hadn't managed to stay in my beanie.

"I'm so glad I met you," he whispers.

"Me too."

A peaceful silence settles between us as the final bars of *All I Want for Christmas* fade out. A couple seconds later, they're followed by the familiar piano intro to *Fairytale of New York*.

"Damn," Isaac says. "That's pretty sick timing, huh?"

"Yeah. We were just talking about this song last week."

"It's a Christmas miracle!" he jokes. "In all seriousness though, thanks for today. I had a great time."

I return his kind smile. "So did I."

20

In my dreams, I'm walking down a dark alley. Someone, though I don't know who, is following me. I hear their shoes crunching against the fallen autumn leaves as I quicken my pace.

"Go away!" I scream. "Leave me alone!"

I break into a sprint until I reach a brick wall. I glance around wildly, searching for an escape, and when I find none, I sink to the damp pavement and helplessly watch as the mysterious figure approaches me, their shadow looming over my trembling body.

"Who are you?" I whisper. "What do you want?"

"Shh, Gracie," a familiar voice says gently. "I'm here. You don't have to be afraid."

"We're lookin' at cloudy skies all day," another voice announces, "with a high of twenty-eight and a low of sixteen. Better bundle up, 'cause it's gonna be a cold one!"

I glance down at my sleeveless ivory nightgown; the same nightgown my father bought me for my tenth birthday, three months before he left. One of the shoulder straps has come undone and blows freely in the harsh wind. If it is twenty-eight degrees, then why am I not cold?

"Now, let's take a look at the traffic."

I fumble around for the OFF button on my alarm clock. It's still dark when I open my eyes, though I'm in my bed, not some alley, the only voice I hear is Jamie's singing *Cheap Thrills* as he uses the bathroom, and my nightgown has been replaced with a grey sweatshirt and plaid pajama pants.

"It was just a dream," I whisper. "You're all right. You're all right."

Even though I want nothing more than to stay beneath my cozy blankets all day, I force myself to get up and walk downstairs. Mom is fiddling with the dials on the toaster, audibly cursing under her breath.

"What happened?" I ask.

"Jamie wanted an English muffin, but this damn thing keeps malfunctioning. I'll have to pick up a new one sometime."

"Try Goodwill." I spoon two-thirds of a cup of vanilla yogurt into a bowl, then add half-a-cup of granola and banana slices on top. "Hey, Mom?"

"Yes?"

"Can I skip school? I didn't sleep well."

"You took your melatonin, right?"

"Yeah, but I had some strange dreams, and I'm really tired so—"

"So, you don't think I'm tired too?" she interrupts. "I have a job I need to be at in forty minutes, a household to run, a broken toaster, and two high-maintenance kids on my hands, but do you see me complaining?"

"I guess not."

"Exactly. Now eat your breakfast and put on something nice. You're not wearing pajamas to school again."

"When did you get so mean?" I ask.

"I'm not being mean," she responds. "I'm being firm. How else do you expect anything to get done around here?"

"Fine. Whatever."

With a sigh, I plunge my spoon into my yogurt and take a bite. I finish fifteen minutes later, then place my bowl in the sink and head upstairs to change my clothes. As I'm brushing my teeth, I use my left hand to send Isaac a text saying: *i had a great time yesterday. still cant get FONY out of my head lol. i hope ur morning is going better than mine is. so fucking exhausted! dont know how im gonna get thru school!*

After some consideration, I delete the last three lines and replace them with: *looking forward to seeing u in program!* That's better. I press the blue arrow and wait for him to respond while I rinse toothpaste out of my mouth.

But he doesn't.

Ten minutes later as Mom drives me to Chuckles, I glumly stare out my window at the melting snowbanks. "Mom, do you think I have SAD?"

"No, I think there's just still so much California in you," she responds. "I didn't even grow up on the West Coast, and I hated winters too when we moved back here."

"And now?"

She shakes her head. "A couple months after we moved—I think it was around New Years—one of my colleagues told me something that changed my mind. He said; 'snowflakes are winter's butterflies, so whenever you long for flowers, remember that only butterflies can touch the sky.'"

"That's pretty," I say.

"It is, isn't it?"

"Do you think we'll ever move back?"

"I'm not sure, but there are a number of excellent colleges out there that I could definitely see you at in two years."

In my mind, two years seems like an eternity. "Depends if I can survive high school."

"Of course you can. I know it seems like a long time from now, but I promise it'll fly by much quicker than you expect."

"You mean it?"

She nods. "I certainly do."

But time does not fly by quickly today—on the contrary, it crawls. My first two periods seem more like four hours than the forty minutes they actually are, so when I finally arrive at chemistry, I'm exhausted. It's Friday, which means that instead of having to endure another mundane lesson on chemical elements, we'll be completing whatever half-ass experiment Ms. Lloyd has slapped together to keep us busy while she browses Target.com on her laptop. She should move her desk away from the window if she doesn't want us to know that she prefers thongs to briefs.

"Where's Michaela?"

Ms. Lloyd, who's struggling to activate a twenty-percent discount code, pauses to shoot me a confused look. "Huh?"

"My lab partner. She's not here."

"Ah, right. I believe she had a dentist appointment."

"So . . . what should I do? I can't do the experiment alone."

"Let's see." Ms. Lloyd scans the classroom, searching for another absence, and when she finds none, she says, "Why don't you join Jess and Tiffany? They look like they could use some help staying on task."

"Are you sure I can't work with anyone else?"

"Is there something wrong with Jess and Tiffany?"

"No, it's just—"

"That's what I thought." She hands me a graduated cylinder

and a thick packet describing the experiment. "Safety goggles and aprons are in the back. I'll be here if you have any questions."

So, after insincerely thanking her, I head to the supply station to collect my apron and goggles. I rummage through the box of leftovers for one without a broken strap, and when I'm unsuccessful, tie the loose ends together so they won't slide down my face.

"Can I help you?" Jess asks when I approach her and Tiffany. Unlike the rest of the class, who have followed Ms. Lloyd's safety guidelines, she's tossed her goggles and apron aside. All it would take, I realize, is one "accidental" mistake to ruin her white Justin Bieber shirt.

"Ms. Lloyd said I should join your group," I respond. "Michaela's at a dentist appointment."

Jess laughs. "Unless that's her twin smoking weed in the bathroom, she's not at the dentist."

"That girl's a hot mess," Tiffany says. "Did you see the picture she posted on Instagram after the Migos concert last week?"

"The one with that hideous see-though shirt?" Jess nods. "I don't know what Matt sees in her. She's such a slut."

"Um, guys?" I say. "We should probably get started. Experiments are worth twenty percent of our semester grade, you know."

"Yes, teacher." Jess hands Tiffany the cylinder. "We need thirty ml of water."

"That's milliliters, right?"

Jess rolls her eyes. "What else would it be?"

"I dunno. I was just making sure."

"Well, it is, so go get the water before Miss Goody Two Shoes here gets all pissy."

"Okay, okay. I will."

While Tiffany waits behind Tommy to use the sink, Jess turns to me. "It's nice to see you back, Edwards."

Her benevolence takes me by surprise. "Uh, thank you?"

"Bianca says you had the flu," Jess continues, "but I'm not so sure. One month is an awfully long time to be out with an illness that usually lasts less than two weeks."

"I was very sick," I respond.

"I'm not saying you weren't. Just maybe not *that* type of sick, if you know what I mean."

I try to think of something clever to say to contradict her blunt assertion, but nothing comes to mind, so I remain quiet.

Jess smirks. "That's what I thought."

"I got thirty ml," Tiffany says. She leans over Jess to set down the cylinder, but her hand slips, and it tips, spilling water all over Jess' notebook.

"What the fuck, Tif!"

Tiffany's blue eyes grow wide with horror. "Oh my God. I'm so sorry!"

"Just—just get a fucking towel, you moron," Jess snaps. "God, I hate this class."

While they argue, I reach across Jess to retrieve my packet, which was thankfully only slightly dampened by Tiffany's spill. Her skintight jeans would look unflattering on ninety-eight percent of girls at Chuckles, but on Jess, they merely show off her annoyingly perfect figure. Even sitting down, her thighs are as slender as ever.

I wish I had Jess' body; I wish I had her lithe legs and her tiny waist and her washboard stomach and her silky hair and her unblemished complexion. I wish for it every day, despite knowing that those wishes will never come true. You can't choose the body you were born into. And now, thanks to Mom and my treatment team micromanaging every decision I make regarding my diet, I don't have much choice in how I treat it either.

Because of my group's inability to focus, we run out of time to complete the last page in our packet by the time the bell rings and have to do it for homework. Mom and I eat lunch—a slice of fresh-baked banana bread with a cup of minestrone soup and seventeen grapes—and then I join her in her office to finish answering questions sixteen to twenty-one before Program. She sits at her desk replying to emails on her outdated PC.

After a while, her noisy typing begins to bother me. "You should get a new computer."

"What's wrong with this one?"

"It's old, and loud, and the other day when I couldn't find my charger, I used yours to work on a Classroom assignment, and it took five minutes to start up. Five minutes!"

Mom's lips twitch, like she's trying not to smile. "I'm guessing that's a long time."

I nod. "The sound makes it even worse."

"The sound?"

"Of your keyboards. It's, like, super annoying."

"Well, I see someone woke up on the wrong side of the bed."

"I already told you, Mom; I didn't sleep well last night."

"Because of your dreams?"

"Yeah."

"Do you remember what they were about?"

"No," I lie. "I just know they weren't good."

"That's too bad. They seemed to be getting better." When I don't respond, she asks, "Have you tried listening to music before you fall asleep? I've heard that helps."

"Yeah, I've tried that."

"And?"

I shake my head. "It doesn't. Literally nothing does."

I'm still in a crappy mood when Mom drops me off at CADE three hours later. Everyone but Miriam has begun preparing their snacks in the kitchen, so I grab a Red Delicious apple from the fruit bin and measure out two teaspoons of soy butter. As I'm slicing my apple into eight slivers, Isaac approaches me. His snack, a bowl of Goldfish and another smoothie, is already plated in his hands.

"Hey, Grace."

"Hey. Did you get my text?"

"No, uh, this is kinda awkward but . . ."

"But what?"

A bright-red blush spreads across his cheeks. "My mom took away my phone when she found out about you."

"I thought she already knew."

"Well, she didn't." Before I can respond, he quickly adds, "But I'll talk to her later, I promise. I'm sure once I explain things, it'll all be okay."

"Why didn't you tell her?" I ask. "Are you, like, ashamed of me?"

"Grace, of course I'm not ashamed of you. It's just, my mom has been super uptight about me dating since I ended things with Holly, and I didn't want her to freak you out."

"Freak me out?" I repeat. "You think she'll freak *me* out?"

Isaac raises an eyebrow. "You say that now."

"I'm serious, Isaac. After CTC, nothing seems so scary anymore."

"I know what you mean. Sometimes when I close my eyes, I still see Jonathan running through the hall at two in the morning claiming that God was trying to kill him."

"I have some pretty fucked up dreams too," I say.

"It's not a dream, Grace," he responds solemnly. "It's a reality."

We spend the first half of snack debating whether Barbecue or Salt & Vinegar is the superior potato chip flavor and the second playing a round of Categories when Teagan implements the "no food talk at the table" rule. Afterwards, we clear our dishes and head to the Group Room for DBT. To our collective surprise, Miriam is already there. She's curled up on one of the couches with a blanket wrapped around her tiny body. Brooklyn sits beside her stroking her pin-straight hair as tears trickle down her mascara-smudged cheeks.

"Mir, what's wrong?" Aria asks.

"I'm going back to residential," she whispers. "I feel like this isn't real; that it's all in my head, just like everything else is."

"Oh, Mir. I'm so sorry."

"Well, at least you already know the staff," Mandy says.

Miriam shakes her head. "It's not in Massachusetts. It's in Utah."

"Utah?"

"Uh-huh. I'm boarding the plane tomorrow morning, so this is my last day."

"Then we should do something," Eva suggests. "Like . . . like a dance party."

"I'm not in the mood to celebrate."

"But you're always talking about how dope your Goodbye Group is gonna be," Aria responds. "Why not have it right now? You can choose a song and—"

"Fuck goodbyes!" Miriam interrupts. She wriggles away from Brooklyn and dashes out of the room.

"Emilia!" Brooklyn calls to her colleague. "Some help please!"

"On it!" Emilia responds.

The six of us listen to her high heels clickety-clack against the floor as she chases after Miriam, followed by an audible *thud* of the entrance door slamming shut.

"You think she'll run away again?" Eva whisper-asks Aria.

"God, I hope not," Aria responds. "The last thing she needs is another trip to the ER."

Teagan clears her throat. "Nobody is going to the ER, Aria. Miriam just needs a little space to clear her head—that's all. In the meantime, would anyone like to make a Process Statement?"

"I guess I will," Aria says. "Mom, when you don't tell me that my hearing was moved, I feel anxious and betrayed."

"Can I reply?" Faith asks.

Tegan nods. "Go ahead."

While Faith is talking, I reach beneath the blanket I'm sharing with Isaac and brush my pinky finger against his. For a moment, I'm afraid he's going to ignore my gesture, but then I feel him press back. We exchange small smiles, then avert our attention to Faith and Aria as if nothing had happened, nothing at all.

The rest of the evening is a blur. When Process Group ends, we gather for dinner, and when dinner ends, we hang out in the kitchen for a couple extra minutes waiting for Miriam to show so we can say goodbye. But when the clock strikes seven and there's still no sign of her, we reluctantly bundle up and head outside.

The city looks beautiful at night with festive lights strung around every tree and street sign in sight. Plastic snowflakes dangle from the awnings of the smaller shops while the larger ones are decorated with illuminated wreathes and more colorful lights.

Mom is waiting in the parking lot of the elementary school next to CADE. "I'll never forget how I felt the day you started kindergarten," she says. "I was so nervous, I thought I was going to throw up. After your bus left, I was overcome with anxiety that something would happen to you; that you'd get hurt and I wouldn't be able to protect you." She chuckles softly. "It seems silly now, but in that moment, that fear was so real.

"When I got in my car to drive home, I turned on the radio, and the song *Breathe* was playing, and I just sat there and listened to the lyrics until I was able to catch my breath. It got easier as the year progressed, but every time I pass an elementary school, I think about that day and it reminds me of how much we've both grown."

"I know what you mean," I say. "Remember that Hello Kitty backpack I used to have?"

"Of course."

"God, that thing was hideous."

She laughs. "Yes, it was."

We're quiet for several minutes as Mom navigates through the busy streets to merge onto the freeway. Finally, I ask, "Did you know Miriam's going back to residential?"

Mom nods. "I heard. Her poor mother's in shambles."

"I keep thinking; what if that was me? What if *I* had to go back to CTC or somewhere else?"

"But it isn't you," she says, "and it won't be, because you're so strong and motivated, and the progress you've made is monumental. You're kicking ass, Grace. We all see it."

My hand slips into the pocket of my fleece jacket, fingering the leftover crumbs of my Clif Bar that hadn't made it down the toilet this morning. Miriam was right about one thing; with so many students to deal with, Nurse Belinda was too busy helping a boy with a bloody nose to notice me pocketing my snack.

"I see it too. It's just that today has been pretty crappy, and that makes things seem worse than they probably are."

"Well, I know something that'll cheer you up," Mom says.

I wait for her to elaborate, and when she doesn't, I ask, "Aren't you gonna tell me?"

"And ruin the element of surprise? Sorry, hon. You'll have to wait until we get home."

"Great," I grumble. "Another freakin' secret."

"Oh, don't be such a Grinch. Is it really so hard to trust your own mother?"

"You don't trust me."

"I don't trust your disorder," she corrects. "There's a difference."

"But you just said I was making progress."

"You are, however recovery doesn't happen overnight or even over the course of several weeks or months. It's gradual. You understand that, right?"

"I guess so," I admit. "That doesn't mean I like it."

"I know, hon. I don't like it either."

The house is dark when we arrive; Jamie must have forgotten to turn on the porch light again. When we walk inside, he's at the kitchen table working on a puzzle of two kittens snuggled in red stockings.

"How was Program?" he asks.

"It was okay. One of the girls left, so that was sad, but everything else was good." I reach for a border piece, but he swats my hand away.

"I can do it myself."

"Right. Sorry." Turning to Mom, I ask, "So, now can you tell us your big surprise?"

That captures Jamie's attention. "What surprise?"

"Wait here," she instructs. "I'll be back in a sec."

She disappears upstairs. Thirty seconds later, we hear a startling bang, accompanied by various clunking and thumping sounds.

"What's she doing?" Jamie asks.

I shake my head. "I have no idea."

Thump. Clunk. Crash. Mom breathlessly drags a bulky, green bag down the staircase and into the living room. "Recognize this?"

"Of course," I say. "It's our Christmas tree."

Jamie's eyes light up. "Ooh, fun!" he exclaims enthusiastically. "Can we decorate it?"

Mom nods. "You two get started. I'll see if Trevor wants to help."

While she searches for her boyfriend, Jamie and I begin assembling the base. It's easy for me, but he struggles repeatedly and has to resort to the manual for guidance.

"Why don't we have a real tree?" he asks.

I shrug. "Environmental reasons, I guess."

"Well, Jack says fake trees are tacky, and that the people who own them are lazy liberals."

"Who's Jack?"

"Zack Ackerman's younger brother. He's in my math class."

"Does he pick on you too?"

Jamie nods. "I think he's angry at me because I got Zack suspended."

"You didn't get him suspended, Jamie. It's not your fault he's an asshole."

"Well, Jack thinks I did."

"You know, I forgot what ignoramuses middle school boys can be."

"What's ignor—whatever that word is?"

"Ignoramus means a stupid person," I explain. "Want some advice?"

"Uh-huh."

"Just ignore everything he says. If you ask me, it sounds like a load of bullcrap."

"That wasn't the advice you gave me last time."

"You gotta pick your battles, Jamie. Not everyone is worth getting stitches over."

"Especially not ignoramuses."

"Exactly."

We're halfway done with the base when Jamie surrenders and begins sifting through a box of miscellaneous ornaments instead.

"Remember this?"

He shows me a poorly decorated snowflake cutout, and I laugh. "Didn't you make that in first grade?"

"Second. And everyone was annoyed, because I used all the pink glitter."

I point at a jingle bell with a red ribbon looped through the top. "Remember that? It's from the time we rode the Polar Express in Essex."

Jamie nods. "That was some good hot chocolate."

"It sure was."

"Did someone say hot chocolate?" Mom, precariously balancing three steaming mugs in her hands, sets them down on a coffee table and tosses me my Exchanges Sheet. "Two starches, one dairy."

"Thanks." I record the numbers, pleasantly surprised when they fulfill my daily requirements. "Where's Trevor?"

"Finishing an important call upstairs. He'll be down shortly."

"He doesn't like hot chocolate?"

Mom shakes his head. "Coffee's his drink of choice."

"And beer," Jamie says.

"Jameson!"

"What? It's true."

Coincidentally, Trevor walks into the room sipping a can of Budweiser. "How can I help?"

Mom hands him a clump of knotted rainbow lights. "You can work on these."

Trevor sighs. "Awesome."

Mumbling under his breath, he begins untangling the lights while Jamie, Mom, and I hang the rest of the ornaments; a blue Rudolph ball with a glowing red nose, a cardinal nestled in its nest, a glass figurine of a girl playing soccer. So on, and so forth.

The final ornament is a small circular photograph of Mom, Dad, Jamie, and me that was taken on the Christmas before he left.

"*Chestnuts roasting on an open fire,*" I hear Dad sing as I snuggle up in a faux-leather recliner and gaze at the palm trees swaying outside the window. "*Jack Frost nipping at your nose.*"

"Do *Little Drummer Boy,*" five-year-old Jamie pleads, tugging on his leg.

Dad smiles. "Of course, Jameson."

I run my thumb over his face and wonder how someone could have the audacity to abandon their own family. I know he and Mom were fighting, and I know I wasn't the perfect daughter and Jamie wasn't the perfect son, but every family has their share of issues. That's life. You deal with them. You don't just walk—or in his case, drive—away when things get tough.

"We don't have to hang that if you'd prefer not to," Mom says. She takes the picture from me and holds it in her hand. "I know you liked it before, but if it makes you sad—"

"No, I want to," I interrupt. "I'm not gonna let the past ruin Christmas. It's time to move on."

"Now that's the spirit!" Mom watches as I position the ornament between a sparkly sleigh and a ceramic black dog. "Very nice. Jamie, hon, come help us with the topper!"

Jamie, who's skimming through *Twas the Night Before Christmas*, places the book down and skips over to us. Mom hands him the star, and we hoist him up so he can reach the highest branch.

"A little to the right," I say.

Following my instructions, he adjusts the star until it's no longer tilted. "Better?"

"Yeah. It looks great."

"Thanks. Mom, can I have more hot chocolate?"

"Sure. Would you like to help me make it?"

"Yeah. Do we have marshmallows?"

"No, but I believe we have whipped cream."

"Awesome!"

While they head to the kitchen to prepare Jamie's drink and Trevor disappears upstairs again, I Snapchat Isaac a picture of our tree. He responds a minute later with a selfie beside his own. He looks exceptionally cute in a red pajama shirt and an oversized Santa hat that conceals the top half of his piercing blue eyes. They're even clearer in the dim lighting, practically resembling the razor-sharp icicles dangling from my roof.

Isaac: i talked to mom. everythings good.

Grace: yay!!

Isaac: :)

"Grace?" Mom calls. "Jamie and I are going upstairs, okay? It's getting late!"

"Okay, I'll be up shortly!" I respond.

Sending Isaac a *goodnight* text, I plug my phone into its charger and leave the room, switching off the overhead lamp so the sole source of illumination comes from the rainbow lights Trevor's strung on our tree. In the kitchen, Mom has left my melatonin on the counter. I wash it down with a cup of lukewarm tap water, then head to the bathroom to brush my teeth. I hum along to a holiday playlist on YouTube while I scrub the lingering taste of hot chocolate out of my mouth.

Chestnuts roasting on an open fire

Jack Frost nipping at your noise

I quickly press the small arrow to the right of the play/pause button. After a five-second Alexa commercial, the familiar intro of *Walking in a Winter Wonderland* blasts through my earbuds. A sigh of relief escapes my lips. It's far from my favorite Christmas song, but at least it's better than the former. At least it's better than thinking about him.

21

"C*ause we're walking in a winter wonderland!*" Lou bellows off-key. She skips down the hall to catch up with me, ignoring the scowls she receives from passing students. "Move! Sorry! Excuse me! Move please!"

"Well, you're awfully excited about something," I observe.

"Are you kidding? Christmas is one week away! If that's not exciting . . . fuck, I don't know what is!"

I grin. "Yeah, I'm excited too."

"I saw your tree on Snapchat."

"And? What'd you think?"

"Not bad. I was particularly fond of Jamie's glittery snowflake."

"You could tell it was his?"

Lou nods. "Grace, the only time I've seen you wear pink was at the Race in the Park. And even then you still had on black sweats."

"Okay, good point. But, Lou?"

"Yeah?"

"Why are you here? I mean, your fifth period is practically on the other side of the school."

"I'm ditching."

"What?"

"Cass and Sam got four tickets to the matinee of *A Christmas Carol*, and since Becca is sick, they said I could invite someone," she explains. "You get out at noon anyway, so I figured missing one period would be no biggie."

"Lou, aren't you forgetting something?"

"Uh . . . I don't think so."

"I have Program!" I exclaim.

"I thought you dropped down to Tuesday, Wednesday, and Thursday."

"*Monday*, Wednesday, and Thursday," I correct, "and plus, Mom would throw a fit if I ditched. Maybe we could go Friday?"

Lou shakes her head. "Can't. Today's the last performance."

"I'm sorry, Lou."

"Don't apologize," she says. "I mean, it sucks that we don't hang out as much as we used to, but at least you're not in the hospital. And I'm okay with putting some stuff off for a little while if it means you never have to go back. 'Cause I really fucking missed you, man. Like, a lot."

"I missed you too." As we exchange smiles, I slip my hand into the pocket of my fleece jacket, where crumbs from the four Clif Bars I pocketed last week, along with the one from this morning, collect. It's really due for a wash.

Lou thumps my shoulder with her fist. "Grace Edwards, kickin' ass as always."

"But the play—"

"There will be others. I bet I could convince Cass' friend Jacob to get us a couple extra tickets to that music festival tomorrow, since he's DJing. You said you had Tuesdays free."

"Seriously? You'd do that?"

She nods. "Definitely. Also, if you're interested, my church needs volunteers for the Christmas Pageant Saturday night. They're short on staff now that half the altar boys are praying the gay away in Utah."

"In Logan?"

"I dunno. Why?"

"One of the girls in my group went there last week. She—" I shake my head. "Never mind. I'll ask my mom if I can help."

"Awesome. Oh, and invite Isaac too. I really want to meet him."

"He might be with his dad that day," I say, "but I'll see if he can come."

"I'm gonna have to meet him eventually, you know? As your best friend, it's my duty to make sure he's good for you."

"He's really nice, Lou. You'll like him a lot."

"Is he a good kisser?"

"Oh yeah."

"But not as good as me, right?"

I shove her playfully. "Shut up."

Before she can respond, her phone buzzes. "Shit, that's Cass. I've gotta go. See ya!"

"Okay, I hope you—" I begin to say, though by then she's already disappeared behind a burly football player. I sigh. "Have fun."

I arrive at history as the bell rings and claim my usual seat in the back. To spare myself from the inevitable boredom, I doodle in my notebook while Mr. Duffy rambles on about Mercantilism. As he's explaining Mercantilist policies, my eyes begin to droop. For the past week, my sleep has been even worse than usual; dark memories make drifting off difficult, and when I eventually do, nightmares ensue.

Last night, it was about cake. Two nights ago, returning to the hospital. I make a mental note to ask Emilia if I can increase my melatonin dosage at our bi-weekly therapy session this afternoon. She shouldn't have a problem with it, I don't think.

However, when I do propose my idea later that day, she tells me that I'll have to discuss it with the psychiatrist when she comes in next week.

"But what about the bad dreams?"

"Have you tried listening to music?"

I shake my head. "My mom already suggested that."

"And?"

"It doesn't help."

"How 'bout relaxation tapes?"

"No, but I could probably find a soundtrack of the ocean or something on YouTube."

"Great. Give that a try, and you can tell me on Wednesday if it's working."

"Okay." I finish my banana and move onto my pretzels. "Sounds good."

"So, how are you otherwise?"

"Fine."

"How's school?"

"It's okay. I have As in everything but math. Since it's the only subject I'm still doing outside of school, Marilyn's been helping me a lot."

"Good. I'm glad you two are getting along."

"Me too. Except for the food stuff, she's actually not that bad."

"Food stuff?"

"She's always making comments about how my mom's cooking is gonna make her fat or that she needs to cut back on carbs so she'll look good when she goes to Miami over break."

"Does that bother you?"

"Not really. I hear that stuff at school all the time. I think I just have to accept that most people have a love-hate relationship with food."

"That's a very mature observation, Grace."

"Thanks."

"And how has your relationship with food been?"

"Fine. Normal."

"Well, according to Brooklyn, you're down a couple pounds. Do you have any idea how that happened?"

Even though I do, I shake my head. "I've been eating the same amount as always."

"Are you exercising more?"

"Besides a couple walks around my block, no. I'm not allowed to."

"Okay, okay. I'm just throwing around suggestions."

"I know, but sometimes this weight thing is just so annoying. I don't understand why you can't tell me my number or at least my range. I mean, Aria already knows hers."

"It was Aria's choice to buy a scale," Emilia says. "We cannot control the choices you make outside of CADE. The most we can do is help you recognize how those choices impact your recovery."

Once again, I picture myself in the Jackson's bathroom on Thanksgiving staring down at their scale. I could have relapsed that night if Lou hadn't knocked on the door when she did. In a split-second, I could have jeopardized months of hard work simply to please the thing inside me that hungers for control.

"But what if I were to find a scale at the gym or—or someone's house? Wouldn't you want me to be prepared?"

"I'm sorry, Grace. The answer is still no."

I sigh in frustration. "Why does everyone always do this?"

"Do what?"

"Treat me like I'm a kid. For my entire life, it's felt like everything I did, everything I felt, was because someone told me it was okay."

"Only you can feel the way you feel," Emilia responds. "There's no shame in emotions."

"Not even fear?"

Emilia's slender brows furrow. "Do you feel afraid, Grace?"

"Not as much as I did when my dad left. It's been almost six years, but I still remember how scared I felt watching him drive away. I kept hoping he'd come back but as days went by, and then weeks, I knew he wouldn't. I think I'd always known. I just didn't want to admit it."

"I'm sorry. I imagine that must have been very difficult."

"It was the first time I cut myself," I say softly.

"What?"

"I've never told anyone, but a month later when my mom started looking at houses on the East Coast, I cut myself with a piece of sea glass. More than once, actually."

"How long did this go on for?"

"Only a couple weeks. I stopped when we moved to Connecticut. I still had urges, but I didn't act on them—at least not until this September."

Emilia reaches across the table and holds my hands. "Thank you for telling me. I'm proud of you."

"Why?"

"Because scars, like emotions, aren't something to feel ashamed of, nor are they something to hide. Time doesn't mend trauma; talking about it does."

"I didn't have anyone to talk to when Dad left. I guess that's why I started cutting."

"Are you experiencing urges to self-harm now?"

"No," I lie. "I haven't in a while."

"That's good to hear. But if you do begin to have them again, please let one of us know."

"Okay, I will."

"Is there anything else you'd like to discuss with me?"

I shake my head. "I don't think so. Can I go to Group?"

"You may—after you tell me whether you'd prefer a chocolate or vanilla shake."

"Are you serious?"

"Rules are rules, Grace. Since you lost weight, you'll need to supplement your dinner."

"Well, I've only ever had chocolate," I say, "and it sucked big time."

"So, vanilla then?"

"Sure. I mean, it can't be that bad . . . right?"

Ninety minutes later, however, as I watch Teagan pour the drink into a plastic cup, I begin to have second thoughts. "Is it supposed to be grey?"

"If you think the color's bad, wait until you taste it," Aria pipes in. "Fucking disgusting."

"Not helpful," Teagan says.

"What? I'm just being honest."

"Teagan!" Faith calls. "Where are the measuring spoons?"

"Have you checked the dishwasher?"

"Uh-huh. They're not there."

"Okay. Let me see if I can help."

While she and Faith search the kitchen for the missing spoons, I face Aria. She's eyeballing a cup of two-percent milk, her hand trembling as she lifts the half-gallon.

"Are you all right?"

With a sigh, Aria sets down the milk. "Not really. There's a lot of shit going on in my life right now, and it's all very overwhelming. I haven't been able to sleep, because I'm worried about my hearing, and when I do . . ." She sighs again. "Anyway, what's up with you?"

I shrug. "Not much."

"It sucks that you have to drink a shake."

"Yeah."

"Aria? Grace? You two almost done in there?"

"Yes, Teagan!" Aria responds. To me, she says, "You coming?"

"I'm right behind you."

With my shake in one hand and a plate of lukewarm soy nuggets and sweet potato fries in the other, I follow Aria into the dining room. I sit beside Isaac, who's slender face breaks into a grin.

"Hey."

"Hey. You have broccoli in your teeth."

Isaac runs his tongue over his upper incisors, then flashes me a second smile. "Better?"

"Yeah." I take a small sip of my shake and grimace at the sickening taste. "Yuck. These things are so gross."

"You lost weight?"

"Just a couple pounds. It's not like I'm dangerously under, so I don't know why everyone is freaking out."

"Eating disorders aren't one size fits all."

"Easy for you to say."

"Grace, you don't have to be super skinny to be pretty. You know that, right?"

"I mean, I guess so." I drag a sweet potato fry through a small pile of ketchup and pop it in my mouth. In California, when Mom had more time on her hands, she used to make them all the time. It was one of my most requested sides. "It's just hard when there are so many people I see at school or around town that I'd rather look like."

"You can't change the way you look," he responds. "Or you can—except then it'd be fake. I know it's easier said than done, but at some point, you've gotta accept what you have, because if you don't, you'll be miserable forever."

I sigh. "I've heard that before."

"Me too."

"And have you?"

"Accepted myself?" When I nod, he says, "Not yet, but I'm getting there. Can I try one of your fries? They look good."

I slide three onto his plate. "They're all right. My mom's are better."

Later that evening as Mom and I drive home, I replay Isaac's words in my head; *you don't have to be super skinny to be pretty.* I wish I could believe him—I really do. The problem is that every time I try, the abusive thoughts return to remind me of how ugly and worthless and pathetic I am. Emilia asked earlier if I still have urges to self-harm. But what good would admitting to her that I contemplate cutting every night as I'm lying in bed unable to sleep do me? She'd just relay the information to Mom, and that wouldn't end well.

Mom looks so peaceful now, humming along to *I'll Be Home for Christmas* as she passes the *Welcome to Connecticut* sign. After the hell I've put her through, she deserves to have a relaxing Christmas. For one day of the year, just twenty-four hours, she deserves to forget.

To our collective surprise, the outside of our house is illuminated with colorful lights when we pull into the driveway.

"Did Trevor put those up?" I ask.

"He must've while we were at Program. He's really becoming a pro, isn't he?"

"Yeah."

"I wish he'd remember to take the mail in too. Here." She

hands me the stack of envelopes that were crammed into our mailbox so she can unlock the door. "Thanks."

"No problem."

Once we're inside, I sift through the mail for Jamie's iTunes gift card, which I'm beginning to worry won't arrive in time for Christmas morning. Instead, I find an envelope addressed to *Grace and Jameson Edwards* in a sloppy, yet vaguely familiar handwriting.

"I thought we got all our Christmas cards," Mom says when I show her the peculiar envelope. "Who's it from?"

"No idea. It doesn't have a return address."

Jamie, who's sucking on a candy cane, peers over my shoulder. "Open it. I call dibs if there's money."

So, I tear open the envelope and remove a card with a silly cartoon Santa drawn on the front. Handing Jamie a twenty-dollar bill, I read aloud; "*Dearest Gracie and Jameson, I'm sorry I didn't reach out sooner but I needed time to clear my head after what happened between your mother and me. Even though my past actions might not have conveyed compassion, I want you to know that I think about you all the time, especially around the holidays. Christmases were always so special when you were younger. No matter what, promise me you won't let that spirit die with age.*

"*I hope you're well and are staying warm. Best wishes for a Happy New Year – Dad.*"

The card slips through my fingers and floats to the ground, where it remains untouched at my reindeer-patterned socks. "Oh my God."

"Oh, Grace. Are you all right?" Mom places her hand on my shoulder, but I shrug it off.

"It's fine," I lie. "I'm fine. I just—I just need some space right now, okay?"

She nods. "Of course. Take all the space you need, hon."

While she picks up the card to reread Dad's note, I head upstairs and lie face-first on my bed with my heart pounding like a drum in my chest. I close my eyes and picture his face; his tan skin, his thinning blonde hair, the small scruff beneath his lips that tickles my cheek when he kisses me.

"I love you, Gracie. Don't ever forget it."

I hear him walk downstairs, where Mom is preparing dinner in the kitchen. I hear her frightened voice, as clear as a bell, say, "William, I'm so sorry. I didn't mean—"

"Shut your mouth, you slut!"

A pan clatters to the floor; in the room beside mine, my six-year-old brother begins to cry. So does Mom.

"William, please—"

"Did you think I wasn't going to find out? Did you?" When she doesn't respond, he raises his voice, "Answer me, woman!"

"It—it was a mistake, I promise. It won't happen again."

"Was I not enough for you, huh? Was he a better fuck than I was?"

"No, we didn't—"

"You know what? I don't fucking care. Save your breath, bitch, because I'm outta here."

"William, wait," Mom begs. "Don't do this."

Her pleads are met with the sound of the door slamming shut. Through my window, I watch Dad get into his Jaguar. I watch him start the engine, back out of our driveway, and take off down the street, his wheels screeching against the smooth asphalt.

The rest of that evening is a blur. I remember sinking to my floor, trying to make sense of what happened but not knowing where to begin. I remember feeling confused. I remember feeling guilty. I remember my mom knocking on my door, and I remember turning her away.

I remember forgetting.

But now the memories are coming back, surging through the barriers in my brain that I've built to keep them out.

Dearest Gracie and Jameson, he'd said. *I'm sorry I didn't reach out sooner but I needed time to clear my head.*

Except no amount of time can erase the pain and fear he caused me when I was just a kid. And neither can talking about it, because words cannot express how devastating this fucked up situation is. My father is gone, and nothing—*nothing*—I do will ever bring him back.

Tears are streaming down my cheeks as I reach beneath my mattress for the pair of scissors I'd stolen from Ms. Lloyd's classroom last week. I press the sharp blade against my wrist and bite my lip, holding my breath as it pierces my skin. It's like Miriam said; that when you're sad, it seems like everyone around you is breathing while your head is submerged underwater. And then you feel different; you feel like you're not good enough to belong.

You feel like you want to die.

But I don't want to die, not really. I just want it to go away; the shame, the fear, the anger, the invasive memories that haunt me all day, every day. Mindfulness and opposite action are nothing compared to the sweet relief cutting gives me. If I can't starve away my emotions, this is the next best option.

I'm about to make a second incision when someone knocks on my door. "Grace, can I come in?" Mom asks.

"Leave me alone," I respond.

Silence from her end. I'm beginning to think she's left when she unexpectedly barges into my room. She sees the scissors in my hand, sees the fresh cut on my wrist, and her lips part in shock. For the first time in the sixteen years and seven months I've known her, my mother is speechless.

Without asking questions, without passing judgment, she sits beside me and wraps her arms around my quivering shoulders. I nestle my head against her chest and continue to sob into her soft cardigan sweater.

"I'm so sorry, Mom. I'm so sorry."

"It's okay, honey," she whispers. "I'm here with you. I'll protect you."

We're quiet for a minute or two. Twice, she clears her throat, as if she's going to say something, but she doesn't. So neither do I.

Our silence is eventually interrupted by Jamie. "Mom, can I have ice cre—" He trails off when he sees us, and concern fills his hazel eyes. "What's wrong? Why are you crying?"

Mom subtly tucks the scissors in her waistband. "Come here, hon. Sit with us."

Jamie squeezes between Mom and me. He gently touches my tear-stained cheek with his lilac-painted fingers. "Is everything all right?"

"Maybe not in this moment," Mom responds, "but it will be. Right, Grace?"

I hesitate. After everything I've been through, part of me stopped believing in happy endings a long time ago. But there's another part, a smaller, yet still accessible part, that reminds me that I cannot know if it's possible to get better until I actually try.

So, dismissing the doubt and the guilt and my crippling fear of the unknown, I nod. "Yeah. It's gonna be okay."

22

The haphazardly strung lights on the tree cast a rainbow reflection against the window. I'm seated beside them on a burgundy couch, surrounded by Mom, Jamie, and Lou, and watching the sun set over New York City. Two stories below, the streets are alive with taxis, charity Santas, and frazzled pedestrians lugging last-minute Christmas gifts back to their apartments. One woman is struggling to carry an exceptionally large stuffed elephant. I keep waiting for someone to offer her a helping hand, but even when she nearly wipes out on a patch of ice, people simply walk by.

I sigh. So much for the season of giving.

On my right, Lou laughs at something Jamie said. On my left, Mom sits quietly, her chipped fingernails tapping against her faded jeans. When our eyes meet, she smiles faintly.

"How are you, hon?"

"Okay, I guess. I started a new medication yesterday."

"I know. How's that going?"

"It has some weird side effects. Dr. Drexel said they're

usually temporary, but if they get worse, she'll consider taking me off. She said sometimes, it takes a few tries to find the right fit."

"You remember that from when you were younger, don't you?"

I groan. "Don't remind me."

"I think I still have a list of the medications you tried. Maybe I'll give it to her."

"Why?"

"It could be helpful."

"Yeah, I guess. I just . . ."

"You just what?"

I shake my head. "Nothing. Never mind."

Out on the streets, the elephant lady is gone. I hope she made it home safely. I wish I could go home too; I wish I could help Lou with the pageant. I wish I could cuddle with Mom and Jamie on our own couch—not this ragged piece of shit—and watch a Christmas movie or two. I wish I could fall asleep beneath my cozy snowflake-patterned covers looking forward to tomorrow rather than dreading it.

A hospital is not a fun place to spend Christmas Eve. I know that now.

When I was admitted to Mistlyn six days ago, I was surprised at how different it was than CTC. Unlike the grey corridors I'd grown used to, the yellow wallpaper and blue-tiled floors provided an otherwise dismal setting with a much-needed burst of color.

The other girls, Alexa, Dani, and Seraphina, are also vastly different from my former inmates; for starters, they're quieter, and they all struggle with food the same amount, if not more, than I do. On my first day, we spent an hour in the cafeteria waiting for Dani to finish her waffle fries. It got to the point where I wanted to shake her bony shoulders and exclaim, "Just eat already! Why can't you just eat!?"

But I didn't. Instead, I played with the new admission bracelet around my wrist and reminded myself that not too long ago, I was her; petrified of every bite, every calorie, that entered my body. Dani eventually finished her fries, then fled the cafeteria in tears and spent the next half-hour on the phone with her mom begging her to "get me out of this hellhole" because "the rules are bullshit and my doctor is a bitch."

Although she's far from perfect, I don't mind Dr. Drexel. When I told her about Dad, she didn't bombard me with questions or cliché expressions like "it will get better" and "this too shall pass." Instead, she listened. She let me vent for an hour straight, interrupting only once to ask if I wanted a tissue, and when I was finished, she told me that when she was my age, she was involved in a similar situation.

"What did you do?" I asked.

"I moved on," she responded. "I'm not saying it's easy; on the contrary, it's quite the opposite. I think the hardest part for me was coping with the guilt. I'd created this assumption in my mind that I was the reason my mother left; that if I'd been a better daughter, she would have stayed. But with time, I realized that was a delusion. She was the problem; not me."

"How much time?"

"Pardon?"

"You said with time. I want to know how much longer it'll be until I'm able to move on, like you were."

"It's different for everyone. My father was an addict, so he wasn't able to offer me the support I needed. I was all alone. You at least have your mother."

"But my mother's the reason he left. If she hadn't cheated . . ." I sighed. "How can I forgive her after that?"

"Everyone makes mistakes," she responded. "All I can say is that your mother loves you. She understands this is a process, and she's committed to helping you work through it if you'll let her."

"It's not like I have a choice."

"You always have a choice, Grace."

"I know. It's just . . . it's just I think about him all the time. His face, his voice—even the songs he used to sing to me. Whatever it takes to make it stop, I'll do."

"That's good to hear."

"Do you think he's the reason I'm sick?" I asked softly.

"I don't know. I think there were a number of reasons that contributed to your eating disorder, him being one of them."

"You're right. I can't blame everything on my parents because I've fucked up plenty too with the eating and the cutting and all that stuff."

"Are you still experiencing urges to self-harm?" she asked.

I was sick of lying, sick of pretending that I was okay when I actually wasn't, that I decided to finally tell the truth. "Yeah. I am."

"And how about suicidal thoughts?"

I nodded. "Those too."

After my confessions, Mistlyn's psychiatrist briefly met with me to discuss medication options. He ultimately selected Abilify, and with one signature, I kissed my emotions goodbye and ventured into Zombie Land, where I've resided ever since.

Even now, sandwiched between my best friend and my devoted family, I'm experiencing that same detachment.

"You guys didn't have to come," I say. "You could've stayed home and done something more fun or Christmassy."

"We wanted to come," Mom responds. "Christmas Eve wouldn't be the same without you."

"Damn straight," Lou agrees, "and when you discharge, we're gonna have an ah-mazing party with lights and music and dancing and—"

"And presents," Jamie says.

Lou nods. "So many presents. You'll legit think you're in Whoville."

"When'd you watch *The Grinch*?" I ask.

"In Psych last week. We're learning about sociopathology, and Mr. Marshall thinks the Grinch is a sociopath. How 'bout you?"

"Three days ago. It was the original, but I like that one more than the remake. Tonight, we're watching *It's a Wonderful Life*."

"You always loved that movie," Mom says. "We all did."

"Except Dad," Jamie reminds her. "He liked *Die Hard*."

"Technically not a Christmas movie," Lou interjects.

Mom winces at the mention of my father. "Honey, perhaps you shouldn't—"

"Mom, it's fine," I interrupt. "I'm not a little kid. You don't have to coddle me."

"I'm a mother," she responds. "Coddling is what we do."

Whereas Lou chuckles, I merely roll my eyes. "Well, don't. I don't like it."

"Okay, okay. I'm sorry."

I glance at the analog clock above the television. The large hand is pointed at the eleven while the small hand nears the eight. "They'll probably make you leave soon. I bet traffic will be hell."

"It can't be any worse than it was driving over," Mom says. "Although, it was beautiful."

"Did you see Rockefeller Center?"

Lou nods. "I'd show you the picture, but you know how the nurses are about phones."

"Where's it from this year?"

"Uh . . . somewhere in Maine, I think. It's crazy tall, like ninety-five feet or something."

"Wow."

Nurse Donna, one of my primary nurses, enters the Rec Room with my pill and a cup of water. She waits until I've swallowed, obediently lifting my tongue for the routine "mouth check," to say, "Visiting hours are just about over. We're setting up snack in the kitchen, so you can join us after you've said goodbye, Grace."

"What are we having?" I ask.

"Iced pumpkin cookies. They're quite delicious, if I do say so myself."

I shrug. "We'll see about that."

While Nurse Donna leaves to round up the others, Mom, Lou, and Jamie begin bundling up in their winter clothing. I don't need to step outside to know it's cold; I can tell from the frost covering the sparse patches of city grass and the harsh wind whooshing through the bare trees. Nurse Donna's colleague, Nurse Angelica, predicted at least ten inches of snow tonight. I wouldn't mind having a White Christmas. It's not like I'll have to shovel.

"Goodbye, Grace," Mom says. "We'll see you tomorrow, okay?"

"Okay."

"I love you."

"Okay."

Mom kisses my cheek while Jamie throws his arms around my shoulders and Lou tousles my messy hair.

"Don't have too much fun without us," she jokes. "We've still got that party to plan."

"Can I help?" Jamie asks.

Lou tosses him his baby blue pompom hat. "Of course. I'm gonna need as much help as I can to make it f-in awesome."

Jamie grins. "Sweet."

I watch them walk away with an ache in my stomach, similar to the one I had after I was forced to eat a slice of chocolate cake for night snack several days ago. "Hey, Mom?"

Mom turns around. "Yes?"

"I—I . . ." I take a deep breath. "I love you too."

Tears well in her eyes, but she quickly blinks them away. "Thank you."

"You can go now," I say. "I just thought you should know that."

"Okay. Happy Christmas Eve, my beautiful daughter."

"Happy Christmas Eve, Mom."

"GRACE? GRACE, WAKE UP."

When I open my eyes, Nurse Angelica hovers above me with her plump cheeks stretched into a broad smile. "Merry Christmas, sleepyhead."

I reluctantly raise my head from my stiff pillow. It's light outside—no, it's white—with a thick layer of snow covering the ground. Nurse Angelica was right; we did get a White Christmas, after all.

"Come on, dear. It's time for your weigh-in."

After I've changed into an itchy paper gown, I follow her through the adolescent wing and into the adjacent adult wing, where I stand behind an emaciated thirty-something-year-old woman to get weighed.

"G'morning." Serafina, accompanied by her NG tube, joins me in line. She's forgotten to tie the strings on the back of her gown, so her spine and scapula are painfully visible.

"Hey. Did you see the snow?"

She nods. "It's pretty, isn't it?"

"Very."

"I just hope the roads are good enough for my parents to drive on. Is your family coming?"

"My mom and my brother are. I think my friend is too."

"Lou, right?" When I nod, Seraphina says, "She seems great."

"She is. I don't know why she puts up with my bullshit, but I'm really glad she does."

"Well, you're lucky. I wish I had a friend like her."

"Grace?"

Nurse Donna beckons me into the Weigh-In room. She closes the door behind me, and I pull down my underwear so she can confirm that I'm not hiding anything in them that could affect my number. Then I turn around and step onto the scale until I hear a shrill *beep*!

"All set," she says.

While Serafina takes her turn, I head back to my room to change my clothes. Alexa is sitting on her bed, humming along to *Christmas Wrapping* on her handheld radio. When she sees me, she lowers the volume.

"Hey."

"Hey." I remove my gown and open the top drawer of my dresser, rummaging through long-sleeved shirts, turtlenecks, and bras until I find my favorite UConn sweatshirt. I pair it with baggy navy sweats, then close the drawer and casually lean against the window. "Happy Christmas."

Alexa snorts. "That's a joke, right?"

"Yeah, it's a joke."

"I heard we're having pancakes for breakfast."

"Really?"

"Uh-huh. I just hope they're not chocolate chip." She wrinkles her nose. "Yuck."

"I like chocolate chip," I say. "My father would make them for us when I was younger. It was a family recipe or something."

"You talk about your father a lot."

"It's hard not to when he's on my mind all the time."

"Do you think you'll ever see him again?"

I shake my head. "Even if I could, I don't think I'd want to."

"How come?"

"I guess . . ." I hesitate. "I guess because I wouldn't know what to say."

"Alexa?" Nurse Donna yells from the hall. "Your mother's on the phone!"

"Tell her I'll call her back!" Alexa responds.

"She's pretty adamant on wanting to talk to you now!"

Alexa rolls her eyes. "Fine, I'm coming!"

She trudges out of our room, grumbling beneath her breath, while I press my palm against the window and watch as snow continues to fall. I close my eyes and see Isaac and me sitting outside the movie theater with tiny flakes clinging to our lashes. I hear Lou bellowing *Walking in a Winter Wonderland* as she skips down the hall at Chuckles. I see Jamie grinning as he hangs his glittery pink ornament on our tree. I hear Mom say, "Snowflakes are winter's butterflies, so whenever you long for flowers or palm trees . . ."

"Remember that only butterflies can touch the sky," I whisper.

"Grace?" Nurse Donna pokes her head into my room. "It's time for breakfast."

"Yeah. One sec."

I listen to her footsteps fade in the distance; I listen to Alexa hang up the phone without saying goodbye; I listen to a door slam, a plate drop, a woman who's been battling her disorder for too long to reclaim freedom curse at Nurse Angelica. I listen to the sound of my heart thumping inside my chest, each beat reminding me that I'm still living even if at times, it feels like I'm more dead than alive.

I crumple my gown into a ball and place it on my desk next to a photo of Jamie and me posing outside of Splash Mountain. If I weren't here, if I weren't stuck in the hospital on my favorite day of the year, we'd be sitting around our tree unwrapping presents with childlike excitement and devouring the peppermint bark Mom religiously slips into our stockings. But we can't because I'm sick, and when someone you love is sick, you have to make adjustments; you have to change your ways. You have to be there for them, to help them remember that they're not alone.

Because when you're not alone, there will always be hope. I don't feel it now, but then again, I don't feel much of anything other than a little hungry. Dr. Drexel warned me that I'd have an increase in my appetite when I began the medication.

Before I head to the cafeteria, I glance out the window one more time, and my eyes grow wide with surprise. Perched on the sill, encompassed by the snow and the cold and the sound of the city gradually awakening for Christmas morning, is a beautiful butterfly.

If you or anyone you know is suffering from mental illness, please call 1-800-950-6264 or visit <u>nami.org</u> for more information.

ACKNOWLEDGMENTS

"Alone we can do so little, together we can do so much."
– Helen Keller

When I began writing *Changing Ways* one year ago, I was determined to do everything on my own. But, as time progressed, I realized that writing is not a solo career, and that in order to achieve my goals, I needed support and assistance from others. So, I want to thank all the kind and amazing people who helped me make my dream a reality.

Thank you to my two wonderful mothers for unconditionally supporting me in both my writing and my recovery. Thank you for tolerating me when I was at my worst and never giving up on me—even when I'd given up on myself. Thank you for your willingness to read and critique my work time and time again. *Changing Ways* would not be where it is today without you, and neither would I.

Thank you to my kick-ass team of editors. Thank you to

Karin Stahl, author of the hauntingly beautiful memoir *The Option*, who so willingly took me under her wing when I reached out to her for guidance in the beginning of this process. Thank you to Kate Conway, author of the best-selling *Undertow* series, who in addition to editing *Changing Ways*, designed my spectacular cover, formatted my novel inside and out, and voluntarily mentored me through the complications of self-publishing. Thank you to Kari Karp, my local librarian, Diedra Dietter, my social worker, and Ben Cramer, my quirky best friend, for not only offering me suggestions on how to improve my writing but also for helping me understand and appreciate the benefits of teamwork.

Thank you to Cedrick Ekra for photographing me in an outdoor park on one of the hottest days of the year. Although my limbs were covered with sweat and bug bites, I've never felt so beautiful in a photo before.

Thank you to my treatment team for helping me get to a place in my recovery where all of this is possible. Four years ago, even the idea of living to eighteen, much less self-publishing a freakin' novel by that age, would have seemed preposterous, but it's because of your constant support and encouragement that I've been able to achieve both.

Lastly, thank you to my cat Chibi for making me smile even on days when my depression was suffocating me. I love you, Baby Bop-Bop.

ABOUT THE AUTHOR

Julia Tannenbaum discovered her love for writing when she was thirteen, and since then has been featured in the anthologies *Dear Mr. President*, *Girls Write the World*, and *Inside My World*. Drawing from personal experiences, she often incorporates her struggles with mental illness into her fictional work.

She is a currently a high school senior and lives in West Hartford, Connecticut with her family and four cats. *Changing Ways* is her debut novel.